Pay Back

Pay Back

MALCOM CHESTER

PAY BACK

This book is written to provide information and motivation to readers. Its purpose is not to render any type of psychological, legal, or professional advice of any kind. The content is the sole opinion and expression of the author, and not necessarily that of the publisher.

Printed in the United States of America.

ISBN   978-1-64552-150-1   (Paperback)
ISBN   978-1-64552-151-8   (Digital)

Lettra Press books may be ordered through booksellers or by contacting:

Lettra Press LLC
30 N Gould St. Ste N
Sheridan, WY 82801, USA
3035861431 | info@lettrapress.com
www.lettrapress.com

Prologue

Ralph Tager in full battle gear with camouflage paint and a Colt M4A1 assault rifle clutched in his hands scanned the ramshackle cement buildings in front of him. His four fellow Seals anxiously watched and waited for his orders. Ralph's intelligence indicated that an important American Diplomat lay bound and gagged by Al Qaida operatives inside the small school and orphanage in front of him. His and his fellow Seal's job: extract the diplomat without killing or harming the Iraqi children living and studying at the school—a very tall order by any measure. Ralph did not like anything about the setup.

First and foremost, the intelligence could be wrong, the very reason a standard marine patrol hadn't already tried to extract the diplomat. They could be storming into an orphanage with only children and non-combatant teachers. Even if the diplomat lay bound there, they would have to avoid an almost certain ambush to rescue the man. More than likely they would have to fight their way into the school with the loss of life, which might include some or all of them, children and teachers and even the prized diplomat. The phrase heads you lose and tails they win came to mind. Yet, neither Ralph nor his fellow Seals would back away from their assignment.

Ralph crouched low quickly approached the front of the school while he motioned his fellow Seals to approach the school from the right and the left. At his signal, all five of them threw tear gas canisters into the school. The noxious odor soon reached them as they waited patiently for those inside to come outside, their backs against the school walls. Soon, children and teachers poured out of the school. Then quite suddenly a soldier with an AK-47 clutched in his hand tumbled out of the school. Almost the moment he caught his breath, the soldier raised his gun toward the huddled children and teachers. With a single shot to his head, Ralph dropped the soldier before he could fire. Several more minutes passed. No one else came out. The gas would slowly dissipate. They had to make their move now.

Putting on their gas masks, the five Seals ran in the front door, spreading to the right and left and staying close to the ground. Another AK 47 came to life spraying the entrance. Ralph caught a painful bullet in the top part of his bulletproof vest near his neck but returned fire immediately as did his comrades. The firing abruptly ceased. Three bodies lay sprawled on the floor in front of the Seals, their AK 47's pointed outward. The gas had mostly disabled and disoriented the Al Qaida fighters. The five Seals quickly searched the rest of the small school locating the diplomat in an unused classroom. Although cut, bruised and singed with cigarettes, he still breathed. The window next to him lay open. Ralph left Cole in the room to protect and untie the diplomat while he, Rafael, Sean and Edward ran back out of the door. The last Al Qaida soldier stood there with his AK-47 pointed at the head of a whimpering eleven-year old girl. His eyes looked like wet red orbs from the gas, but he managed to keep his weapon steady. Only a small portion of the soldier's head peeked above the girl's head. Ralph did not hesitate. He immediately took the shot. The top part of the soldier's head exploded and the girl dropped to the ground crying but unhurt.

Chapter I - History

Many years later, a depressed and despondent Ralph Tager, sat in near total darkness crossed legged on his living room floor. His large knife, throwing knife, assault rifle and handgun lay in front of him. Ralph assembled the guns many times while sharpening his knives. He examined every piece of his guns and oiled them. Ralph also carefully checked the balance of his knives. If they deviated even a little from what he considered optimal, he would replace them. With a sudden fury, he disassembled his guns once more doing so with only the feel of his hands. Ralph had a timer in front of him counting out the seconds. He reduced the handgun to its pieces in 30 seconds and reassembled it in 40 more. The ritual continued for almost two hours before he finally stopped. Sighing Ralph placed his weapons in the locked drawers where he kept them and stretched his body, which cramped a little from the rigid position he held on the floor.

On a sudden impulse, Ralph ran out his front door, carefully locking it and headed for the base track and gym. Ralph would run and work out until he could no longer. Ralph wanted his muscles to hurt so badly that this normal pain and soreness would replace the extreme emotional pain he felt. Ralph delivered death a hundred different ways to his enemies and gladly accepted the possibility of his own demise. Death brought no shock or fear. It became part of his daily existence. Yet, Ralph experienced more loss in this month than all of his previous thirty-two years.

First, his Seal Unit, Cole, Edward, Sean and Rafael, under the leadership of Chief Petty Officer Sean Terzich, his brothers far more than the real brother he had, caught an ambush the moment they parachuted into Afghanistan. Twenty Al Qaida fighters shot at them on their way down to the ground and kept shooting at them the moment they landed. Despite what amounted to an execution his team managed to take out ten of the enemy before they succumbed to the overwhelming fire. While he occasionally took assignments with his team now, a promoted Ralph Tager gave up his regular leadership role on the field. Yet, from the very moment the news reached him, Ralph blamed himself for the fiasco. They were his brothers in arms, who had faced and cheated death a hundred times but now the moment he left them, death found them. He literally couldn't function for a week after receiving the news. While Ralph knew intelligence sometimes failed, this incident reeked of betrayal and treason. These Al Qaida knew where his team would land. Somebody told them but despite his best efforts Ralph could not find the responsible party. He continued to look but reluctantly began to accept the terrible truth that he would never find the traitor. Yet, this tragedy paled in comparison to what happened next.

A predator abducted his nine-year old daughter, Melissa and killed his beloved wife Trudy when she attempted to prevent it. Ralph's very soul cried out in severe emotional pain. Despite his pain, Ralph hadn't been able to truly grieve for Trudy, who the predator savagely stabbed and Melissa, who had been sexually abused before being strangled. He had only one thought since the murder of his wife and daughter: torture and kill the man responsible. While he waited patiently for his GPS trace to reveal the location of this monster that went by the name of Ted Wiggle, Ralph reflected on the events that brought him to this day. The rhythmic impact of his sneakers on the track helped him remember the details well.

Ralph from the time he could first remember wanted to be a soldier. A good athlete and a good student particularly in math and science, Ralph from birth grew to be that soldier. Unlike other boys, he had no fear of anything and maintained his cool demeanor regardless of the challenges that faced him. Two incidents in his childhood probably best demonstrated these unusual traits.

When part of his Boy Scout troop became separated from their guides and adult leaders and lost in the Rocky Mountains, ten-year old Ralph calmly organized the six boys with him into two teams and conducted a grid pattern search for the trail. After locating the trail, he decided that with nightfall only a half an hour away, descending the trail to base camp would be foolish. Instead, Ralph found the group shelter for the night in a defensible position inside a shallow cave. When a pack of wolves threatened them, Ralph defended the rest of the boys with a spear he fashioned from a strong branch and his hunting knife. Accessible only from the front, the wolves had to squeeze through some thick brush Ralph piled in front of the cave entrance to reach Ralph and his fellow scouts. As they tried to wiggle though the brush, Ralph stabbed them in the eyes with his spear. After the third wolf fell, the others broke off the attack and went in search of other game. After a good night's rest, Ralph led his team of boys out of the mountains and to the safety of the base camp.

In an even more famous incident while a sophomore in high school, a deranged student, Wilbur Morris, attacked the school with an AR-15 and ten spare clips of ammunition. While most students, teachers and administrators cowered in various rooms and closets, Ralph went on the hunt for the gunman. Although unarmed, he had neither fear for his safety nor concern for the fate of the disturbed boy. He merely regarded Wilbur as a threat that needed to be eliminated. Following the dead and dying victims, gunfire and screams, Ralph moved silently along the walls of the high school's second floor, ducking into doorways and classrooms to maintain his cover. He already excelled in moving soundlessly and had achieved black belt status in several martial arts disciplines. Ralph as usual wore his all black outfit. On this day, he knew it would help obscure his profile. When Ralph neared the end of the north south corridor over which he traveled, he heard Wilbur's boots approaching his corridor from the intersecting corridor on his left. He quickly ducked in the doorway of the last classroom and waited. Ralph placed himself in as much shadow as the recessed doorway allowed, squatting down on his knees to further conceal himself. He carefully controlled his breathing.

As Ralph expected, Wilbur passed him without looking in the doorway or seeing him out of the corner of his eye. Just as he passed, Ralph leaped. Wilbur turned toward the onrushing Ralph but could not bring his rifle to bear on him in time. The already muscular Ralph hit Wilbur with a powerful punch to his Adam's apple with his left fist and ripped the rifle from the gunman with his right hand. As Wilbur gasped for breath, Ralph brought the rifle to bear on him. Not knowing whether the boy had additional weapons like a handgun or hunting knife, Ralph calmly emptied the remainder of the assault rifles clip into Wilbur's chest. The boy died before he hit the floor. Ralph threw the rifle on top of Wilbur and quietly and confidently walked out of the high school, carefully raising his hands to show he posed no threat. Ralph then explained to the officers gathered there that the gunman lay dead on the second floor, his assault rifle on his chest. Hailed as a hero, Ralph attained a special status in his high school and community, but at the same time people while being outwardly nice to Ralph maintained their distance from him. They all wondered whether the obviously deranged Wilbur could have been taken without the loss of his life.

After finishing high school in Highland Park, Illinois, Ralph attended the University of Illinois with a partial athletic scholarship. He played on the football team as a safety and linebacker. Although relatively small at six feet and two hundred and ten pounds, Ralph had a great ability to read offenses and as a result always seemed to be at the right place at the right time. When a hapless receiver or runner encountered Ralph his ferocious tackles brought them down immediately and on more than one occasion injured them. Ralph acted as much like a warrior on a football field as he would later in combat. Ralph while at the university joined the ROTC program, where his superior military skills earned him very high marks. He majored in mechanical engineering, believing this degree would best advance his career in the military. After he graduated from college, Ralph put off accepting his commission to train as a Seal. Excelling at his very difficult and challenging Seal combat training, Ralph became a member of an elite Seals unit. As a Seal, Ralph undertook clandestine missions for the Navy in many of the hot spots of the world. As most people expected, Ralph proved himself to be a great and courageous solider. After several years of dangerous combat, Ralph finished his officer training becoming an ensign overseeing Seal units.

As the ultimate alpha male, Ralph attracted many females and dated frequently. Yet, Ralph could not find a woman he loved. For some reason, the short-term attractions he felt never evolved into anything more permanent. Ralph worried that his soldering ways had hardened him so much that he couldn't love a woman or have a woman love him in return. While outwardly he seemed unaffected by his dating problems, inwardly Ralph found his time out of combat very stressful. During these times, Ralph felt his loneliness very acutely. As a result, he volunteered for more and more missions, where Ralph could achieve success and enjoy the camaraderie of other members of his Seal team.

Then ten years ago, Trudy, a nurse in a field hospital completely changed his life. Ralph visited Trudy's hospital to have a bullet wound in his upper arm examined. He removed the bullet and field dressed the wound while on assignment in the Sudan and wanted to make sure that the wound healed properly. He could not afford to be pulled from duty due to a runaway infection, an all too common occurrence in the filthy places he fought. When Trudy walked into the examination room, Ralph could barely speak. A vivacious five feet five inch brunette with lovely blue eyes and a nice curvaceous figure, Ralph found the young nurse very attractive. Yet, beyond her obvious female attributes, Trudy acted like a very bold woman, who knew exactly what she wanted and had no problem expressing those needs—just the kind of woman Ralph desired.

Without a moment's hesitation, she walked up to him and looked him straight in the eye. Most women shied away from the very strong and powerful Ralph Tager. Speaking directly to him as his drill sergeant once had done, Trudy demanded he remove his shirt. She then carefully examined Ralph and his wound. She extracted blood from his wounded arm and asked that he provide her with a urine sample. After he did so in the bathroom and returned it to her, Trudy just stood there for several moments looking at Ralph. A woman attracted to strong masculine men, Trudy had never seen anything like Ralph. His body looked like it had been carved from marble. He had the perfect male body. Ralph's masculine aura nearly overwhelmed her. Trudy wanted Ralph very badly. After telling Ralph that his wound looked fine but she would conduct tests anyway, Trudy boldly asked Ralph out on a date. He immediately accepted. Within a week, they fell madly in love. Within a month they married. Melissa arrived shortly afterwards.

For nine years, Ralph lived a wonderful life. He accepted a promotion to lieutenant, which placed him in charge of several more Seal units. He spent most of his time at the Great Lakes Naval Base in North Chicago, Illinois, where his command had been transferred. From time to time, he returned to the field to evaluate the units under his command and sometimes head a unit if they found themselves short of qualified personnel, but most of the time he spent with his wife and daughter. He wanted to spend all his free time with these two wonderful females who made him happier than he had ever been in his life. Trudy for her part concentrated on taking care of Melissa, but spent some time nursing at the large hospital on the base. Reading a story to Melissa at bedtime became Ralph's favorite time of the day. When she looked up to him with love in her large brown eyes, Ralph felt his heart would break. Ralph would often go to bed at night thanking god for giving him so much love in his life.

Chapter 2 - Revenge

The fateful day began like any other day. Ralph up at 5 A.M. as usual, checked on his units in the field. One of his units, tasked with doing some surveillance of a new secret Iranian coastal military facility, reported problems escaping after completing their mission. The group's landing craft lost power in the Arabian Sea, leaving them floating helplessly offshore. With each moment that passed, death or capture became more and more likely. Ralph needed to arrange a submarine pickup for his men without creating a major military incident between the U.S. and Iran. He passionately kissed his wife goodbye, hugged and kissed his sleeping daughter and headed out of the door by 6 A.M. He remembered hearing his wife say that the two of them planned to go to Gurnee Mills a large shopping center to look for items they couldn't get at the base PX. Ralph absorbed in the landing craft crisis barely heard his wife.

At 2 P.M. when Ralph took a long deserved break after the pickup of his unit finally took place, an ensign came running up to him with news about an attack on his wife and daughter. A large powerful looking man abducted his daughter and stabbed his wife in the parking lot of the shopping center when she tried to stop him. Ralph literally ran out of Seal headquarters toward the base hospital, telling his C.O., Butch McGregor on his way out that his wife had been stabbed and his daughter abducted.

Ralph paced the hospital waiting room like a man possessed until twenty minutes later when an obviously upset doctor came out of the OR to talk with him. Trudy, although she worked only part time at the hospital, gained the respect and even love of all the workers at the Navy hospital including the surgeon standing before Ralph. Ralph knew before the doctor even opened his mouth that Trudy died. He had given the same speech to love ones killed in the line of duty. Ralph barely heard the doctor's explanation that the wound bled too much and caused too much damage to Trudy's liver for her to survive. Ralph quickly walked into Trudy's room to save goodbye to the woman he loved. He promised to avenge her and their daughter or die trying. Barely able to contain his emotions, Ralph ran out of the hospital and headed straight for the police department. He still hoped that his daughter might live.

Unfortunately, the detectives assigned the case had very few leads to search for his wife's killer and daughter's abductor. Because of his training, Ralph offered to help the police in their search. The detectives didn't really want his help, but Ralph could not be very easily pushed aside. The investigation lasted hours and then days. With each passing hour, Ralph knew Melissa's chances for survival fell. Ralph couldn't sleep. He just kept up his own investigations and coordinated as best as he could with the police detectives. On the third day, the raped and battered dead body of his daughter turned up in a public park. The rage began soon afterwards. Ralph felt it consume his body and soul. He would get even with the man who did this to his family. Ralph had taken too many punches. He needed to hit back.

Ralph used all his free time tracking the police investigation of his family's murders and conducting his own investigation. After two weeks, the police finally received a break when they identified Ted Wiggle as the likely perpetrator. Ted had a long record as a pedophile and had been arrested but not convicted of murdering a child. According to the arrest reports, Ted struck everyone as a nasty intimidating man. He stood six feet two and weighed two hundred forty pounds. He boxed regularly, collected guns and knives and could bench press three hundred pounds. Ralph's independent investigation also led him to the same man. Eyewitnesses had seen him walking through the Gurnee Mills Mall on several occasions staring at small girls. Although his activities generated several complaints to the police, little could be done about his creepy stares. Ted had committed no crime. When the detectives identified Ted, they brought him in for questioning and then searched his home after obtaining a search warrant. The search of Ted's home yielded no incriminating evidence and Ted's questioning led to nothing. Even after several hours, Ted refused to answer any of the detective's questions and requested a lawyer to be present. The detectives with no evidence to tie him to the murders reluctantly let Ted go.

Ralph, however, anticipated these problems and patiently waited for Ted to leave the police station. When he did, Ralph shot Ted in the back of his arm with a tiny transmitter dart he often used on his missions. He then quickly disappeared. Thinking the dart a mosquito bite, Ted ignored the embedded transmitter. Ralph's investigation and training convinced him that Ted conducted his rape and torture of girls at a site away from his home. He now patiently waited for Ted to go to this site.

A day after Ted's release from the police station, Ted headed for a location in Waukegan. Ralph carefully tracked his movements. When Ted finally stopped, Ralph quickly ascertained through the use of Google maps that he appeared to be in a warehouse. Already on his way to the area, Ralph expected to reach the warehouse in ten minutes. He already wore an all black uniform with a Kevlar bulletproof vest underneath. He also had a dark black mask on his face that he created from an old Halloween mask. Various weapons lay hidden in his uniform, including a small and light 22 caliber Beretta 21 Bobcat with a silencer and an M 16-14 River Knife. By the time Ralph reached the abandoned warehouse his transmitter indicated as his location, night fast approached.

Ralph carefully examined all the entrances to the isolated warehouse. The warehouse appeared to be little used even abandoned. Other than the three loading dock doors, the warehouse had one small door leading inside. The warehouse also had some small very dirty windows high up on the walls. Ralph took a few moments to consider his best access. The high windows while easily accessed would leave him exposed and framed once he moved through them. In addition, they might make noise when he opened them. Also, a descent to the floor would leave him exposed until he reached the floor. He ruled out the windows. As to the loading doors they would be noisy to open and definitely alert his opponent that someone stalked him. This left the small door as the best point of access, but it might very well be alarmed or somehow tied into an identification system. Ralph needed to turn the power to the building off before he tried the door.

Ralph quickly located the building's outside electrical box, installed a small charge to disable it and gave himself three minutes to reach and open the door before the charge disabled the electrical line. Reaching the small door in two minutes, Ralph quickly picked the lock and used a special tool to slide the interior bolt back to the open position. Seconds after the charge detonated he rolled through the door next to the ground moving to his left and out of the doorway. A heavy caliber pistol, probably a 44 magnum, fired, shattering the door moments after Ralph rolled through it. Ted must have picked Ralph up before he approached the door. Ralph saw no cameras after his initial inspection but somehow Ted detected him in the darkened warehouse. Ralph inched his way along the left wall and while doing so pulled out an infrared night scope and searched for Ted. He found him close to the place where the shots came, standing and listening for his prey. Ralph quickly moved to a place where he could obtain a clear shot and quickly fired off five shots at Ted, one at each shoulder and each leg and the fifth directly at his heart. Ralph used hollow point ammunition, which packed a wallop despite the small size of the 22-caliber bullet fired by his pistol. After being hit, the big man managed to get off two more shots from his magnum in Ralph's general direction. One of the shots more out of pure luck than any careful shooting caught Ralph in his bullet proof vest and knocked him into the wall. Ralph quickly recovered and resumed his approach along the wall. As he moved, Ralph ignored the pain of the big bruise on his chest just to the right of the center of his rib cage. In Ralph's mind pain became an issue after a mission but during the mission a good Seal ignored it. Only injuries that prevented a Seal from performing became matters of concern.

Seconds after Ralph's bullets found their mark, Ted collapsed to the floor in agony. As Ralph suspected, Ted's bulletproof vest stopped the bullet fired at Ted's heart but the other bullets hit areas as Ralph hoped they would not covered by the vest. Ralph quickly made up the distance between him and Ted, carefully watching to see if the big gun moved in Ted's hand. Quite suddenly it did as Ralph drew near. Firing and moving to his left, Ralph shot Ted in his gun hand as a bullet sailed by his head. Ted dropped the weapon screaming as he did so. Within seconds, Ralph leaped on the writhing big man, pulling his arms behind his back and secured them tightly with a pair of handcuffs concealed in his uniform. Ted yelled in agony when Ralph bound his arms behind him. Then Ralph removed the big man's long sleeve shirt and located the tiny location dart. He removed the dart and placed it in a plastic bag inside of his backpack. Removing his flashlight, Ralph searched the warehouse area and located a chair in the far corner. He dragged Ted to the chair and nearly displaced Ted's arms as he pulled them behind the chair. Tired of hearing Ted moan, yell, curse and threaten him, Ralph put a gag in Ted's mouth. Then he used small strong thin cord to securely bind Ted to the chair and to spread his legs as wide as they would go. Without a moment's hesitation, Ralph removed his river knife and cut off Ted's pants and underwear. Ralph paused for a moment then in a loud voice addressed Ted, looking in his eyes with pure hatred.

"Now you will pay for your crimes in the only way that begins to atone for them."

But before, Ralph could use his river knife; he heard a whimper behind him. Taking his flashlight out of his pack, he examined the area to his left. The area had a filthy bed and a long table with a number of sex items and knives on it. Next to the bed he saw a nude nine-year old girl with her hands bound behind her. She showed some bad bruises and cuts. Ralph could tell that Ted had hurt her very badly. He quickly located some of her clothes and gently redressed her after cutting the rope binding her hands. Speaking softly to the girl just as he used to talk to his little girl, Ralph wrapped a blanket around her. Then an idea came to him. Leading the girl to a bleeding Ted, Ralph addressed the scared little girl.

"The monster that did this to you is bound to this chair. He can no longer hurt you. This monster also killed people close to me. He is bleeding from gunshots wounds to his shoulders, legs and one shot to his hand. One of the shots to his leg appears to have cut an artery. He will eventually lose consciousness. Shortly thereafter, he will die from a loss of blood unless he receives first aid. What shall we do with him?"

Ralph did not expect the girl to participate in the torture of this man, but it felt right for him to ask. In his grief-racked mind, this little girl became his little girl. To Ralph's great surprise, the girl stopped whimpering and a hard expression formed on her face. The girl spoke in a soft hoarse whisper.

"This monster killed my parents and hurt me in my private place many times. I do not want to kill him but he must not be able to do what he did to me ever again. The piece of himself that he used on me must be cut off. Give me the knife and I will do it."

After this brief announcement, Ralph quickly cut off Ted's private parts with his river knife. He did not want the girl to do so fearing it would cause her emotional pain later in her life, but Ralph wanted nonetheless to do what she asked. To Ralph the mutilation meant nothing. He had seen far worse. Carefully sidestepping the blood squirting out of the area where Ted's private parts once protruded, Ralph placed the bloody items in Ralph's left hand. Ted tried to scream his eyes as wide as they could possibly be, but the gag allowed him to say very little. Ralph quickly cleaned up after himself, whipping the blood off his knife with Ted's torn underwear. Ralph would thoroughly clean the knife later and burn the tight rubber gloves on his hands. Almost on a whim, Ralph ignited a stick that lay near him and cauterized the wound he just inflicted with his knife. He did not know whether he did so to save the man's life or to prolong his pain while he died.

Leaving a slumped over Ted where he sat, Ralph wrapped a blanket around the little girl and carried her out of the warehouse to his car. She clung on to him with all her strength asking Ralph whether the monster had gone away. Ralph assured her that he had. Ralph could call the police and/or an ambulance on his throwaway cell phone, but this little girl couldn't wait for the police or an ambulance. He couldn't wait with her either because in doing so he would be turning himself into the police. But if she died as a result of him leaving her, he would never forgive himself. Without really thinking about it, he quickly located a hospital nearby through one of his phone applications and headed for it as fast as he could. His emotions churned inside of him. Ralph quietly talked to the little girl, hoping that she could respond.

"I'm taking you to a hospital. The monster back there hurt you very badly. To save you, I had to hurt the monster. For this reason, I cannot go into the hospital with you. The police will arrest me for what I did to the monster if I do. If I drop you near the door of the hospital, can you walk inside the door? By the way, I'm Pay Back. I kill all the monsters that hurt children like you. I would like to know your name if you will tell me."

"My name is Cindy. I'm glad you hurt the monster. I have no sympathy for him. I think I can walk into the hospital, but my private place really hurts as does the rest of me. It even hurts for me to talk." Cindy paused a moment and then looked directly in Ralph's eyes, melting his heart as she did so. She said, "You have to promise me that you will come and see me when I get better. You are my hero. "

"Okay Cindy I will, but I need to ask you one favor. The police will try to persuade you to identify me so they can arrest me for hurting the monster. I would appreciate it if you tell them you can't remember what I look like."

"I promise I won't try to identify you. I want you to kill all the monsters out there that hurt kids. Anyway, with that mask on I can't be sure what you look like."

"I will kill the monsters for you Trudy and for all the other children the monsters hurt."

Moments later, Ralph reached the hospital emergency room area and helped Cindy get out of the car. As soon as she began to walk unsteadily toward the door, Ralph took off but called the emergency room on a burner phone he kept for situations such as this, telling them that a badly injured and raped little girl walked into their emergency room. They needed to find her and take care of her as soon as they could. An hour later, Ralph also called the police to tell them where the monster sat with his private parts in his hands.

Shortly after Ralph arrived at his house, the story of the little girl reached the press. Her ordeal became a media sensation. Everyone wanted to know who abducted Cindy and how she escaped. They also wanted to know whether she would recover. The doctors announced rather quickly that Cindy would recover, but they also told the press that they did not know whether she would be able to have children when she became an adult. She suffered severe trauma in this area of her body. At first the hospital protected Cindy from the press and the police who wanted to interview her, but after some treatment and proper doses of painkillers, Cindy indicated she would talk to the police. She gave the police her name and address and said that the monster killed her parents in their house before he abducted her. Then Cindy told them that a man she could not identify killed the monster that took her and dropped her at the hospital. He had a mask on his face. The police nonetheless pressed her to reveal the identity of the man who saved her using every trick they could devise but she stubbornly maintained she could not identify him. Using the information they acquired from Cindy, the police quickly located her house and identified the remains of her parents. Using Ralph's call, they found Ted's warehouse. While Ted clung to life for a while after being found, he died shortly after being taken to a hospital from a loss of blood. His condition created a whole new media sensation.

The press criticized Pay Back, their name for him, for mutilating Ted, but most of the letters the newspaper and electronic media received praised the actions he took. One distraught woman, who had her daughter abducted ten years ago and hadn't seen her since, said she would have gladly taken a knife and done the same thing. Not surprisingly, the investigation of Ted's demise quickly focused on Ralph. As police briefly held Ted as a suspect in his wife and daughter's deaths,

Ralph undoubtedly killed Ted to avenge his family's deaths. Ralph's service as a highly decorated Seal made him an even more likely suspect. The police arrested Ralph but got absolutely no information from a Seal trained to resist giving information under the most severe torture. Eventually they let him go when they could produce no evidence that he moved through the scene of the crime or find any weapons used by the mystery man in killing and torturing Ted. After thoroughly cleaning his knife and filing the edge to change its imprint, Ralph buried it in a box in the Lake County Forest Preserve. As to his Beretta, Ralph re-filed the barrel after dropping Cindy at the hospital. When the police seized the weapon after obtaining a warrant, they could not match the markings of the test bullet fired from his gun to the slugs taken out of Ted.

Cindy

Terrified and feeling very alone, Cindy sat in her hospital bed waiting for the police detective to interview her. She had an IV in her arm and looked tired and worn. A woman Thelma, from the Department of Children and Family Services waited with her. Cindy did not wish to talk with anyone. In particular, she didn't want to discuss her rape and torture. She would shake and her heart would pound when her mind focused on the ordeal. Her dreams also tortured Cindy. Her murderer became a vicious beats in her dreams, frightening her more than he did as her actual torturer. Finally, Thelma spoke.

"Don't worry about the police interview. I will be here to protect you. If you answer the detective's questions, this will be over quickly. Oh I almost forgot to mention. In interviews, you should always try to tell the truth."

"I will. I don't tell lies." Cindy answered.

Moments later, Helen Peterson a detective from North Chicago walked in the door.

"Hi Cindy I'm detective Peterson, but you can just call me Helen. I just want to ask you a few questions. Will that be okay?"

"I guess but I don't feel like talking or answering questions. I'm full of drugs and can't sleep very well. I have nightmares."

"I won't take long. Did you know Ted the man who died in the warehouse incident?"

"You mean the man who brutally murdered my parents and then raped and tortured me?"

"The man who allegedly did these things, yes."

"I don't know what that means but I didn't know this man until he broke into my house and repeatedly shot and hit my parents with a baseball bat."

"Okay, I suppose that answers that. When did you first see the man who took you from the warehouse?'

"I saw my torturer, I guess his name is Ted, fall down after bullets hit him. I was tied to a table where Ted had been assaulting me in my private place. I hurt all over my body. I felt like I would die. When Ted fell down, a man in a mask tied him to a chair and drew a knife. Then the man with the knife saw me, put down his knife and untied me. The man helped me get up and took me over to Ted. He picked up the knife on the way back. He asked me if I would mind if he cut off Ted's private parts. I said I wouldn't. The man in the mask then cut off Ted's private parts with a knife. After that he took me to the hospital and left me next to the emergency door. That is pretty much it. The man in the mask saved my life. He comforted me and tried to make me feel better. He is my hero."

"Cindy the man in the mask murdered Ted in a horrible way. He is no hero. We have laws in this country. He broke those laws. Do you understand?"

"Yes but you arrested Ted and then let him go. Your laws didn't help my parents. They didn't help me. I would be dead if I depended on your laws."

"The law isn't perfect but it is the best we have. We can't allow private citizens to take the law into their own hands. What do you remember about the man in the mask? Can you describe him for me?"

"He was very strong and brave. I don't remember much else about him. He had a mask on. I couldn't see his face and the words he spoke sounded funny through the mask."

"Do you remember how tall he was? Do you remember how much he weighed?"

"No not really. He was strong but smaller than Ted. That is about all I remember."

"Was he injured in any way?"

"No not that I could see but he did have a tear in his shirt."

"Cindy I'm going to show you a picture of Ralph Tager, the man we think saved you. Does he look familiar?"

"No. I told you the man had a mask on his face."

"I have also brought a recording device. I'm going to play part of a police interview with Ralph Tager. After you listen to it, tell me if his voice sounds familiar."

After listening to the recording, Cindy responded.

"I don't recognize his voice. As I told you, he spoke through a mask."

"Cindy, did you know that it is a crime to lie to a policewoman? You don't want to get in trouble do you? Now please look at Ralph Tager's picture and listen to his voice again."

After doing so, Cindy said.

"No as I told you the first time, I don't recognize this man or his voice." Cindy said as tears began to form in her eyes.

"Now Cindy. You need to be honest with me." Helen said angrily.

"I am. You're mean. You are trying to force me to give you the answers you want. I don't feel like answering any more of your questions."

"Wait a minute. That is enough. You are battering and bullying a little girl who has suffered unspeakable horrors. She has told you what she knows. This interview is over." Thelma responded in a hostile tone as she protectively moved between Helen and Cindy.

"Okay, but I will be back. Cindy knows more than she is saying. I can feel it." Helen said as she abruptly stood up and left the room.

Chapter 3 - Law Enforcement

The media sensation created by the crimes of Ted Wiggle, his surviving victim Cindy and his mutilation in the most graphic manner possible created a law enforcement nightmare. Detectives from Gurnee, the kidnapping location of Ralph's daughter, North Chicago where Cindy and Ralph lived, and Waukegan the location of Ted's warehouse, all became involved. Because Ralph still served as an active member of the Navy, NCIS gained jurisdiction as well. Finally, the FBI joined the case when they discovered an outstanding warrant for Ted Wiggle in Iowa. Two FBI Agents, Sarah Thelon and Malcolm Rodgers, two NCIS Agents, Terry Peters and Cynthia Whitcomb, a Gurnee detective Helen Peterson, a North Chicago Detective Rufus Wilson and a Waukegan Detective Thad Gonzales sat a table discussing the case. They could not decide what to do next. Each of their bosses placed intense pressure on them to bring this case to a close or to produce some further results.

"We local guys want to close the case and move on to other problems. We all know Ralph tortured Ted to get his revenge and saved Cindy, but we can't prove it. Trudy could probably ID Ralph but she won't. The fact that he wore a mask gives her great cover. We could try to brow beat her into fingering Ralph but doing so to a young girl rape victim will not do wonders for our popularity. Also, a defense attorney would have a field day discrediting the testimony of a nine year old girl intimidated by the police and trying to identify a masked man," Thad Gonzales said with a certain resignation. After Thad finished his speech, Helen and Rufus nodded their heads in agreement.

"Well that is fine for you local guys but my bosses hate vigilantes. Taking the law into his hands, Ralph undermined law enforcement and the court system. The papers are making this guy Ralph into a folk hero, which he is not. Our job is to catch everyone breaking the law including Seals like Ralph, not just the ones we want to catch. The next thing you know when we have a pedophile under investigation a crowd will show up with pitchforks and take care of him before we can even bring a case. We have to stop this guy anyway we can. I want to know what you guys at NCIS found. After all, Ralph is a Seal," Malcolm Rodgers said with disgust.

"No cooperation that is what we found. The hospital staff loved Trudy and refused to say anything about Ralph, which might tie him to the torture of Ted. They felt Ted got what he deserved. The Seals in his unit are even less cooperative. Just so you know what we have to face, this is a direct quote from Ralph's CO, Butch McGregor. I wrote it down. "I don't know if Ralph was involved in that deviant's death but if it had been me after I cut off the guy's balls and cock I would have stuffed them in his mouth and watched him choke to death." When they invented the word macho I think they had the Seals in mind. As a matter of fact, I think the Seals would have lost respect for Ralph if he had let the murder of his family go. Ted made a big mistake when he attacked the family of a Seal. Frankly, my bosses while outwardly mouthing the vigilante line have similar sentiments. They want us to drop the case and to move on just like the locals do," Terry Peters said with resignation.

"Great. We are nowhere. What if Ralph decides to take out some more pedophiles? What will we do then? I somehow have the feeling that Ralph is just getting warmed up. I'm not sure he has satisfied his need for revenge. When we talked to him, I could see the rage behind his eyes. He is a frightening man. I suppose I can try to talk with Cindy again. Maybe I can persuade her to talk to us before Ralph strikes again," Sarah Thelon said.

"Good luck with that. Cindy is now with the Department of Children and Family Services waiting for adoption. If you interview her there, I can guarantee you that one of their lawyers will be present. You will get even less out of her than I did the first time, which was basically nothing. She may be lying, but I don't know how to get her to change her story. She is so traumatized that even if I persuaded her to say something to incriminate Ralph, I doubt it would stand up in court. As to Ralph or whoever else mutilated Ted, there is a part of me that would like to encourage him to keep up the good work. Seeing all the perverts I do and the damage that they do to little girls like Cindy, I would like to castrate them myself," Helen said a little too seriously.

"Great. Malcolm it looks like just you and I are going to be in this fight. Even our federal brothers at NCIS are going to pull out. While you can close your case files, we won't. We're going to continue to follow this guy until we nab him," Sarah declared with some authority.

"A word of caution to you both. Navy Seals in general and Ralph in particular are very dangerous people. They can track and kill almost anyone without leaving a trace. They can kill a man a hundred different ways and are very single minded when they are on a mission. In your zeal to catch Ralph remember just how lethal he is," Cynthia Whitcomb warned.

"Okay Sarah and I have got it. Macho man can be and will be subdued like any other man when the time comes. This meeting isn't going anywhere. The FBI will take this case from here, while the rest of you tuck your tails between your legs and leave the field," Malcolm chided in an irritating way.

"Well since you have already written us off good luck with the case. By the way don't expect any cooperation from us. If you guys are as superior as you think you are, you won't need our help," Thad Gonzales said getting up out of his chair and walking toward the door. Helen and Rufus followed behind Thad heading for the door as well. Without even hesitating, the three locals walked out the door, leaving only the federal agents.

"I think we ought to go too. We will cooperate with you guys at the FBI for as long as they leave us on the case. Is there anything we can do to help for the time we have?" Terry asked.

"Nothing specific but we would appreciate it if you continue to watch Ralph for a while. Maybe he will make a mistake and we can use it to go after him," Sarah said.

"Okay we will," Terry says with Cynthia agreeing. After the FBI agents left, Cynthia turned to Terry and said.

"Sarah and Malcolm are stuck up assholes. With our brass already giving us not to subtle hints to lay off, I think we are better off leaving this case alone until we can close it. I'm not going to trail after Ralph anymore," Cynthia said with some commitment in her voice.

"Funny, I was going to say the same thing. Even though they are federal agents, they are still civilians. They don't understand military people like us. Ralph is a hero in my book. Wiggle murdered his family and tortured his daughter. Ralph did what he needed to do to send a message to other perpetrators that there is a cost for doing that. For the military which we represent this case is closed," Terry said with equal intensity.

A Pleasant Meeting

After Ralph left police custody, he continued to have serious emotional problems. He could still function at work but the time he spent at home haunted him. Ralph kept expecting to see his dead wife and daughter. When they didn't come, rage would consume him. Ralph thought the death of his wife's and daughter's killer would bring him some relief but he still suffered. To move away from the memories, Ted decided to sell his house and move back into base housing. Before he did so, Ralph needed to do one more thing. He needed to visit Cindy. Ralph wanted to adopt her as his daughter and had persuaded his mother to live with them if the adoption became a reality. For reasons Ralph did not understand, Cindy's relatives did not wish to take custody of her. Still Ralph needed to find out whether Cindy wanted to live with him. Also, Ralph wondered whether the state adoption agency would allow him to adopt Cindy even if she wanted to be his new daughter.

The day finally arrived for his adoption appointment. Ralph had already filled out all the necessary state forms and felt optimistic about his chances when he secured the appointment. After spending some time with the state person assigned to Cindy, Terry, Ralph walked into a small room with couches and chairs. Cindy sat in one of the chairs with her hands in her lap. Ralph marveled at the very beautiful little girl looking at him. She had blond curls, deep blue eyes, soft creamy complexion and a perfectly formed little face. As soon as Cindy saw Ralph a big smile crossed her face. She ran to Ralph and hugged him as hard as she could.

"I knew you would come, I knew it. I spent all day dressing up so you would want me. You are my knight and my hero. I want to be adopted by you. I have told all the others wanting to adopt me no. I would never feel safe with anyone but you," Cindy said with tears and hope in her eyes.

Ralph's heart suddenly filled with love for Cindy. Ted had made both of them victims. She lost everyone close to her while he lost the people closest to him. She needed him as much as he needed her. He gently untangled from her embraces and looked in her lovely eyes.

"Cindy I very much want to adopt you. I have convinced my mother to come live with us to make my case stronger to the Children and Family Services people. After we're done here, I'll call my mom. She can call Terry and make our case. And by the way, any girl your age who could survive an ordeal like you did and be standing here in one piece is a hero to me. I have seen grown men collapse mentally and physically when confronted with the terror you endured. "

"Thanks for saying that. I still have bad nightmares and miss my mom and dad very much, but I'm doing alright."

"That's great. Why don't we take a walk on the grounds? It's a beautiful day. They told me I could before I came in here."

"I would love that. Please take my hand. I want to feel your strong hand in mine," Cindy said still looking into Ralph's eyes.

Ralph and Cindy walked on the grounds of the state facility. The sun blazed and the spring flowers bloomed. After a while, Ralph spoke.

"Cindy, one thing is bothering me. You know that I cut off the monster's private parts. I don't want you to think that I'm a monster for doing that."

"No it was only fair. He hurt me in my private place. He hurt your daughter there. He killed my mom and dad and your wife and daughter. He deserved what he got. Anyway, maybe other monsters like him will not hurt little girls there if they think the same thing will happen to them."

"Cindy, we think alike, that's exactly why I did it."

"You know with you here I feel better. I haven't thought about that terrible time since we started talking. I just want to come and live with you. I want to be a normal little girl and start living my life again. I want you to be my dad. "

"Cindy that is what I want too."

Navy Acts

The day after Ralph spoke with Cindy; Captain Butch Macgregor sat in his office. Fortunately, the NCIS investigation into Ralph's involvement in the torture and murder of that pervert seemed to be finally ending. They never proved he had anything to do with the crime and they never would. He worried since the investigation began that the brass would lean on him to get rid of Ralph, his best Seal. If his superiors forced him to move against Ralph, Butch's command would be finished. His Seals wouldn't follow him anymore. They all supported and respected Ralph. He would be expected to have Ralph's back. All Seals thought this way. The brass often didn't understand this.

At just this moment, the phone rang. Butch's secretary a marine sergeant named Bill came rushing in the office.

"Butch, it is Admiral Templeton. From the way he sounds, this does not seem like a social call."

"Okay I've got it." Butch reluctantly put the phone to his ear. Butch did not like the bureaucratic Intelligence Admiral who had somehow become his boss. "Yes Admiral what can I do for you sir."

"I'm not going to beat around the bush. Ralph Tager has to go. I don't care how you get rid of him, but I don't want him in the Navy any longer."

"Sir, I have absolutely no reason to push Ralph out of my unit. He is my best Seal. His record is exemplary and filled with medals and commendations. If you're upset about the murder and torture of the pedophile, NCIS has been unable to tie Ralph to the murder. He has an alibi provided by his mother. There is no forensic or eyewitness evidence putting him at the scene. Also, the little girl rescued by the murderer of the pervert has not identified Ralph as the man responsible. Anyway, Ted Wiggle hurt a lot of kids. Any of those parents could be involved. It's all in the NCIS report. You should have a copy. I'll send one to you if you need one."

"Bullshit. Ralph Tager did it and you know it. A Seal and only a Seal could have done this job and not left any trace. It's what he is trained to do."

"Maybe but that does not change the facts. I have no reason or justification for moving against Ralph and as a result I will not do so."

"Butch you don't understand the problems this incident creates. Seals operate at the edge of if not outside of the law. As long as we operate on foreign soil, we get a pass, but not when we do so in the U.S. Nobody wants us to assassinate U.S. citizens no matter how justified it seems to be. This crosses the line. As long as Ralph stays where he is, the Navy appears to be condoning what he did. We just can't have that."

"Admiral, Ralph is my second in command and extremely well liked and respected by the other Seals in my unit. If I move against Ralph without justification, I will lose the respect of my men. It will undermine my command. I just can't do it."

"What if I order you to do it?"

"I can't obey that order."

"If you don't, I can and I will bring you up on court martial charges for disobeying a direct order."

"Yeah you could, but you won't. I don't think it would do your career a whole lot of good if you have to explain to a number of senior officers what the order was. This isn't the Spanish Inquisition."

"Then you leave me no choice. I'm relieving you of your command and transferring you to the Pentagon. You have one week to pack up your things and move."

"Does Admiral Richter know about this? Who is going to be my replacement?"

"That is my business not yours. As the new CO, I 'm putting Jerry Stevens in your spot."

"I think I met him. He is an Annapolis guy, but I don't remember him having any combat experience. I know he wasn't a Seal."

"Maybe it is about time we had a non Seal in your spot. Anyway, the decision has been made. Now you have plenty to do. I want this transition to be as smooth as possible."

"Yeah I will work on the transition alright but I don't expect it to be smooth. The men will not like your choice. They won't respect this Stevens guy."

"It isn't up to them and you know it. I have to go. I want a report on your transition plan in my office in two days. "

With that statement, Admiral Templeton hung up the phone. Butch started to form a transition plan in his head. Even though he had done the right thing in refusing to push Ralph out, he had to do his duty and prepare for a change in command. He would talk to Ralph first thing and warn him of the problems he faced. Jerry Stevens would have orders to push Ralph out. But as Butch started to swing into action, this whole incident felt very wrong to Butch. Something else took place here but he couldn't' put his finger on what it happened to be.

A New Direction

After talking to Butch, Ralph decided to retire from the Navy. When they found out what happened with Ralph and Butch, several of the remaining senior Seals at Great Lakes planned on doing the same thing. They as well as he could collect some good pensions after they left. The others would also have left if they had better retirement options. The remaining Seals would apply for transfers but knew the new guy would probably not process their requests. All the Seals resented having a paper pusher as their new commander. They respected and admired Butch and Ralph. They would go to hell and back for them. They wouldn't go to the neighborhood store for the new guy.

After Ralph filed his retirement papers, he spent his time at home trying to decide what to do next. He had several offers from security firms at double his Navy pay. Ralph had a job if he wanted it. Unfortunately all the jobs required him to move. He didn't care about where he lived but his adoption of Cindy still hadn't happened as yet. He wouldn't move until Cindy became his daughter or he knew that she would never be his daughter. At the same time, Ralph had to have a stable job to support the adoption. He would just have to convince one of the companies offering him a job to leave him here until the adoption came through.

As these thoughts swirled through his mind, Ralph's cell phone rang. The man on the phone surprised Ralph.

"Is this Ralph Tager?"

"Yes, but I 'm surprised you have this number. I don't give it out to many people. Who are you?"

"My name is Sydney Worth. You may have heard of me. I certainly get my share of publicity whether I want it or not."

"The Sydney Worth; the multi billionaire. Who hasn't heard of you? But how do I know that I'm really speaking to you?"

"You are asking the right question. My office number is 212-921-1789. I have left instructions with my secretary to patch you through when you call. Say the number 1597 when you call and talk to me, that way you will know that it is I who is talking to you. I will wait for your call on this line, which is absolutely secure."

"Okay I will." Ralph followed Sydney's instructions, but first he checked out Worth Industries on line. The general number on line matched the number the caller gave Ralph. When Ralph called the secretary, the operator identified the number as Worth Industries and asked what person or division he wanted to reach. When he asked for Sydney Worth, the operator asked for his security code. Ralph told the operator 1597 and the operator patched him into Sydney's private line. When Sydney's now familiar voice came on the line, Ralph finally decided Sydney Worth spoke to him.

"Alright Mr. Worth. I now believe it is you. What can I do for you?"

"I want you to work for me. Officially, you will be employed as a Vice President of Secure Network, but that is just a front. I own the company. In fact, I bought it so I could employ people like you. "

"What do you want me to do?"

"Even though this network is secure, I need to discuss my needs with you in person. I will have a private jet waiting for you at Executive Airport tomorrow at 3PM. They will bring you to New York where my limousine will take you to my private office. Oh and just so you will take the trip, the job will pay triple what you earned as a Navy Seal. You will also have access to a very large expense account and be paid large bonuses for the projects you complete. Most importantly, I will make sure you have the one thing you want more than anything else."

"What is that?"

"Cindy. The Illinois Department of Children and Family Services never had any intention of allowing you to adopt Cindy. The FBI talked them out of it. I, however, have made arrangements to override these objections. One week after you sign with me, the adoption will be approved."

Ralph could say very little for several minutes. Only mildly interested in the job until Sydney brought up the Cindy adoption, he now had to take this job offer seriously. Ralph never would have known that the FBI trashed his adoption attempt. If Ralph ever wanted to have Cindy as a part of his life, he would have to do as the man asked. Ralph had no doubt that Sydney could make the adoption happen. He gave the only answer he could to Mr. Worth.

"I will be there. I don' really have any choice."

"Good I will see you tomorrow."

Twelve hours later, Ralph sat down in Sydney Worth's immense office overlooking the Hudson River. After some brief introductions, Sydney launched into his carefully rehearsed speech.

"Before we begin, this office is absolutely secure. My professionals swept it for listening devices thirty minutes ago. It is one of the few places I can talk with candor and without fear someone will find out what I said.

"Good Mr. Worth. Security is always an issue with me."

"Okay. Mr. Tager I'm going to tell you a story. I think it will be somewhat familiar to you. I grew up in a lower middle class house in Queens. My father worked on a garbage truck for the city. At an early age, I showed remarkable mathematical ability. Some people labeled me a genius. Through hard work, I obtained a scholarship to Columbia University and then to Columbia Business School where I obtained my MBA. While in business school, I met and married Sarah, the love of my life. She also attended Columbia. Beautiful, funny, brilliant and above all a wonderful caring person, Sarah lighted my world. When I went off to Wall Street to earn my fortune she always sat beside me. She worked at the Metropolitan Museum of Art to help us make ends meet. In my rise to prominence, there were many times when I thought

I would fail or even have to declare bankruptcy. These times of great stress barely affected Sarah. She merely said that as long as we had each other things would turn out all right. If we had to declare bankruptcy we would merely start again. Well as you can see I didn't fail. In fact, I succeeded beyond my wildest dreams but only because she stood there beside me. Without her I wouldn't have made it."

"Then Rebecca came along and my world became even brighter. The spitting image of her mother, Rebecca brought both of us great happiness. I woke up each day thinking that I must be the happiest man in the world. Then, quite suddenly two years ago, my wife developed bad headaches. The doctors I retained, the best money could buy, diagnosed Sarah with brain cancer.

"Despite the expenditure of enormous amounts of money on treatments, she died six months later. I felt like killing myself, but since I still had Rebecca, I didn't. But I did become somewhat obsessed with her safety. I hired a security firm to watch her very carefully. I feared someone would kidnap her and take her away from me. For a year everything appeared to be normal. I missed Sarah terribly but as long as I had Rebecca I made it through each day.

"Then what I feared most happened. Someone kidnapped Rebecca, as it turned out the security man assigned to protect her. He demanded $20mm as a ransom and as proof that he had her; he put my screaming daughter on the phone. Every night I go to sleep I hear my daughter screaming as she did on that phone call. I dropped the $20mm at the designated site and the former guard picked up the money some time later. The FBI followed and arrested him, but he didn't have Rebecca. He had turned her over to another man who paid him $10,000 for her. The arrested man gave the police the man's name but no such man existed. The kidnapper mentioned that the man who paid for Rebecca acted strangely. He thought he might be a pedophile. Desperate to help the FBI and the local police as they promised to help reduce his sentence if he cooperated, the kidnapper offered to help in any way he could. After being shown a list of known sex offenders, he identified Tom Thompson as the person who had Rebecca but at the same time said that he couldn't be absolutely sure, as the man had changed his appearance. Before Tom Thompson could be brought in for questioning, the kidnapper caught a bullet in the head while in the company of US Marshalls. Tom Thompson probably did it, he had been a sniper in the army, but no evidence linked him or anyone else to the crime. Then the unthinkable happened. The battered, raped and tortured body of my ten-year old Rebecca turned up in a city park. The police arrested Tom Thompson for the crime, but without the kidnapper to testify, law enforcement had to drop their case against him. They had no other evidence linking him to the crime.

"In the six months since my daughter died, I have been consumed by rage and revenge. It is the only reason I have to live. At first, I thought hiring an assassin to kill Tom Thompson would serve my needs but I soon realized that wouldn't be enough. Tom Thompson needed to suffer as my daughter suffered. In fact, as I researched who could do this work for me I realized that the mere torture and killing of Tom Thompson would also be insufficient. I needed to do more. I needed to kill and torture every deviant sexual offender out there who tortures, sexually assaults and kills kids. I needed to do this to save other parents like me from the torment of having to see their children abused and murdered in this way. I needed to honor my Rebecca's memory by stopping these monsters once and for all. When I refined my research with these new criteria your name immediately topped my list. You have the training and the skills to do the job and best of all you have the motivation. Well I have talked long enough. What do you think?"

"Well as you must know I had similar experiences. A violent sex offender killed my wife and tortured and raped my young daughter before killing her. Like you I'm consumed by rage. I thought my monster's death would bring me that relief but it did not. Unlike you I found Cindy who suffered as I suffered. In my mind, she has already started to become my little girl. When I look at her, I feel that the job that needs to be done is unfinished. Of course what you are doing and what you are asking me to do is illegal even criminal. As a Seal I did these kinds of things all the time but I did them outside this country, against our enemies and with the blessing of the Navy. This is different. How do I know that you aren't just trying to set me up for the FBI? I am sure that you do a lot of government contracting. They could be recording this conversation and waiting to arrest me."

"Do you really think I care about a hundred million in government contracts that I probably wouldn't lose anyway? I would gladly lose this money and more if I just could get one night of decent sleep. I have to avenge my daughter's death or my rage will kill me. Look as an act of good faith; I will push through Cindy's adoption papers. If I don't, she will be haunting me along with my daughter. When Cindy is your legal daughter, then you will know that you can trust me."

"Okay if Cindy's adoption goes through, I will sit down with you and discuss your offer further. You have my word as a Seal on that."

"That is good enough for me. My secretary will show you out. I look forward to our future discussions."

As Ralph left Sydney's office a smile formed on Sydney's face. Sydney had his man, the sword of his revenge. He and Ralph would drench the world in those deviants' blood. As long as he had breath, he would kill and torture them. When death finally took him, he would be able to tell his daughter in the afterlife that he had stopped all the monsters out there that he could.

For a week after his visit with Sydney, Ralph's Seal units experienced chaos. The Seals leaving including Ralph had no desire to risk life and limb on missions. They focused on their new lives not their old ones. So they refused to go on any missions in their time remaining on the job. Since 80% of the Seals remained on active duty, they should have by simple mathematics had the ability to put 80% of their eight teams into the field. Yet, the Seals remaining had the least experience. They could only muster three teams for field assignments. Three additional teams did go into the field but everyone knew that putting them there risked their lives and their missions. Ralph fumed at the danger faced by his Seals but he had no sympathy for those in charge. If they wanted better performance, those paper pushers could take on the missions. They could dodge AK 47's, rocket propelled grenades, handguns, knives, swords, and yes even baseball bats. They would also know how it felt to go to a place where the insurgents or native soldiers wanted to kill you and the rest of the population hated you and would probably kill you too if they felt they had a chance to do so. One more week of being a Navy Seal then he would leave these bureaucrats forever.

While busy during the day winding up his Seal work, Ralph spent his nights thinking about Sydney's job offer. To do this job he would need heavy logistical support, intelligence, and non- traceable weapons. Without question, the FBI would be hunting him, while the deviants of this world, would find a way to organize and protect them from the Pay Back he would become. There would be risks, but he had lived his whole life taking risks. This wouldn't be any different. Still if Cindy did not become his daughter, he would not accept Sydney's offer. The extra money didn't really mean anything to him. He would have enough to live on accepting his other job offers. Also, the satisfaction Ralph would gain from killing more of these monsters didn't justify the risks. He had already tortured and killed the monster that took his wife and daughter. If Cindy did become his daughter, he would accept the job. He would owe Sydney for giving him a new daughter to love. Also, each time Ralph performed a job he would avenge not only his dead daughter and wife but also his adopted daughter as well. And too, Ralph would be able to put a great deal of money away to take care of Cindy. After what she had suffered Cindy deserved some of the comforts money could buy her. So in the end, the Illinois Department of Children and Family Services, IDCFS, would decide whether Pay Back came to life once more or not.

Seattle

Seven days after Ralph left Sydney's office and on his final day as a Seal, IDCFS called and told Ralph that his adoption of Cindy had been approved. Ralph celebrated. The decision had been made. He knew now what he would do with the rest of his life.

The next several months went by quickly for Ralph. He left the Navy something Ralph thought he would never do. Cindy came to live with him and his mother and Ralph went to work for Secure Network at the princely sum of $250,000 per year. So far, Ralph had consulted with a number of local companies on their security protocols, legitimate work, which he found himself very qualified to do. He also bought a nice home in Lake Bluff, a wealthy suburb with fine schools near the base. While Ralph did not personally care whether they lived in Lake Bluff, he wanted the very best schools for his new daughter.

Ralph spent all his free time with Cindy. He read books with her, played games and sports with her, took her to concerts and plays and taught her self-defense. A black belt in ten oriental fighting disciplines, Ralph wanted Cindy to have a fighting chance if another monster came for her. Ralph constantly worried about Cindy's safety. Ralph also spent thirty minutes just before Cindy went to bed just loving her. He kissed and hugged Cindy and went over the day's events with her. Cindy gratefully returned Ralph's affection, even climbing into bed with him on nights when her nightmares became too stressful for her to handle. Each day that passed Cindy and Ralph loved each other more. Then, three months after Ralph's new life started, a package arrived at his house. The package contained detailed instructions and information on his first hit as Pay Back.

Ralph's first assignment, Tom Thompson, killed his benefactor's daughter, Rebecca. A former Army Green Beret and Sniper, Tom had earned the right to be respected and feared. His apartment in Seattle would be a fortress. There would be physical traps and electronic surveillance. A frontal assault on his apartment would be suicidal. The man would pick Ralph off before he came near. Ralph needed to intercept the man in the open. Using the same blowgun he had with Ted, he would drug Thompson and follow him home. Then he would do his boss's bidding: cut him fifty times with a knife and remove his private parts.

Consulting with Microsoft only in the morning, Ralph would locate and kill Thompson after lunch. His briefing sheets informed him that Tom had taken on a new identity as Bill Lawson, a mild bespectacled operator of an ice cream truck. With a few inquiries, Ralph discovered the probable route of Thompson's ice cream truck. He located the truck moving through a wealthy Seattle neighborhood at around 4 pm.

Thompson's actions of course made sense. He hunted children. His truck attracted his targets to him. Thompson would be in a position to select his target without raising suspicions. When he had his target, Thompson would rape, torture and kill him or her to satisfy the evil inside of him. Yet as a former Green Beret, Tom should have recognized that his cover also made him an easy target. Ralph could approach him as a customer without arousing any suspicions.

Ralph patiently waited for the right time to approach Tom Thompson as he finally parked his ice cream truck for an extended period in a nice park. With Seattle almost as far north as you could go in the continental US, dusk came early and quickly on this Friday in early March. With alarm, Ralph noticed that a pretty twelve-year old girl purchased an ice cream cone and started to munch on it as she walked away from the truck. From his hiding place, Ralph could tell the park had no one else in it. After walking about twenty feet, the girl began to sway a little, clutching her stomach. Moments later she fell to the ground. Tom placed drugs in her cone. Ralph had his chance. Moving quickly and quietly, Ralph moved within range. As expected Tom left the truck and headed straight for the girl, but somewhat against his training he concentrated so intently on the young girl that he did not notice Ralph move near him. When Ralph moved close enough, after putting on his surgical gloves he always wore for missions, he quickly shot Tom in the neck with a drug dart. After the dart struck him, Tom whirled, firing three shots from his Beretta at the place from which the dart cane. Ralph, however, already hit the ground and rolled to his right as Tom fired. The bullets didn't come anywhere near Ralph. Tom continued to scan the terrain until he located Ralph but in the seconds it took him to do so, the powerful fast acting drug began to work. Tom fired his gun again but the bullets went way wide as his body began to shake. The highly classified drug attacked the cerebellum in a way that left the victim without any muscle coordination. The drug also quickly broke down in the blood leaving no trace. Ralph quickly walked up to Tom, who by this time could no longer control, any part of his body, knocked away his gun and dragged him to the truck.

After binding and gagging Tom in the back of the ice cream truck, Ralph carefully removed the dart from Tom's back and placed it in his disposal bag. Ralph then quickly retrieved the truck keys from Tom's pocket and drove the ice cream truck away from the park. After driving to a deserted factory area a few miles away, which Ralph scouted earlier, Ralph parked the truck, pulled out his river knife and approached a shaking and gyrating Tom. On the way to the deserted area, Ralph called the police on one of his throwaway phones and told them that a young girl lay unconscious in the park he just left. As Tom moaned and looked at him wildly, Ralph cut away his clothes. Following Sydney's instructions, Ralph said simply and plainly,

"This is for Rebecca."

Then without a hint of emotion or pause, Ralph cleanly and quickly cut off Tom's private parts and placed them in Tom's shaking hand. He found that his technique already improved from the first time. Seconds later, Ralph made shallow cut after shallow cut on Tom's naked body.

Within a matter of minutes, Ralph cut him over fifty times. Tom tried to respond but he could not do so with a gag placed firmly in his mouth. He could only mumble and shriek in a barely recognizable way.

Finished with his assignment, Ralph drove the ice cream truck to a deserted street area near where he left his rental car. During the ride, Tom passed out from a loss of blood. Unlike last time, Ralph did not cauterize the area between Tom's legs. Leaving his Pay Back outfit on, Ralph left the truck and walked a few blocks. Finding a very large tree at the end of a deserted block, Ralph disappeared behind it. He watched the area carefully. When he saw no one, Ralph re-emerged wearing a business suit he used earlier in the day. Ralph placed his Pay Back suit along with his weapons and bulletproof vest in his disposal bag, which he now carried over his shoulder. Reentering and starting his car, Ralph drove to another part of the city. There, Ralph found a dumpster in a secluded alley. He removed the bag from this trunk, placed the bag in the dumpster, re-entered his car and returned to his hotel. With Sydney's backing, Ralph no longer had to worry about the cost of replacing these items. He would have new ones available for the next mission.

Roberto "Bob" Prandini, a tough good looking Seattle detective, saw the worst of human behavior and developed a wry sense of humor to deal with it. Now in his mid forties, Bob an avid weightlifter, Martial artist and runner still had a rock hard physique. He had never lost a fight on the job. He knew that staying fit might very well be the difference as to whether he lived or died. Not everyone Bob tried to arrest warmed to the idea.

Bob examined what remained of Tom Thompson, the real identity of the corpse in the ice cream truck. With his cell phone, Bob sent a picture of the victim's fingerprints to the national database. When the rap sheet came back on this guy, the vicious torture he suffered made sense. A dangerous child sexual predator and murderer, Mr. Thompson finally pissed off someone who knew how to fight back. Justice prevailed if not in the way society wanted it to happen. If this monster went after one of his kids, he would have no problem killing him even though he probably wouldn't torture him this way. Simple death would suffice. Still, Bob had to admit that once these pictures and information hit the media, Seattle's sexual predators would be lying low for a while. His detective friends in the sexual crimes unit would be happy campers while they did so. After today, the children of Seattle would be a little safer.

Still, Bob had a job to do. He needed to investigate this crime and find the killer of the man in the ice cream truck. His bosses wouldn't give him a pass. They hated vigilantes. Bob's phone rang. Fellow murder detective Hilda O'Malley, every bit as tough as Bob, came on the line. Bob had been thinking about asking the attractive strawberry blond on a date. Bob had finally stopped grieving over the death of his first wife from cancer. He needed a woman in his life, but still worried about a workplace romance. Bob smiled as Hilda spoke.

"Hey Bob your nutless wonder sold something other than ice cream earlier in the day. Squad got a call that a twelve-year old girl passed out in a nearby park. They found the girl, all right. She had been drugged. They think your dead pervert put the drug in her ice cream. Some residents who had been there earlier confirmed that the ice cream truck we found parked there for an hour in the late afternoon. Looks like our victim drugged the girl and planned on taking her when our killer showed. He got pissed and took him out."

"Well I can't really ask our vic if this is what happened. If I did, his voice would be so high I wouldn't be able to understand him."

"Very funny Bob. I don't care if this perp or vic or whatever the hell you want to call him lost his equipment but it would be a real shame if you lost yours."

"Well my equipment is just fine. In fact, if you will go out with me Saturday night, I'll show you."

"Are you asking me out on a date? Well it's about time. Even though you look at me all the time, I was beginning to think you liked guys."

"Me a fruit-no way. I have been fantasizing about you ever since you first walked into the office. So how about 7? I have a nice little Italian place I'd like to take you."

"Yeah okay, but don't think I'm easy. As tough as I am, I'm still a girl and want to be treated that way."

"Don't worry. I'm Italian. We know how to romance girls. It's in our blood."

"Well I'm half Irish and have a devastating right hook if you get fresh."

"No problem. I'm not that kind of guy."

"Okay Italian Stallion, we will see about your approach but you still haven't said anything about my theory."

"Well it doesn't quite fit, the part about a guy just passing by and taking out Thompson. Thompson was a badass Green Beret and sniper-- one tough son of a bitch. Whoever took him out had to be equally tough. An ordinary person wouldn't have a chance against him. I suppose a pro might have been walking by at just the right moment but I think it is much more likely someone hired a pro to take him out. A guy like Thompson probably pissed off a number of people in pursuing his sick ass ways."

"Yeah that makes sense. If you're talking about a pro, there isn't going to be a hell of a lot of evidence."

"Yeah forensics isn't done yet but so far we have nothing. I'm going to knock on all the doors around here. Maybe somebody saw something. Then I'm going to head back to the barn and look up all of Thompson's victims. I bet one of them is going to stand out. When are you heading back?"

"I don't know. Jerry my partner is taking a bunch of sick days before he transfers out to financial crimes. He says he is sick of homicide. Claims that he can't make lieutenant here. I can't say I'm sorry to see him leave. He has grabbed my ass a couple of times lately. I almost filed a complaint against him. He knows I'm pissed about it. Maybe that is why he is leaving. Any way with him gone, I have twice the work to do."

"Well at least Jerry has good taste. By the way, if we get together, you won't have to worry about anyone grabbing you anymore. If they do, I will punch their lights out. No one treats my woman that way. Anyway, I'm glad Jerry is going. Maybe now we can become partners. Manuel my partner has been weird ever since he took that slug in the shoulder. Lost his nerve, doesn't want to chase perps anymore. I think the lieutenant is going to make him a desk jockey. Lieutenant has already asked me about it. I'll put in for you as my new partner if you put in for me."

"Yeah I hoped you would. Everyone in the barn knows Manuel has lost it, happens to the best of us. I would love to partner up with you. I know you will have my back, but that doesn't mean you can try and take advantage of me Saturday."

"No I told you that all I'm going to do is romance you and I meant it. See ya beautiful. Can't wait till Saturday."

"Yeah me too."

A week later, Bob sat at his desk daydreaming. He and Hilda got together Saturday night and had been together ever since. Turned out she loved him as much as he loved her. He would never have guessed. Bob hadn't been this happy in years. He just wanted to spend every moment of every day in her arms. Bob's cell phone quickly brought him back to reality. He picked it up and gruffly replied.

"Prandini"

"This is FBI Special Agent Malcolm Rodgers. I understand you have been working on the Thompson case. Let's cooperate. I have information you want and I'm hoping you got something I can use."

"Is this one of those cooperating with bureau things, where I tell you everything and you promise me something but give me nothing?"

"No, the more people who go after this vigilante guy the better."

"Okay if you go first, I will play. I just have had some bad experiences in the past."

"Fair enough--this is what I got. A pervert named Ted Wiggle killed the wife of a very tough Navy Seal named Ralph Tager in the process of raping and killing his daughter. After the police arrested Wiggle for the crime but put him back on the street because of a lack of evidence, Wiggle turned up dead in his own warehouse with his private parts in his hand. At the time, Wiggle had raped and tortured a little girl named Cindy, but hadn't killed her yet. A guy in a mask, who killed Wiggle, dropped her off at the hospital. She claimed she couldn't recognize him. The Chicago media really played up the incident. It generated a lot of heat for the FBI and local police. A few months ago, Ralph Tager adopted Cindy. The state's Children and Family Service Department allowed the adoption to go through, even though we told the state that we suspected Tager of being the masked man. We think someone put heat on the Children and Family Services Department to allow the adoption but we don't know who did so. Whoever it was, they must have had a lot of juice. By the way, this guy Wiggle was a tough guy-weapons expert, vet and body builder, but from what we know about him not in the same league as Tager. Despite months of effort, we produced no evidence connecting Tager to the murder and mutilation. Yet my gut tells me he is the man in the mask."

"Yeah sounds like the same guy. Our own pervert, a nasty guy named Tom Thompson, took on a new identity as a seller of ice cream out of a truck. After the service, he apparently did some accounting work and saved up the money to buy the truck. The day he met his maker, Thompson sold a twelve-year old girl a cone laced with a sleeping drug. We think when he left his truck to pick up the girl a masked man jumped him. A woman with a house facing the park saw a masked man there but did not see the actual incident. When we found Thompson, he was tied up in the back of his truck with his private parts in his hand. He also had over fifty small cuts on his body. Some of his skin fell of when we touched him. By the way, this guy Thompson sounds like your guy, an army sniper and Green Beret, real tough son of a bitch. We found a gun he apparently owned that had been fired but other than the torture marks and the loss of his parts; he shows no other signs of injury. We suspect drugs made him defenseless and are testing for them. Also, I looked up a list of Thompson's known and suspected victims. I didn't find anyone named Tager on the list, but there is one guy of interest: Sydney Worth the billionaire. Thompson allegedly kidnapped, tortured, raped and killed Rebecca his daughter."

"Bingo that's it. It all fits. Tager went to work for Secure Networks, one of Worth's companies. Worth has the kind of muscle to push through Cindy's adoption. Sounds like they made a deal. Also, I forgot to tell you. On behalf of Worth's company, Tager consults for Microsoft. He stayed at the Seattle Ritz at the time of the murder and met with Microsoft employees."

"Well that is great but we still have to tie Tager to this murder. I'll talk to Microsoft and then I will go over to the Ritz and see what I can find. By the way, do you know how Tager got around? The Ritz is about five miles from the crime scene."

"No not yet. We have his flights but no record of a rental car. Someone must have lent him a car or drove him. I doubt he took a cab but you should check it. I don't suppose you have any more ID's close to the scene?"

"Nah just the woman who saw a guy in a mask from a distance. That is all we have so far. The little girl, who the pervert drugged, recovered from the drugs but she doesn't remember seeing anything. Maybe a picture of Tager and a description of the car will help. We will see. Anyway the information you just gave me is a big break. At least now, I know what I am after."

"Yeah me too. The two of us working together could actually make this arrest happen."

"A good thought but we still have a long way to go. I don't think this guy left much for us to find. I guess this cooperation thing is not so bad after all."

"Yep but I agree the celebrating might have to wait for us to find more evidence. Theories only go so far. "

A Meeting

Ralph Tager sat in an empty dark warehouse, waiting for Sydney. He didn't like being here but Sydney insisted. Ralph could feel a man walk to his table and sit down. The new arrival's voice reached out to him as a faint light illuminated their area.

"I'm sorry I arranged for this meeting but I just had to talk to you in person. I have to know what Thompson looked like near the end."

"I can understand that. Revenge needs a little personal treatment to be at all satisfying. Well, at first, Thompson, looked like a soldier, badly affected by the drug I gave him but still defiant. I had a gag in his mouth so he couldn't say anything or draw attention to the truck. Then when I sliced his private parts off his expression changed. First I saw shock, then terror. As I began cutting him, you could see the pain on his face. Then he passed out from loss of blood. He died a short time later. His blood covered the inside of the truck. That is about it. Death is never pretty."

"Great, terrific. Thompson suffered, that is what really counts. I'm in your debt, more than you will ever know. I might even get a good night's sleep for a change. By the way, I put 200 grand in your Swiss account. I could never pay you enough for what you did but the money out to help you take care of Cindy."

"Okay that is good. So what do we do next? Both of our monsters are dead."

"Well as I told you I wanted to keep on killing the monsters for Rebecca, but maybe I need some time to think about it. There are thousands of them out there. We can't kill them all. It 's really law enforcement's job not ours. Also, the more monsters that are killed the more enemies we will make. More law enforcement on top of what is already out there will pursue us; the sexual predators we hunt will be more wary and better armed. Heck they might even become organized against us. They already talk on the Internet through codes to hide themselves. Even though we are both good at what we do, sooner or later our enemies will probably either catch or kill us. You of course run the greatest risks." Sydney said.

"Yeah you're right. As Seals, every time we went on missions we knew there was a chance we would be arrested, captured, tortured, injured or killed. Even though our planning and training were superb and our support system terrific, you learned very quickly that random events took place despite your best efforts. Sometimes things would just go wrong. Real life is not like the movies. The bad guys win sometimes. At the end of the day, the risk each Seal took had to be personally worth it to them. That is the question we will both have to answer. Is it worth the risk?"

"Honestly right now I don't know. I will contact you in a month with what I want to do. We need to let the furor over the last mission die down a little. With two incidents out there our enemies, the police and the media will begin to see a pattern. When they do, the will put the heat on you and maybe me as well."

"A month then. I will have my answer. If I feel some heat I will let you know."

"Okay but let's limit these private meetings as much as we can."

"I couldn't agree more. I didn't want to come to this meeting in the first place."

"Wait a minute Sydney, before you leave you should know about some of my suspicions about what has happened. I lost my Seal Team my brothers in an Afghanistan ambush. As a Lieutenant Commander I gave up the day-to-day leadership of my team, which is why I am still alive. Obviously a traitor revealed their arrival location, but I haven't been able to find this traitor. Worse yet, no one in the service seems interested in looking for him or her. Then a mere two weeks later a sexual predator kills my wife and daughter. These two terrible events happening so close together seems like a plan directed at me. The predator I killed, Ted Wiggle served in Special Forces. He would have known that such a rape and murder would motivate the entire Seal organization to pursue him. Why would he pick on a Seal and his brothers who could fight back? It cost him his life. The only explanation is that someone put him up to it and promised to protect him, but who would do this and why is a mystery. In your case, your actual abductor gave your daughter to a predator, a far different situation."

"I don't know Ralph. You can drive yourself crazy following conspiracy theories. It could have just been bad luck. Ted Wiggle may have killed your family to challenge you, the ultimate macho challenge. Sometimes the simple answers are the correct ones." Sydney replied.

"Okay Sydney, you might be right. Contact me when you make up your mind. There are more Ted Wiggles out there waiting for divine judgment."

"Yes there are."

Two weeks later, Ralph sat in his living room reading some alarm system technical manuals when the doorbell rang. Ralph often spent time at home preparing for his trips to companies that needed his consulting work. He planned on taking a flight to New York the following day to consult with GE on an upgrade to its current laboratory alarm systems. Cindy probably sat in class this very moment. His mom paced the local grocery store. Ralph stretching his legs a little went to answer the door. As trained, he carefully examined his caller through the peephole in the door. As he did not recognize the big man on his doorstep, he called through the door.

"Who are you?"

"My name is Bob Prandini. Here is my badge. I'm a Seattle detective investigating the murder and torture of Tom Thompson two weeks ago. I understand you were in Seattle at the time. I need to ask you some questions. Can I come in?" Bob showed Ralph his badge through the window.

"No, I will come out. I don't allow strangers in my house."

Ralph stepped out of his house and shook Bob's hand. Then said,

"Okay, ask your questions."

"Well, were you in Seattle the 13 through the 15th and did you stay at the Ritz?"

"Yes".

"On the morning of the fourteenth, you attended a meeting at Microsoft."

"Yes".

"Where were you on the afternoon of the 14th?"

"I was in my room."

"Can anyone verify that?"

"I made a few phone calls on my cell and had room service deliver some food around 4:30 but beyond that no."

"What were you doing in your room?"

"I was preparing materials for my 15th morning meeting at Microsoft."

"Did you leave your room?"

"Not that I recall."

"Did you know a Tom Thompson?"

"No never heard of the guy until you spoke his name through my door."

"Did you kill Mr. Thompson?"

"Come on get serious, a guy I didn't even know--of course not. You flew 2000 miles to make these ridiculous accusations. I answered your questions. We have nothing more to discuss."

"I am not through asking you questions, Mr. Tager."

"Yes you are. You have no jurisdiction here. You are trespassing on my property. As a courtesy I answered your questions. I don't have any more time for your games. Good day."

Ralph moved back inside his house and attempted to close the door. Bob wouldn't let him. Ralph's voice took on a hard edge.

"If you don't get out of my doorway, I will call the Lake Bluff police who do have jurisdiction here and have you arrested. Now get off my property!"

"Okay I will but this is not the last time we'll talk. I can assure you we will continue this conversation if you ever come back to Seattle. "

Bob reluctantly moved out of the doorway and the door closed in his face seconds later. He blew the interview by being too confrontational. He might have asked some other questions and obtained an impression from the responses. Now he would get no more out of Ralph. Unlike in Seattle, Bob had no right to take Ralph in for questioning and even there he probably didn't have enough to take Ralph to the station house. Nothing he had put Ralph anywhere near the murder scene. Still in his gut, Bob knew Ralph killed Thompson. He just needed to prove it.

For Ralph the rest of the month passed with little fanfare. He soon put the incident with the Seattle Cop out of his head. He liked his job and the travel involved. Ralph felt that his knowledge of security helped his clients better protect their people, their information and their assets. The President of the Company Wilbur Sieges had even remarked that Ralph already earned his salary. The clients really liked him and his work. For Ralph, this complicated his thoughts about Pay Back. He could make a very good life with Cindy and perhaps a woman he might meet without having to resort to the torture and murder of violent sexual offenders and pedophiles. Ralph felt his mission days should be coming to an end.

Yet, Ralph had other thoughts too. Every time he looked at Cindy, Ralph saw his own daughter and the terrible suffering she had to endure and of course Cindy's own suffering. How could he leave the monsters out there to do more of this to other children and not do anything about it? Ralph had no good answer to this question.

Also, Cindy continued to have problems from her rape and torture. While now the doctors believed Cindy could have children, when she met new men, Cindy would visibly flinch. Her reaction to boys, girls and women showed a certain reticence as well. Her wary attitude made social interactions at school very difficult. Unlike normal children of her age, she did not have friends over to the house or visit other children's homes. Cindy instead lavished all her attention on Ralph. She constantly hugged and kissed Ralph and insisted on sitting on his lap whenever she could. Also, now every night at home, Cindy crawled into bed with him. She said she could not sleep unless he lay next to her. Otherwise her nightmares kept her up at night. While Cindy's affection did not appear to be sexual, Ralph knew that puberty would change the situation. The ways things stood, Cindy could never experience normal teenage years. Ralph also worried how he would react to a fully mature Cindy. She grew more beautiful by the day. Cindy would almost certainly become a gorgeous woman. He loved her very much. If somehow sexual feelings worked their way into their relationship, Ralph feared the damage it might do to her already delicate condition. She needed intensive psychiatric help. Ralph provided that help to Cindy but at some point the cost of it would become an issue particularly if he had to fund more sessions. The high salary he received at Secure Networks and the cash payments Sydney placed in his Swiss account for missions provided the kind of resources he needed to absorb these costs. If Ralph refused to do any more missions and as a result had to leave Secure Networks for a lower paying job, he might not be able to make ends meet.

Ralph also needed Cindy to reach a point where he could date women. She reacted badly to any suggestions he made along these lines. Cindy worried out loud that any woman he might date would take Ralph away from her. While Ralph tried to reassure her on this point, Cindy refused to support any dating he might do. Despite his male needs, Ralph had as a result not dated another woman since his beloved wife died.

While all these factors might force him to go on missions again, Ralph worried that he might be killed or injured. As a Seal, he had always calmly accepted this risk, but what would happen to Cindy if he couldn't help her anymore. He had no answers to this question. Whatever decision he made, Ralph had to help Cindy find a normal life as a woman. Ted Wiggle had already destroyed his wife and daughter. He wouldn't allow him to destroy Cindy from his grave.

The Predator Network

Pete Ramirez, of both Hispanic and Anglo Saxon heritage, had from puberty obsessed over young girls. He could think of little else. At first he only fondled them but as he grew older he increasingly used them to fulfill his sexual fantasies. In order to do this, he had to abduct, hide and eventually kill them. To do any of this on the street or in someone else's space led in his experience to arrest and prosecution. Of course, his activities attracted law enforcement. As a youngster, he had been arrested and convicted for sexual crimes, but as Pete grew older he learned how to avoid the law. Possessed of a brilliant organized mind, he meticulously planned and executed the abduction and murder of these children. In the years since he left prison at age 18, the police had not even come close to arresting him. To support himself and his obsession, Pete did free lance software programming work. He had a particular talent for this work and made large amounts of money at it. Best of all, Pete could perform the work from his elaborate home computer equipment. To pursue his sexual passions, the fewer people he had to interact with the better.

Pete developed one more interest outside of his sexual predation and computer work: assembling a network of like-minded sexual predators. With his computer knowledge and expertise, Pete erected an almost untraceable web site. He also used codes to mask the conversations taking place. Pete carefully scrutinized each new member of the site to make sure they belonged in the brotherhood. After exhaustive vetting, he provided this predator with the sign up code. On several occasions, Pete caught law enforcement trying to use the site. In each case, he blocked them. Even so Pete insisted that no member ever admit to any criminal behavior and that all conversations be phrased as hypothetical's. Pete learned an enormous amount from his site: from techniques to enhance his sexual enjoyment to ways to minimize exposure during abduction, incidents which the site called taking home the package.

The site now had 512 members and in code adopted the name, the Hunter's Fantasy. Pete spent at least two hours a day working and maintaining the site as well as participating in the discussions. Over its two years of existence, Pete came to identify many of the members through their discussions. Although pictures could not be uploaded to the site, Pete still pictured many of the members in his mind. When Day Rider logged on, he knew exactly with whom he spoke.

The discussion today and indeed for many months concerned Pay Back, a name the papers gave Ralph following the Waukegan mission. He threatened the predator community in a way that no law enforcement agency or any relative of a package ever had. As time passed, it became clear to all the members of Hunter's Fantasy that Hard One, believed to be Ted Wiggle and Puff the Magic Dragon, believed to be Tom Thompson had been tortured, mutilated and killed by this vigilante. As long as Pay Back still lived the members of the predator community would never be safe. Potent One spoke.

"We have to eliminate this hypothetical Pay Back guy. I'm scared to even look at a cute package, thinking some GI Joe is going to walk up to me and cut my essentials off. I haven't had a package in several months. This can't go on. What is the plan?"

"Well I hope you noticed that this hypothetical Pay Back guy if he exists is one tough son of a bitch. Hard One and Puff were probably the best warriors in the Fantasy. If any of us confront this hypothetical Pay Back guy, we can expect to lose a bunch of parts." Big One wrote.

"No we can't seek this hypothetical guy on our own. Like these complicated modern cars we drive, you hire someone to work on them. You don't do it yourself. The same applies here. We need to hire a hypothetical expert for the hypothetical Pay Back. I figure we need about 100 k. We don't need a 99 cent blue light special here. He has to be the best of the best if he exists. Also, not everyone likes what we do and us. Not all the hypothetical people we may try to hire may want the job. A fat fee will help us find the hypothetically right guy. To raise that kind of cash, each of us hypothetically is going to have to put in a thousand, really pretty cheap when you think of the alternative. If you are in, respond and transfer your money into the hypothetical special account. I'm transferring the hypothetical money as I speak, putting my money were my mouth is." Day Rider, Peter's screen name, said.

"Hey do you know the hypothetical name of this guy," Potent One asked.

"Yeah the papers put out a hypothetical name when Hard One had his problem. If there is a guy to seek, he is it."

"Good enough for me. The papers are our best friends. They give out information that we would otherwise not have. I guess they are grateful. We sell a lot of newspapers for them," Puff joked.

"Yeah good enough for me too, but we haven't discussed Hard One's package," Big One said.

"Yeah the papers identified a hypothetical package. When Pay Back leaves, the hypothetical package may need a new home." Day Rider replied.

"Yeah you're right. Even though this is a used hypothetical package, it is supposed to be a nice hypothetical package. Anyway, we need to take this hypothetical package in honor of Hard One," Vibrate a new participant added.

"Why don't we talk about it after the Pay Back leaves? We all want to honor Hard One's memory." Day Rider replied.

The Fantasy all agreed with Day Rider, many e-mailing their thoughts but the e-mails made it clear too many members wanted the Pay Back's package. They couldn't all have her. Pete would have to figure out how this would be handled when the time came. Still in the next several hours, fifty more members e-mailed back saying they made a hypothetical donation. By the next day, Day Rider had the 100 k he needed in his special Swiss account. He started looking on his computer for a hit man who could do the job.

Shortly after the Fantasy discussion and three months following his first meeting with his boss, Ralph walked quietly to a single chair in the near darkness of another lonely warehouse and patiently waited. Ten minutes later Sydney's voice reached out for him.

"Pay Back as you might expect I want to keep going but in a different way. I hired another Seal and sent him after a target. Since your wife and daughter died, you've attracted too much attention. I put a big bull's eye on your back and endangered Cindy. I want you visible in another place when this warrior strikes. The perverts and law enforcement will start to question whom the real Pay Back is just as we want them to do. Still, I want you involved. You are still my best warrior. If you are up to it, I will call on you again. "

"You anticipated my problems with our arrangement. The papers already fingered me for the Wiggle killing. If the perverts have any sense they will hire someone to kill me. Your new assassin may throw them off the scent. He can also eliminate more perverts, a good thing by any measure. Still, I wouldn't care if the perverts hired someone if it were not for Cindy. I accepted my death long ago. Each day I live I feel I'm cheating Mr. Death a little. But if I'm killed, no one will be there to look after Cindy. The perverts will likely target her. I can't stand this thought. As a result, I have to undertake my own mission: hunt down and kill my potential assassin before he kills me. I need your help for that. Also, I want you to promise me that you will protect Cindy if the perverts kill me. If you make those promises, I will kill whatever perverts you want me to kill."

"It's a deal. I will protect Cindy no matter what happens. I wouldn't be able to live with myself unless I did. I owe it to Rebecca. As to help tracking down any would be assassin, I will give you whatever help you need. This is war. A would be assassin is as much a target as any pervert. In fact, I will even pay you bonus money if you take an assassin targeting you out."

"Good. We have a deal. I will need all the information you have on sexual predator groups. I need a place to start my hunt."

"I will get you everything I have which includes every web site they sponsor and the encryption they use to protect their identities. I will also give you a list of my IT professionals and investigators who have worked on this information. These people and their files should give you a good start. By the way do you know what one of these web sites calls their victims: the package. Every time I think of my Rebecca being some package for one of these monsters it makes my blood boil."

"Don't worry Sydney. As long as I am alive, the only package they'll get is a bullet and the sharp edge of my knife."

"Good. That is exactly the kind of package I want them to receive."

Over the next several months, Ralph dedicated several hours a day to his search for a likely assassin. Of the thirty-four sexual predator websites he examined, two stood out for their size and sophistication, the Hunter's Fantasy and the Ecstasy of Youth. They both used sophisticated encryption and complex codes to hide their discussions and activities. After carefully studying both of these sites and the decoded transcripts from their recent discussions provided by Sydney's decoders and IT professionals, Ralph decided that the Hunters' Fantasy catered to the more violent and aggressive predators likely to hire an assassin. Also, he came to believe that the two predators he killed participated in the site. Yet, at this point, despite extensive discussions on all the sites about Pay Back, he had no record of any conversations about hiring anyone to kill Pay Back. Essentially, he had nothing to pursue. Then he received a phone call from Bert Rodriguez, one of Sydney's decoders.

"Ralph this is Bert. I just decoded a conversation on Hunter's Fantasy that lays the whole thing out. They raised $100 K to hire a hit man to kill you. The site leader Day Rider will hire the hit man but there are no further details about whom he will hire. We have been trying for almost a year to find a location or identity for Day Rider but so far we have had no luck. Also, they plan on attacking your daughter Cindy after you're gone. They're actually fighting over who will have the honor of abducting her. I'm sending you the whole conversation, but basically this is it."

"Ted do you have the location or identity of any of the people on this site?"

"No not yet but we're working on it."

"Okay thanks. Unfortunately it's exactly as I thought it would be. I hoped that Cindy and I might not get targeted, but now I know I have a fight on my hand."

"For what it's worth, we all support what you allegedly are doing here. As far as I'm concerned, all these predators should lose their equipment."

"As I dig further I may need your help."

"We're all here for you."

Moments later, Ralph quickly read the Fantasy discussion about hiring an assassin on his computer. In addition to what Bert said, the perverts worried about his fighting skills. They would not want to risk hiring someone who did close in work. They did not care whether he suffered or not. They just wanted him dead. They also wanted to make the hit as clean and untraceable as possible. By far the best person for this job would be a sniper. For a 100 k they could hire a good one. Bill Theodore an old Seal buddy won the best shooter title at the Seals many times. Ralph heard that he went into the assassination business. Ralph saved his life more than once. Bill would almost certainly be able to give him some leads as to which assassin Day Rider might hire.

The Assassins

ﺡﻭﺡ

Steven Tomkins from the time he touched his first plastic gun at age four, knew what he wanted to do with his life: shoot guns. In the thirty years since, he had done exactly that: first for the military, then in tournaments and now to support himself. Quite simply, Steven rivaled the best shots in history. When he shouldered one of his sniper rifles he could hit anything regardless of its size or whether it moved or stood still. If he could see it, he could hit it anywhere he wanted to hit it. While at first he lived modestly off his winnings from shooting competitions after leaving the military, he soon learned that he could live lavishly with a minimum amount of effort. If Steven simply killed people rich and powerful people wanted killed, they would reward him handsomely. He earned more on one of these jobs than he had from all his tournament victories. To his great surprise, Steven also discovered that he enjoyed killing people. To him they represented challenging targets to be eliminated. He didn't care who they were. Steven would gladly have killed Mother Teresa if the fee attracted him. He simply had no conscience, none at all.

His latest job offer certainly fit into this category. A bunch of perverts at least he assumed they were perverts wanted to kill the Seal the papers had dubbed Pay Back. Steven relished the challenge of killing one of the best soldiers out there. No matter how good a Special Forces soldier Pay Back happened to be, no one could defend against a bullet fired from a mile away. Still, Steven realized that killing this man would only be easy if he didn't know Steven targeted him. If he knew, Steven could become the hunted rather than the hunter. Well, he already deposited $40 k of his $80 k fee, the rest of whatever the handler charged going to him. Steven must hurry up and earn this and the remainder of his fee before the Pay Back knew what came for him. He already scouted shooting sights. Steven would strike soon, very soon.

Bill welcomed Ralph with a big bear hug to his luxury apartment on Lake Shore Drive. After a drink and a few shared memories, Ralph stated his reason for calling.

"Bill, as you no doubt suspected, I'm here for a reason. I think a group calling themselves the Hunter's Fantasy has hired a sniper to kill me. The Fantasy is a group of sexual perverts who suspect I killed one of their own as payback for killing my wife and daughter. I have adopted a new daughter Cindy and I'm afraid if this sniper succeeds she will not have anyone to protect her. I need to hunt this sniper before he kills me."

"Yeah I've followed some of the articles about Pay Back. I don't know if this is you or not, but I support what this guy is doing. They ought to slice the nuts off every one of these sexual predators. Just so you know. I don't take jobs like this. Just as we used to say in the Seals I only kill who needs killing. Most of the people in my profession are like me: they choose their jobs carefully. Yet there are some snipers who don't care who they kill. I will e-mail you what I have on these members of the profession but as you might expect we don't share much information with each other. You'll still have to do some digging. Ralph you know I owe you my life, as do many of the other guys who served with you. If you decide who you are hunting, I'll help. I think many of the others would too. We're brothers for life."

"Thanks, Bill. I appreciate that. I may need that help. As long as this sniper knows who I am and I don't know who he is, he has the advantage. I may call you after I study your e-mail. I don't know how much time I have before this sniper strikes."

"Yeah. Just remember to avoid open places with any high structures nearby. Think like a sniper and you can probably avoid him for a while."

"I have already put a high fence around my property, installed bullet proof glass in my car and am wearing a new style bullet proof vest that is hard to detect. I'm doing everything I can, but you know and I know that eventually the sniper will find a place to kill me. It is just a matter of time."

"I know but I'm going to attach the sniper's manual to my e-mail. It is our bible written by one of our own. The manual may have some tips and suggestions you haven't considered. Whoever comes after you, he'll act like the sniper in the manual. Knowing his tricks will help you avoid him."

"Thanks Bill. I'll read it." Ralph said as he stood. He continued. "Anyway, I need to get going. I have to pick Cindy up at school. I don't want her walking home from school anymore."

"Yeah I can understand that. Stay in touch and remember that I'm here for you. No matter what happens we're brothers for life."

"Brothers for life," Ralph said to Bill as he walked out his door and onto the street below.

Steven tried to stretch his sore muscles. Crouching on the top of a building for six hours in a way that kept his head below the railing on the edge did that to him. He lovingly cradled his new Barrett 99 sniper rifle, reputed to be the finest sniper rifle in the world. He couldn't wait to use it. Any minute now, Ralph Tager would emerge from the front of the suburban office building where he worked. When he did, Steve would have a clear shot. Ralph Tager would die quickly as had all his targets when a 41.6 caliber bullet pierced the center of his forehead. We all die. Ralph would die sooner than most.

Ralph Tager almost reached the front door of his Schaumburg office complex when the hairs on the back of his head stood. This always meant danger lurked nearby. In the more than 50 Seal missions he undertook, Ralph always relied on this early warning indicator. Ralph had no idea how or why this occurred. The indicator could not even be called foolproof. Danger had occurred without it happening. Yet, when it did, danger had always been near—every single time. Ralph immediately knew from where the danger came. A sniper now lay in wait on a nearby office building waiting for him to come in range. Ralph already identified three possible shooting locations. He would now seek the most likely shooting sight. The one he would use were he the shooter and not the target. Ralph moved back from the door and took the stairs to the garage. His alternate route took him this way. Once he exited the garage, he would hunt his hunter. His loaded and silenced 22 caliber Beretta lay hidden in a secret compartment in his briefcase.

Steven became nervous. Ralph Tager did not emerge from his office building within the time window Steven established for him. He knew Tager worked in the building. Steven observed Ralph Tager entering the office building this morning but did not have a good shot at him. Others lay in the way. He could have killed these others, so called collateral damage, but if he had done so, Ralph would have been alerted to the threat and dove for a place Steven could not hit him. Also, his new super rifle had to be loaded one bullet at a time. Tager might have escaped before he could shoot again. From what he knew of his target, Steven did not want to be hunted by this man.

Ralph worked his way to the flight of stairs below the stairs leading to the roof of the office building across from his own—the one he believed had the best shooting solution. Ralph carefully examined the roof of this building from a safe vantage point and believed he saw the glint of metal or glass near the edge. Unfortunately, he had no safe vantage point, which would give him a clear view of this area. The glint would have to be sufficient. Instead of climbing to the roof, Ralph decided to wait for the shooter, if indeed he lurked there, to descend to his position. The shooter would make his move soon. Ralph's scheduled time for leaving his office had already long passed. The shooter would not want to be exposed too much longer. The moment the shooter opened the door to the roof, Ralph would have a clear shot at him. If he attacked the shooter on the roof, the assassin would have the advantage.

There would be traps. Also, he would be in a position to see Ralph before Ralph saw him. The minutes slowly ticked away.

Steven could not wait any longer. The target would not exit the front of the building today. He had left the area by another exit. Quite possibly, the target now stalked him. Steven carefully packed his Barrett sniper rifle and disabled the traps he laid. He approached the roof door carefully. Instead of merely opening it, Steven cracked the door and fired six 9mm bullets from his silenced Beretta into the space beyond.

Ralph, crouching at the bottom of the stairs leading to the roof of the building across from his office, saw the door crack open. He knew what came next. Moving back out of the line of fire, he waited until the shooter fired off a series of shots. Fortunately, none of them hit the small glass mirror Ralph placed against the wall in such a way that Ralph could see the sniper open the door. Moments later, the assassin fully opened the door and fired several more rounds down the stairway. After the bullets hit the area around his mirror, Ralph rolled on the ground to a firing position on the stairway landing and fired four shots at the figure in the door, two aimed at the man's shoulders and two at his knees. The man fired the two shots left in his extended magazine wildly and tumbled down the stairs. When the shooter reached the bottom of the stairs, Ralph kicked his gun away and threw his Barrett sniper rifle into the corner. The shooter moaned in pain, but remained awake. He probably broke some bones on his way down the metal stairs and the bullets created a great deal of pain as they bled. Ralph placed his Beretta inches from the shooter's mouth and calmly addressed him.

"If you tell me who hired you, I will leave you here. You might live. If you do not tell me, I will pull the trigger of my Beretta and paint the wall with your brains. The choice is yours."

"I, I receive hiring calls from a throw away untraceable phone. If I accept, the money is wired to my Swiss account, half up front half on completion once again from an untraceable source. I do not receive the second payment until the media publishes the name of the kill. I never know who hires me. I think a guy called the handler is behind the calls. He is the one that deals with the clients."

"Can you reach the handler in the case of emergency or for any other reason?"

"Yes there is a number in my wallet written in red ink. If you call this number from my phone, he will call you back from what I assume is another untraceable throwaway phone. When you make the call, you must hang up immediately after it is answered. If the call is made and there is not a good reason for making it, the handler will never give you another hit."

After putting on some gloves, Ralph searched the sniper's wallet and removed the number written in red ink. Then he pocketed the sniper's cell phone. After doing so, he continued.

"You know I believe you're telling the truth. If you killed people who needed killing, I would leave you here. I might even call 911. I have killed many men like that. But you kill anyone no matter how good they might be for money. You have no principles, no morals. You do not deserve to live in a civilized society. You will only kill more people if I let you live, including me and my precious daughter."

With that statement, Ralph pulled the gun away from Steve's mouth and walked a few steps away. He heard movement from the assassin and then with great speed Ralph whirled and fired a bullet into Steven's forehead. Ralph acted wisely. Despite the great pain he suffered moving his arms, the assassin began to raise a small pistol toward Ralph he had concealed in his shoe. Carefully, cleaning up the site, Ralph descended the stairs and left the building. He needed to get home for Cindy. For the first time in weeks, Ralph would sleep well. For a time, they would be safe, but another assassin would soon be after him. The new one could not afford to fail as this one had today.

The next day, Ralph shared the contact protocol with Sydney's technical experts. With them monitoring the call, Ralph called the number in red ink. He hung up as soon as it connected. Ten minutes later, the sniper's cell phone rang. Ralph answered.

"Yes."

"You called."

"I'm frustrated. I've tracked the target for days but I still have not been able to acquire a firing solution."

"Time is important. If you don't take care of the target in the next 5 days, you must return the money wired to you. After doing that, you'll never receive another contract. I don't accept failure."

"I need more time than that."

"You do not have it. Never call me again to discuss your problems."

Before Ralph could issue another word, the handler hung up. The technical experts found a location for the call, but the call came from fifteen miles away. Ralph hurried to the location but he as expected found nothing but a busy street. At least, he now had a location, even though he could do little with it.

A Performance

Ralph moved nervously in his seat at the small grade school gymnasium. Now ten and in the fifth grade, Cindy would play her guitar and sing a song in a few minutes. Cindy practiced her singing and playing every day but refused to allow Ralph to listen in her presence or comment. She repeatedly told him she wanted to surprise him by singing in the talent show this evening. Apart from whether she did well or not, the little Ralph heard through her bedroom door sounded pretty good to him; Cindy faced one of the most challenging events of her young life. Just performing in front of a large number of people including her new dad would be a huge achievement for her. When Cindy first returned to school, she could barely make it through the day without experiencing panic attacks. Her psychiatrists pushed her very hard to enter and perform in the contest feeling it would help her social standing at the school. Ralph would be less nervous on a Seal rescue mission in Africa than sitting here waiting for Cindy to perform. Ralph moved around a number of work assignments to be here this evening. He knew how important this moment would be for Cindy. Finally her time arrived. Ralph literally clutched his seat.

Cindy walked slowly to the microphone. She looked gorgeous, her luminous blond hair cascading down her back but she also looked very nervous. She tried to say something into the microphone but when the words did not come, Cindy started to play her guitar instead. Slowly the fear started to leave her face. She played very, very well, like an adult entertainer. Then, quite suddenly her beautiful sweet voice filled the room. She sang on key with perfect rhythm and pitch. For a few moments, Ralph just laid back and enjoyed Cindy's performance. She easily outclassed all the other performers. Ralph looked with pride at the reaction of the parents near him. They clearly marveled at her performance as he did. But her courage impressed Ralph even more than her performance. From the edge of both physical and mental death his Cindy just made a giant step toward a normal happy life.

Easy Rider carefully monitored the discussion about Pay Back's package on the Hunter's Fantasy but did not participate in the conversation. He needed a new package but had difficulty finding one he liked. This Cindy seemed to be ideal for his needs, beautiful, and already broken in. Easy Rider also liked the recognition it would bring him in the community to kidnap this special package. Better yet, unlike many of the members of Hunter's Fantasy, he lived in the Chicago area where this girl lived. He had easy access, they didn't. Also, unlike the other members of the Fantasy, Easy Rider had no intention of waiting for the assassin to eliminate Ralph Tager. Easy Rider would move on the package as soon as he could. Using the information supplied by the newspapers, Easy Rider located the girl's house without too much difficulty but unlike other packages she never left the house without someone with her. Entering the house also appeared to be very difficult. The house had a sophisticated alarm system and the wall surrounding the house made observations of the inside of the house almost impossible. When she left school, the package also had company, usually her very scary new father who obviously could not be directly confronted. Still, even though access presented problems, an opportunity to snag her would present itself. He merely had to be patient and persistent.

After several frustrating weeks of shadowing the girl, Easy Rider devised a strategy to get close to her. Clever with computers, he carefully monitored the arrival of new students at her elementary school. When a new fifth grader transferred into the school, Easy Rider would pose as the child's parent, knowing full well that the school would not know what the father looked like until parent teacher meetings took place. Waiting for gym time, he walked into the principal's office and introduced himself as Rodney Wentworth the father of Steve Wentworth, a student who entered the school the previous week. After a polite chat, an aide, Nancy, took him on a tour of the school including the fifth grade classroom. Easy Rider told the aide that he did not want to go to the gym, fearing Steve would become upset about his father spying on him. As Easy Rider toured the building he looked for something anything that would give him better access to the girl. He found it. Her name appeared on a signup sheet for a talent show the next week. If Pay Back attended, he would be in the audience and the package would be backstage. He could drug the girl and remove her before Pay Back even knew she had been taken.

The night of the talent show, Easy Rider waited anxiously backstage for the package to finish her performance. A pharmacist, Easy Ryder had a powerful sleep inducer tucked away in his pocket. One whiff of this and the package would be sound asleep. Easy Rider really enjoyed the package's singing and playing. He would make her perform for him as he fulfilled his fantasies. Finally, she finished. Loud applause followed. Cindy ran backstage with a smile on her face. Several teachers and kids surrounded her. Easy Rider could not wait for them to leave the package. Pay Back might be working his way back here this very moment. Using the nice voice he always used during his abductions, he stepped out from the curtain where he hid and addressed Cindy.

"Well Cindy that sounded wonderful. My name is Mr. Wentworth, Steve's dad. Your dad Ralph and I are old friends. He asked me to take you home with me. He had other pressing business to attend to."

Cindy's smile quickly left her face. She responded angrily.

"You're lying. I'm not going anywhere with you. My father told me never to leave with anyone that he had not first introduced me to."

"Cindy that is Mr. Wentworth. I gave him a tour of the school last week," Nancy declared with some certainty. She waved to Mr. Wentworth earlier.

"I don't care who he is. I don't know him. I'm only leaving with my father."

Easy Rider did not have any more time to play this game. He pulled a colt 32-caliber revolver out of his jacket. He snarled at Cindy as he reached for her.

"You 're leaving with me now or I'm going to start killing people including you if you continue to fight me."

Meanwhile, Ralph with a big smile on his face worked his way backstage. He just wanted to hug, kiss and praise his daughter for her wonderful performance. As Ralph drew close to backstage, the hair on the back of his neck stood. Danger lay near. Adopting his Seal persona, he moved quickly to a place where he could view the stage behind the curtain without being seen. Ralph reached for his throwing knife that he always kept in a heavily shielded holder above his shoe as he did so.

Without really thinking about it, Cindy swept her left arm outward pushing the man's gun away from her, stomped down on the arch of the man's foot and punched him in the Adam's apple-just as her new father taught her to do. The gun went off but did not hit anyone. The man began to choke and then stumbled a little, but soon regained his composure. Easy Rider began to swing the gun back toward Cindy, rage suffusing his face. Just as the gun began to move a metal object flew right past Cindy's head into Easy Rider's throat. Stunned, Easy Rider clutched his throat; started to wobble, then fell heavily to the ground. He wheezed and bled for a few seconds, then his eyes turned glassy and he died. Cindy ran into Ralph's arms sobbing. Ralph held her tightly and spoke softly to her.

"Cindy my love I came back here to congratulate you on your great performance and for having the courage to stand in front of all those people and do what you did, but I'm even prouder of you for facing down this predator. You didn't let him make you a victim."

"Dad he almost killed me. I was so scared."

"Yeah but you faced your fear. That is what counts. I'm taking you away from here.

The cops will want to talk to us but they can wait a while." Addressing the other three adults and two children standing there Ralph continued.

"Please tell the police that Cindy and I will come to the station tomorrow to make a statement. I need to have some time with my daughter to calm her."

"We will. I will make sure they wait. You saved our lives. I don't know how to thank you." Helen said embarrassed that she tried to encourage Cindy to go with the man lying dead at her feet.

"Yes thank you," another parent said, followed by the third person, the drama teacher who put on the show. The two children just stood there silently, too shocked to speak or move.

"Well you're all welcome. I'm just glad that this evil man can no longer terrorize young girls."

With that statement, Ralph quickly left the backstage area and then the school. As he did so, two men climbed in a plain black car. After a few minutes they left as well.

The Aftermath

***

ater that night, the doorbell rang. Ralph gently disentangled himself from a sleeping Cindy, pulled his Beretta out of his locked side table, placed it in the specially made pocket inside his robe, and descended the stairs to the front door. After looking carefully at the two suited men through his peephole, Ralph reluctantly disabled his alarm and answered the door. They looked like cops and had a reason to be here despite the message he left for them with the people at the talent show. Ralph, however, kept the door mostly closed. Caution still ruled his every thought and movement. The interior of the door consisted of two-inch thick steel. It would stop most bullets. The men spoke through the crack.

"Are you Ralph Tager?"

"Yes."

"We need to take you downtown for questioning."

"Let me see your identification."

The men hurriedly showed their ID'S through the crack in the door, but Ralph instantly recognized them as fake. He carefully studied local and state police badges to avoid just this kind of setup. Ralph had a decision to make. He could merely close the door in the men's faces but if he did so they would return. He would not be safe; Cindy would not be safe. No he would end this here and now. Their assumption that he had bought their ruse would be the assailants undoing. Walking calmly back from the door, Ralph studied the men in his hall mirror. He spoke casually as he did so.

"Okay let me get my coat."

Ralph could see the men push the door open and reach into their coats. Ralph fell sideways, twisted back toward the door and pulled his silenced

Beretta as he did so, all in one motion. He shot the two men in the forehead before he even reached the floor. The suited men both shot their silenced guns at Ralph the moment they entered but their shots went where Ralph had been not where he ended. They two men did not fire another shot. Instead the two men collapsed on the floor, their eyes glassy and wide.

Ralph, putting on the plastic gloves he always kept handy, quickly stripped the dead men and put their clothes in a black plastic bag. Next Ralph placed their naked bodies in the trunk of their car after obtaining their keys and driving their car close to the house. He then parked the assassin's car four blocks away in a grade school parking lot. He left the keys in the ignition and the door open. He hoped some stupid kid or adult for that matter would see the keys and decide to take the car. After parking the car, Ralph removed the plastic bag from the backseat and placed it in a dumpster next to the school. If he remembered correctly, the city would empty the dumpster tomorrow. Ralph took a calculated risk in doing what he did. The better option would have been to drive the car to another part of the city and to dispose of the bodies there. Yet, he could not and would not leave Cindy that long. His mother had left to return to her home for a few days.

Before calling it a night, Ralph carefully cleaned the area where the men bled. By the grace of god, Cindy did not waken and come down to see what happened. Ralph would re-file his gun's barrel and then dispose of the gun. He had already purchased several spares. The bullets they would pull out of the men would not match his Beretta but he could not continue to re-file the barrel without at some point affecting his gun's performance. He would dispose of his assailant's guns tomorrow. Ralph hid them in a place under the floorboards.

As Ralph walked wearily up his stairs, he wondered when all this violence would end. Maybe he and Cindy needed to find new identities and a different place to live. Ralph knew the people who sent the sniper to kill him would send someone else to finish the job, but he didn't expect them to come so soon. New ones would be sent for the same reason these men came. Their job remained unfinished.

Cindy

indy entered school this day as she usually did frightened and alone. Very upbeat and popular in her last school, she could not relate to anyone in her new Lake Bluff School. Slowly her panic attacks lessened but they still came. She could barely look at any of her fellow students and the closer she came to adults or children the more anxious she became. Cindy hoped her performance at the talent show would break some of the ice surrounding her but with the predator attack overshadowing her performance it had not. Her fellow students just didn't know how to react to her. In truth, Cindy preferred to be home schooled but her therapist had strongly recommended against this option. So she dutifully entered the school everyday, concentrated on her schooling and returned home as quickly as she could. Many of the school bullies tried to attack her but even they withdrew after she faced down an armed predator. Even the biggest and loudest boys shrank a little when they stared into her eyes. They saw no fear there, just an angry determination. So Cindy expressed some real surprise when Priscilla a popular pretty redhead approached her on the playground after lunch. Cindy often looked at Priscilla as the Cindy who would have existed had the attacks on her never taken place. Priscilla as soon as she drew close started talking.

"Cindy I really admire you. You are so pretty talented and smart. You were incredible at the talent show. The other kids think you are weird, unfriendly and unapproachable, but I think I understand you."

"Really, how could anyone understand me? I don't even understand myself. I try to be just a normal kid but I just can't be. What happened to me changed everything. The attack at the talent show made it even worse. I want to have friends but I don't know how to do it anymore. Before the attacks, I like you had many friends. Because of all this, coming to school is very hard for me." Cindy said.

"Well I'm going to tell you something that I haven't told anyone else. I think you may be the only one I can tell this to. I put on a good act at school but my home life is terrible. My father beats my mother. The police have come several times. My father has never touched me but I have seen the anger in his eyes. He can't control himself particularly after he has been drinking. I know he will eventually come after me. The older I get the greater my risk. My mom is planning on leaving my dad and taking me with her but she hasn't done it yet. I'm so afraid when I go home after school that I peed my pants in the third grade. I just want to know how you became so brave. You even faced down the school bully. I would like to be brave like you." Priscilla said.

"Maybe we can help each other. You do well here. I do well at home. I lucked out. My new dad is handsome, very brave, and loves me completely. Despite all the evil out there, I know my dad will protect me. He is my whole world now. I love him with all my heart. His mom stays with me when he has to travel for work but most of the time he is there for me. I guess he makes me feel brave. Before he adopted me, I couldn't sleep at night. I was a complete wreck. This is where you will be if your dad beats you. The fear is actually worse than the physical injuries. They heal; the fear does not. You can come over to my house and meet my dad. Maybe he can help you." Cindy replied.

"That would be great. The later I get home the better. My dad is a car salesman. Sometimes when sales are slow he will come home early before mom gets home from work. He starts drinking right away when he comes home then. I'm terrified when this happens." Priscilla said.

"Okay we have a plan. I want to be your friend. I hope you will become mine." Cindy said.

"I will." Priscilla replied.

For the next several months, Priscilla and Cindy became inseparable. Priscilla came over to Cindy's house whenever she could. In turn,

Priscilla became Cindy's greatest advocate at school. With her help, Cindy's school relationships improved. She actually felt happy most days. Unfortunately, Priscilla's home life did not improve. Her father became more abusive. For the first time, he put his hands on Priscilla throwing her into a couch when she tried to stand up for her mother. Priscilla only received some minor bruises but became more anxious.

The whole issue came to a head when Priscilla's dad Barry came to pick up Priscilla at Ralph's house. Barry had been drinking heavily and just missed crashing his car into Ralph's garage. Then, Barry tripped walking up the steps to Ralph's front door but managed to catch himself as he fell. Despite the bruises and scrapes from his fall, Barry knocked as if nothing happened. When Ralph answered, Barry stumbled into Ralph's house already angry from his difficulties in reaching the house. In a loud and hostile voice he said.

"Priscilla, where the hell are you? I'm picking you up and taking you home."

Ralph calmly answered.

"Barry I think we met briefly before. I'm Ralph, Cindy's dad. I think the girls are in Cindy's room listening to music and talking. I'll tell Priscilla you're here."

Ralph walked upstairs, knocked on Cindy's door and entered. He spoke quickly to Priscilla.

"Your father is here to pick you up but he is very drunk. I don't think you should go anywhere with him in this condition. Can you call your mom?"

"She won't be of much help. She doesn't leave her job for another hour. Her boss doesn't like it when she leaves early. I can ask her to pick me up when she gets off work but I don't think my dad will go for it. He is a violent and angry man and doesn't listen to reason when he is drunk."

"Okay let's try." Ralph said.

Ralph led the girls down the stairs and spoke with a wobbling Barry when he drew within earshot.

"Barry, the girls want to play for another hour. Your wife can give Priscilla a ride home then or if she doesn't want to do it, I can give her a ride. We weren't expecting you so early.' Ralph said pleasantly.

"No way. Priscilla is coming with me now. The little bitch is just like her mother. She never wants to do anything I want to do. I'll carry her to the car if I have to." Barry bellowed.

With that Barry advanced on Priscilla but Ralph stepped in front of him saying.

"Nobody threatens anyone in my home. My home my rules. Unfortunately, you're drunk and in no condition to drive anyone anywhere. I'm a retired Navy Seal lieutenant commander and have led many Seal teams. With what we faced, many Seals drank too much on leave or at the base. We took care of them and made sure they didn't drive or get into fights. This is no different. If a cop catches you, you'll lose your license for a long time. We will get you and your daughter home but you won't be the driver."

"Get out of my way. I'm bigger than you. I'll squash you like a bug." Barry said as he tried to grab Ralph. In a flash, Ralph grabbed Barry's arm and drove him into the ground.

"Now Barry, I can dislocate your arm or break it. Your choice--or I can let you go and we can work this out." Ralph calmly said.

"Let me go." Barry bellowed.

After Ralph let Barry go, he lunged for Priscilla.

"You goddamned bitch. This is your fault. I'll teach you a lesson."

Moments after Barry crashed into Priscilla, Ralph grabbed Barry and forcibly removed him from Priscilla. Then Ralph put Barry up against the wall. Ralph spoke with a steely voice.

"Barry I could have killed you the first time you threatened me. I thought I could reason with you. But apparently I cannot. Now listen to me very carefully. If you ever touch Priscilla this way again or harm her mother, I will find you and break every bone in your body. You will be an invalid the rest of your life. Now I am going to let you go again but please don't come at me again. If you do, I will knock you out." Ralph said as he once again let Barry go.

Barry immediately took a swing at Ralph, which he easily ducked. Ralph responded with a powerful punch to Barry's jaw that knocked Barry to the floor. He lay on the ground twitching. Ralph turned to the girls.

"I knocked your father out. His jaw will be sore but he will recover. I'll put him in his car with his keys under the mat. I will take you to your mother's place of work. She can take you home. I will also call the cops and have them deal with Barry from this point forward. I'm concerned if he comes at me again, I will hurt him. I have a tape of everything that happened. Barry will not be able to charge me with anything. He tried to hit me in my home. I'm very sorry I had to deal with you father this way. He could have badly injured both you and himself had he driven you home."

""It's okay. My father is crazy when he drinks this much. He needed to be put in his place. My mom and I need to find someplace else to live until dad can find a way to control himself." Priscilla said.

"Well said Priscilla. Your dad needs help but he can't be allowed to threaten you and your mother. That is out of bounds." Ralph replied.

Ralph did as he said and took Priscilla to her mother. He returned to greet the police and showed them the video of Barry. The police took Barry to the police station and kept him there until he sobered up enough to speak with them. Ralph refused to press any charges against Barry, but from this point forward paid very close attention Priscilla to make sure her dad didn't come after her again.

The Handler

The handler buried his head in his hands. One of his valuable assassins lay dead in a morgue and in all likelihood two more would also be found dead. For a fifty thousand dollar fee and the promise of another fifty thousand dollar fee of which he only kept $20,000 the handler had seriously damaged his business. He needed to return the $50,000 and cancel the hit. He couldn't afford to lose any more of his assassins who were difficult to find and recruit. The handler knew his reputation would suffer from his failure to eliminate Ralph Tager, but he really had no one left who would take this kind of job. No one liked assassinating a war hero for sexual predators least of all the ex military types who made up most of his operation. The handler also trembled when he remembered the phone conversation with the Seal, who killed his assassins. He certainly did not want to motivate this dangerous man to continue looking for him. If the man ever identified him he would be the dead man. Perhaps the handler could send Tager a message that no more of his killers would come after him. From another throw away phone the handler texted the sniper's phone: "Contract is canceled."

Day Rider also had second thoughts. According to an article placed on his web site, Ralph Tager killed Easy Rider when the rider attempted to abduct the package of the late Hard One. Also, on his site an article mentioned the death of a sniper by some unknown assailant, who almost certainly had to be Ralph Tager. Finally and perhaps worst of all, a predator on his network, Macho Man, had been killed and castrated two thousand miles away in Washington shortly before the time Tager killed the sniper locally. Even if he killed Tager, others would probably be hunting him and his fellow predators. Day Rider and his community still faced a serious threat, but at the moment Day Rider had no strategy to deal with this threat. Eliminating Tager might make some sense but the rest of the community in light of these new facts would need to sign off on this continued assassination effort. He would not make the decision alone.

A ringing phone pulled Day Rider out of his thoughts. He answered and heard this followed by a click.

"I'm cancelling our contract and returning your $50,000. I no longer have the resources to do the job. "

Day Rider attempted to continue the conversation then tried to call back but to no avail. He quickly went on line for a chat.

"Gentlemen, we have a problem. Our hypothetical contract has been canceled and our hypothetical money has been returned. Also, if you have been reading the blog you will know that the hypothetical contract doesn't cover all the threats we face."

Monster replied. "Maybe we are going about this thing the wrong way. Tager is a soldier. Soldiers take orders. We need to find a hypothetical guy who gives the orders, the so-called head of the snake. The hypothetical snake's head has to come off if you are going to stop this killing of our kind. Otherwise we will continue to face threats no matter how many hypothetical soldiers we kill."

"Yeah. That makes sense. Without money and resources, the alleged killing will stop. We just have to find out who this head of the snake is. Even better, he will probably not be a scary special forces guy who can duck assassination attempts." Potent One interjected.

"I agree. The head of the snake can call on the scary guys to shield him but if he is alone the head is vulnerable as you say. The key is to attack him before he knows he is being targeted. I, for one, vote to use our hypothetical resources to attack the hypothetical head of the snake." Big One said.

"I second that," Potent One agreed.

"Alright I will poll each of our hypothetical contributors and see what they say, but I like you support this hypothetical plan."

Meanwhile ten miles away, Ralph walked into a secluded warehouse and sat in a chair underneath a dangling light. He waited patiently for Sydney to speak from the darkness.

"Pay Back you probably haven't seen the new intercepts of the Hunter's Fantasy website but if you have you will know why I'm here. These perverts after failing to kill you are targeting me. I have already beefed up my security but this provocation needs a response."

"Yes it does. I have been thinking about a new approach. As Seals we fought in teams. I led Seal teams for years. Sydney you need to fund some of your own Seal teams with the sole purpose of eliminating sexual predators. It will of course require a major financial commitment from you."

"An interesting idea—the best defense is a good offense. One thing for sure, I'm not going to sit around and wait for these perverts to come after me. Okay draw up some plans. I'll take a look at them."

"I will sir. I like your approach of going on the offensive. "

Confession

Raised as a Catholic, but absent from church most of his adult life, Ralph quietly sat in the confessional with Father O'Brien. Ralph addressed the middle age priest with some caution.

"Father, bless me for I have sinned. I have not confessed since I was a child. As a warrior for my country, I have killed many people. I thought this would end when I left the military but it has not. I no longer know the difference between right and wrong."

"Please continue my child. You are not the first soldier to sit in my confessional."

"Father, do you believe in good and evil? Society condoned what I did as a soldier but I killed other soldiers whose character I did not know. They may very well have been good family men and upstanding citizens of their communities. Now, I'm killing violent child predators that are the very embodiment of evil and the scourge of their communities. For this, society would brand me a murderer and kill or imprison me. I could stop killing these evil men and women but if I do not kill them, they will kill and enslave more innocent children. I can't allow them to do that. If I go to hell for what I have done and what I will do, at least I can save others from the torment of losing their child."

"My son these are not simple matters. As a young priest, I would have asked you to stop killing or otherwise endanger your mortal soul. After all, thou shalt not kill is one of the Ten Commandments and Jesus teaches us to love our enemies not to kill them. He also said blessed are the peacemakers for they shall inherit the earth. Yet, I have also come to believe in evil and that all of us must do what we can to fight it. One of my most devout and supportive families lost a son to a sexual predator, just as you lost both your daughter and wife to one. I spent countless hours counseling them but their pain and torment eventually tore them apart. Their daughter ran away from home and became a drug addict. The mother divorced the father and then committed suicide, one of the deadliest sins a Catholic can commit. The father never remarried and spends most of his time at home in isolation. He has not attended mass in over a year. While this family did not resort to violence as you did to give them a measure of peace, they certainly did not come to terms with their loss. Evil spread its wings and took them inside. So who I am to judge you should you prevent the destruction of another family through your actions? My church has often employed warriors to fight the evils they perceived around them."

"Father I feel I am caught in a trap. I do not know how to be anything but a soldier. It is who I am and what I do. My enemies are the sexual predators out there who prey on children. I will fight them the rest of my life. Yet, I fear that I will endanger my adopted daughter Cindy by continuing to do what I do. I sometimes wish that we could go somewhere and hide so she could be safe. Yet, in my experience hiding from your enemies rarely works. They always seem to find you. All I can do is train her to protect herself and be there to protect here as long as I can."

"Your adopted daughter has also been brushed by the wings of evil. The devil already counted her as one of his victims when you snatched her away. He will continue to seek her. You cannot protect her by hiding. She must fight alongside you."

"Yes I agree but I can't stop worrying about her. I just wish she could live a normal life."

"My son not all of us are fated to have a normal life. God has other things in mind for us. So it is with you and your daughter."

Pay Back Crew

Ralph welcomed the ten men who entered the secluded warehouse where he had spoken with Sydney. Nine of them worked for him as Seals before retiring from the military, the tenth Trevor, also a Seal, eliminated the third sexual predator. Ralph did not know him. After some slaps on the back and jokes, the men finally found seats on the boxes surrounding the single chair where Ralph sat. Ralph left the chair and began to walk in a circle talking to the men who he considered his close friends and colleagues.

"Even though we have left the military, we are still Seals. We give no quarter. We take out our enemies."

"Hoorah," they all answered, using the Marines response.

"In the Seals, we considered foreign hostiles our enemies. Just before I left the Seals, a sexual predator killed my beloved wife and raped and killed my daughter. He also raped my now adopted daughter and killed her parents. This sexual predator no longer lives having lost his equipment to a river knife, but others like him still live. They continue to rape and kill our children. They have no right to live in our society. I have made it my life mission to kill as many of them as I can. They are my new enemies. I'm forming two Pay Back teams patterned after the teams I used to run in the Navy to do just that. Each member of these teams will be very well compensated by our wealthy benefactor and given the tools and intelligence to do their missions. I have chosen you ten, the best men I know, to be members of these teams. What I ask of you is not easy. I wouldn't blame you if you walked out that door never to return. Law enforcement will consider us vigilantes and try to arrest or kill us. Our targets will try to organize against us and kill us if they can. No one will give you a medal for what you do. The question is will you fight with me to rid our society of these vermin?"

The question hung in the air for almost a minute before one and then the rest loudly responded. "We will sir. We will consider it an honor and a privilege to fight with you again. These targets are our enemies as well as all of mankind's enemies."

"Then it is settled. We will form two teams, Pay Back 1 and 2. Trevor who is the most senior Seal other than me will take one team; Collingsworth will take the other. I will oversee the entire operation. As law enforcement already believes me to be the killer of these predators, I cannot accompany you on your missions. So I will serve as a diversion. When you target a predator in one city, I will make sure that I visit another. There are tens of thousands of dangerous sexual predators in the U.S. We have targeted for elimination the cruelest and most depraved two hundred of them. We will kill them fast and efficiently. Our goal is to kill them all within the next two years. Then we will develop a new set of targets. Are you with us?"

"We are. We will keep killing them until they are all dead."

"Then let us get down to business. We have a great deal of planning and work to do."

First Job

Trevor, the head of Pay Back team 1, sat on top of a three-story building studying the third floor San Francisco apartment across the street with a powerful set of binoculars. Buck Sanchez, a man of mixed Hispanic and Anglo heritage, occupied the unit at the edge of the building. Buck had spent most of his youth in and out of jail and mental institutions. He killed three little girls and two little boys after brutally raping and assaulting them but because of his mental state and some problems with his various prosecutions, he remained a free man. Buck made a living doing forensic audits for a consulting company. In his sane moments, he proved to be a good accountant.

On this job, Trevor worked as a spotter and set up man for the shooter. Wilson his other set up man had left the observation site to procure a specific sniper weapon that Sydney had made available at one of his many companies. Van the shooter would soon disembark from a commercial airliner and drive to the site in an older but well maintained car parked at the San Francisco airport. Wilson would be here in thirty minutes; Van within an hour.

Buck would be home from work in an hour and one half. Before then, Wilson and he would leave the rooftop after carefully briefing Van on the job. Trevor would then head to the airport before the job took place. Trevor would need an alibi and the taxi driver would provide one for him. Wilson would walk the street waiting for Buck. When Buck walked up to his building, Wilson would call Van and let the phone ring once. If at all possible, Wilson would brush Buck to target him. If not,

Van would quickly find Buck based on the detailed descriptions and pictures provided to him by Ralph and Wilson. Once Van identified Buck, he would kill him with a bullet to the head from his sniper rifle. Van would then leave the gun, which would bear no fingerprints from Van's tight gloves, in as hidden a place as he could find on the roof before exiting. At a later date, if the gun remained hidden, someone not associated with the team would retrieve it. All three of the team would after the shooting leave San Francisco on different flights to different cities.

On the next job, Terry would take Trevor's place; then Bill would take Van's place on the third job. On the next job, Wilson would be the shooter and Terry and Van would be the spotters. Ralph had already made sure law enforcement knew he travelled to a city other than the one where Buck lived. He would do the same on the next job.

An hour and twenty-five minutes later, Wilson walked casually on the street in front of Buck's apartment. Buck suddenly appeared on the street from around the next corner. Wilson called Van's number let it ring once and then cut the connection. Wilson walked causally by Buck, making sure he brushed him as agreed. Buck barely noticed the brush. After leaving Buck behind, Wilson talked with a convenience store owner. He wanted a witness in case one was needed. Wilson then hailed a cab and took off for the airport. Van carefully lined up his shot as Buck suddenly appeared on his scope. Without hesitation, Van shot Buck in the head watching him fall to the pavement. Van did so without displaying any emotion. He killed many of the nation's enemies in the same way. Van quickly left the sniper rifle in an old box on the roof. He then walked quickly down the stairs of the high rise and flagged down a taxi. With a few minutes of shooting Buck, Van rode a taxi back to the airport. When the news reported the sniper killing of an alleged sexual predator, the entire team had already boarded their flights for different cities in the U.S.

The Last Target

For the next eight months, Pay Back teams 1 and 2 eliminated their targets with ruthless efficiency. They encountered few problems. Eighty-three sexual predators died in different communities throughout the US. Then the advance teams began to see law enforcement traps everywhere they went. Their advance work took more and more time. They often had to switch targets to avoid the stings. The whole operation slowed. Only eighteen predators died in the next eight months. Ralph no longer served as an effective distraction. Law enforcement already knew he would not be present at the shootings.

The media and the public became obsessed with the Pay Back killings. Consequently, law enforcement became equally obsessed. They targeted Sydney and Ralph but they could not tie either one of them to the killings. Ralph always turned up in cities other than the one where the assassination took place. Sydney conducted his business as usual with no contact to anyone who could have been associated with the killings. The flow of money and weapons could not be traced back to him. After sixteen months and one hundred and one dead predators law enforcement had very few valuable leads.

Still, law enforcement would not allow either one of them to go anywhere without some kind of law enforcement tail or attempt to intercept their communications. Law enforcement also spent a great deal of time trying to question Cindy. Ralph became so upset by these constant attempts, he obtained a court order limiting law enforcement questioning of his daughter to only those times he would be present. In a perverse way, the harassment he and Sid suffered benefited their cause. When law enforcement resources concentrated on them, they expended fewer resources to search for the Seals who actually undertook the missions.

The 102nd mission in Chicago began like all the missions before it, but this predator differed from the earlier ones in many respects. A blond thin 28-year old man with a nice sweet smile and pleasant face hid the demon that lay inside. This man Victor Simone sexually abused, tortured and then killed his victims 12 and under with absolutely no remorse. To the contrary, he became ecstatic and even sexually aroused while performing his evil acts. While not a powerful man, Victor possessed a very high IQ and showed outstanding organizational skills. Consequently Victor left no traces of his abductions, tortures or murders. Law enforcement had not even come close to arresting him. Victor ridiculed law enforcement as a bunch of bumbling idiots. Thirty children died horrible deaths at his hand and more would surely follow.

Victor, however, possessed with a strong sense of self preservation wanted nothing to do with Pay Back and his team. All his intelligence and cleverness wouldn't provide much protection against these highly trained killers. So on a bright sunny day in May, Victor walked into a local Chicago police station and offered to serve as a lure for the Pay Back teams.

The police as expected spent almost two days trying to convince Victor to admit to some of his crimes as a tradeoff for police protection from Pay Back. Victor simply refused. He even laughed at the police attempts. Victor knew that at some point the police would see the wisdom of using him for bait. Finally, Bob Prandini, who had been assigned to a special FBI unit charged with arresting the Pay Back crew, paid Victor a visit.

"Okay Victor I get it. You keep your freedom and we get Pay Back. Of course, we will not rest until you are tried and convicted for your crimes, but this will come another day and in another place. You came to us. You must have a plan."

"As a matter of fact I do. The Bay Back Teams rely on speed and ruthless efficiency. We never know where they will hit and when. When they do, they complete the job in minutes. No police force on earth can react fast enough. This is why you must use bait like me to catch them. The problem is that these Pay Back Teams are very good at seeing the traps laid for them. So we will use deception. We will dress several people like me and place them at places I am likely to be. Each look alike will have a team of police ready to pounce on the Pay Back Teams if they show. We have to make sure the targets are in poor target locations without good lines of site. Also, they will be heavily covered with body armor. I will be one of the targets. That is my contribution." Victor said.

"This may have some merit, but what makes you think the Pay Back team will target you. We will have to use a lot of resources to implement your plan." Bob said.

"The Pay Back teams have killed all the predators with reputations similar to or even less fearsome than mine. I'm the next logical target. My precautions have kept them away. By skipping some of those precautions, a Pay Back Team will come after me."

"Okay. We will use your plan but only for a month. If a Pay Back team hasn't showed by then, we stop working together. As you said, they may smell the trap." Bob said.

Pay Back Team One spent many days shadowing Victor their top remaining target. Victor who inherited money used a new technique. He hired people who resembled him to throw the Pay Back team off the scent. From a distance, one Victor looked like another. But the Pay Back team received in their military training techniques in how to overcome this substitution game. No two people walked the same way. So Pay Back Team One spent considerable time studying the walk of Victor long before the so-called clones started showing up. They always knew through observation who the real Victor happened to be. Still, the real Victor went out of his way to be a poor target. He traveled in a bulletproof car and did not expose himself to fire from any remote structure. He never took walks without his hired bodyguards. Victor also wore body armor including bullet-deflecting helmets when he ventured outside. Trevor expressed his frustration to Buck and Wilson the other members of Pay Back 1.

"Victor isn't going to give us a shot at him from a distance. We have to move in close. This risks detection and of course makes our escape much more difficult. I'm not so sure we should suddenly change to a close in kill model. It could bring the whole operation down."

"He is goading us into attacking him. You can bet he has teams of law enforcement waiting to arrest our team members. A close in model will allow these guys to move on us before we escape. I'm thinking that our ultra small assassination dart covered with concentrated poison from an Australian Funnel Spider could work. He won't even realize the dart has entered into him. It will feel like a mosquito bite. I can hit him at 30 yards," Butch responded.

"Yeah that might work. I'd hate to give this guy a free pass. Still, I think our hunting days may be coming to an end. These kills are just getting too hard. You're going to have to shoot him in just the right place. All of us need to get out of this city as soon as possible." Wilson said.

"I'll use the distraction technique." Trevor said as he walked away from his colleagues, who nodded their heads in approval.

After a frustrating day of disregarding the clones, Trevor the spotter finally fell in behind the man he knew to be Victor. He had a couple of guards near him and a law enforcement team not far away. Butch crouched behind a window on the second floor of a store in the next block. Wilson had already left town. He wouldn't be needed for this kill.

Trevor conveyed all his information on the target to Butch and waited for Victor to approach Butch's position. When he did, Trevor knocked over a garbage can across the street. When Victor turned toward the noise, Butch shot the dart in the back of his neck. Victor noticed the small pinch from the dart but kept on walking. He didn't even turn toward Butch's window. Butch then quietly closed the window and slipped out the door. Trevor hailed a cab and left the seen as quickly as possible. Butch did the same, exiting out the back of the store he just occupied. He disposed of his dart tube in a garbage can in the back. The whole operation took only minutes. Meanwhile Victor began to walk erratically as the poison took effect. He screamed that he had been hit. As Butch left the scene in an orderly fashion in his plain Toyota rental car, several unmarked cars after receiving notice of Victor's problems roared past him to the building where Victor pointed his finger. Meanwhile, Butch donned his long grey hair wig and mustache. The police in the approaching cars looked at him but kept going. Butch's car came from a parking place on the street not directly behind the building. He did not look like he fled the scene. Butch didn't really care whether they stopped him or not. He no longer had a weapon of any kind on him.

Three weeks later, Sid and Ralph met at another one of Sydney's abandoned warehouses. Each had to spend over an hour losing their tails. This new warehouse had two chairs in the middle of the dimly lighted space. It looked very much the same as the first warehouse they used. Ralph spoke first this time.

"Sid I don't think we can conduct any more missions safely. Law enforcement has surveillance on almost every target left on our list. They are posing police officers as predators. They have traps laid everywhere we go. The local police detained two members of Pay Back Team 1. The target we selected turned out to be an FBI plant. All the intelligence we collected on him proved to be fake. I pulled the team a minute before our shooter retrieved his assassination rifle and only five minutes before he would take his shot. When I double-checked a child this predator allegedly killed, I discovered the child died of cancer. I just got lucky. We had no suspicions until I did this extra check. As good Seals, these arrested members withstood hours of questioning. The police made it clear that they had full files on every member of Pay Back 1 and 2, including pictures. The police eventually had to let our team members go. They didn't have any solid evidence and our attorneys threatened to sue the police department for false arrest.

The operation before this one proved to be difficult as well. Several law enforcement cars roared past our dart shooter minutes after his attack. They could have stopped him but his disguise fooled them. I'm becoming fearful that this police activity will result in us killing a target that does not deserve to be eliminated. We are extremely careful in vetting our targets but with the misinformation we are receiving, mistakes will eventually be made. Also, as I mentioned before, I think I'm being targeted by an organization. It could be the government for reasons unrelated to the predator killings "

"I knew this would happen at some point. Still I would hate to shut down our operation. I have been thinking about new targets, the human traffickers. They sell young girls into sexual slavery, mostly illegal immigrants and runaways. In my book, they may even be worse than our sexual predators." Sydney said.

"Yeah but they also are affiliated with cartels and gangs. They have many soldiers. If we go after them, they will come after us. Then we will have both them and law enforcement to fight. I don't shy away from a fight but if you want to go there you will have to know what we face. We will need a lot more soldiers. You are talking about a war here."

"You're right maybe it's not feasible, but emotionally I've come to depend on the news that another predator has died. Maybe you can pursue the government angle while we wait for the heat to die a little on our current mission. If the government is somehow involved, we need to know how and why. They represent a much larger threat than a bunch of perverts."

"Okay, I'll devote the majority of my time trying to resolve my federal government issue, whatever it might be. Meanwhile I will shut down our operation for six months but please continue to pay our people. They have earned the money."

"Paying them is fine with me. They have done a great job and I'm grateful to them."

Beautiful Woman

Ralph couldn't help but notice the beautiful woman in the foyer of his office building. She had a perfect curvy figure, beautiful long legs, slightly brown skin, a perfect sculpted face and beautiful long wavy dark hair. She looked like a super model. The woman waited for someone as she kept looking toward the elevators from which Ralph just emerged. The woman stood on the other side of the security desk, presumably searching for a man to exit the front doors. After the incident with the sniper, Ralph no longer went that direction. So as usual he turned toward the door in the back leading to the garage. Before he reached the garage, the woman stepped in front of him. She apologized, a little out of breath from running to intercept Ralph.

"Excuse me. I'm looking for Ralph Tager and from the pictures I saw on the Internet that is you. I like macho men and when I looked you up online you seemed like the perfect match for me. I know that I am being a little forward but I'm a modern girl who likes to take what she wants when she wants it. My name is Tina."

Ralph moved backward to give himself room to move if he had to do so. In his experience, women didn't behave this way. Something didn't seen quite right. When the woman first came up to him, Ralph could feel the tension in her muscles, liker a tiger before it attacks. He finally found his voice.

"Tina pardon me if I am little taken aback. As a security professional, I'm accustomed to looking at everyone I meet as a potential threat. Beautiful women are particularly dangerous adversaries."

"Well that is not the romantic response I expected, but I read up a little on your background and can understand your caution. My name is Tina Reynolds. Google me if you like. I model a little but my main occupation is marketing women's clothes and accessories. I work freelance. In my line of work, the men I meet tend to be pretty boys, who don't attract me in the least. So there you have it. Work time is over. Would you like to go for a drink?" Tina said hopefully.

"No, not tonight. I promised my daughter Cindy I would be home. Anyway, I also promised Cindy I would seek her approval before I dated any woman. I'll have conversation with her tonight after we review your material on Google. If you want to see me again, you know where to find me."

"Okay, I'll be here again tomorrow. Once I have my mind set on something, I don't give up very easily." Tina said turning toward the door and walking slowly and seductively out of the office foyer. The men in the area followed Tina out of the office foyer with their eyes. Ralph just looked puzzled. Tina intrigued him but she wasn't who she pretended to be.

The Black Widow

ina relaxed her breathing on the way out of the office complex. She nervously fingered the handle of the poison needle she intended to stick into Ralph Tager. Ralph's sudden move backward when she approached him made the needle stick impossible. If she had moved forward to strike, the powerful Ralph Tager would have stopped the needle thrust and then hurt her very badly. Tina noticed the river knife and gun concealed on his person, but this man obviously didn't need either to hurt her. His powerful hands could snap her neck in a matter of seconds. Worse of all, she saw no hesitation in his eyes. This man had killed many times before and her beauty, which usually disarmed men, would not disarm this man. Ralph Tager would strike without a second thought. Tina suddenly felt sexually aroused. She hadn't lied to Ralph when she said powerful macho men attracted her. Unfortunately, Tina would kill Ralph before she could enjoy him as she had done to so many men before him. She had two reasons this time. Her employer the CIA black ops group and her brother Pete Ramirez both demanded it. Still, Tina would need to build this man's trust before she struck. If she moved too quickly, she might lose her own life. Tina would have to be patient to complete this assignment, a trait she as well as her employer ordinarily did not display. Tina would wait a little longer to see if Ralph asked her out. She would have the advantage then. If Ralph did not ask her out, Tina would focus her attention on his daughter Cindy. While Ralph had no apparent weaknesses, he, according to her briefing notes, fiercely protected his daughter. Tina would do whatever it took to complete her assignment.

Tina still felt agitated when she relaxed in her small but attractive apartment an hour after leaving Ralph's company. She carefully removed her three weapons, the River Knife, 22 caliber Beretta with a built in silencer, and her CIA issue poison stick and placed them on her coffee table. Beginning with the River Knife she carefully sharpened the blade until it could cut one of her hairs. Tina could not be satisfied with a weapon that operated any less than 100% of its maximum design capacity. After sharpening her knife and checking its balance, she tore apart her gun and carefully oiled each of its pieces. Even the best guns could jam or have one of their mechanisms stick. Tina worked on her gun everyday and had never experienced a problem with it. Next Tina examined her poison stick to make sure the retractable mechanism worked smoothly and that the poison glistened on the end of the sharp edge. Just to be safe, she added some fine oil to the mechanism and refilled the poison reservoir. Tina spent an hour on these tasks. Finally satisfied, Tina ordered some Chinese food. The deliveryman would be there in forty-five minutes.

Unfortunately, Tina struggled with her sexual desires. Ralph awakened them and once someone did so, she had difficulty turning them off. Tina would need to do so. If she picked up a man tonight, Tina would have a hard time not killing him during or after sex. To her the two acts went together, the ultimate sexual climax. Her Black Ops handlers told her after she killed her last lover Tina would have to stop killing non-targets if she expected to continue in her job. Tina had promised to do so, but in fact had only stopped killing her sexual partners during assignments by refusing to find such a partner during these times. When Tina successfully killed a target, she would find a young man to make love to her and then kill him. Still, tonight Tina would have a sexual dream about Ralph and would continue to have such dreams until she killed him. Then finally she would be able to seduce and kill a man to satisfy this burning desire in her.

Dating

Cindy now a pre teen surprised Ralph one evening after they ate some pizza together on a Tuesday night.

"Dad, I've been thinking. You need to find a wife and I need a mother. Your wife has been dead a long time. In fact, I've already researched a number of women on dating sites. I've compiled a list of the ten best in this area. I thought we could choose the woman for you to date together. I'd have to be comfortable with any woman you bring into our lives."

"Wow, I've been thinking of how to approach you on the very same subject. I like the idea of us doing this together. We want to create a family here. Although I must confess, I'm interested in a woman I recently met named Tina. She comes everyday to meet me after work. She is very beautiful and a little mysterious. I don't completely trust her yet, but I researched her background and can't find anything wrong. I wanted to introduce her to you but I feared you wouldn't approve."

"Bring her to dinner and I'll tell you what I think. If we can't agree on her we can try some of the women I've identified." Cindy said cautiously.

"Okay, it's a deal. I'll bring her this Saturday night. I can make some pasta and you can make your sauce."

"Perfect dad. I'm sure it'll be a great evening. I really want my life to be more normal that it is, but I'm afraid that I will be jealous of any woman you date."

"I will always love you Cindy. You are my girl no matter what happens."

Dinner

The dinner went well. Tina looked stunning in a tight short skirt and loose fitting blouse, showing off some of her cleavage. She made conversation easily and looked relaxed. Cindy and Ralph warmed up to her but not completely. Ralph drank very little of the red wine on the table, Cindy none and Tina only sipped the wine in her glass. Due to an earlier agreement, Ralph and Cindy never let Tina out of their sight and kept her away from the food and drink preparation. They knew this bordered on paranoia but considering their past experiences they both felt it warranted. Tina showed no apparent concern with the way either of her hosts behaved. She just smiled, ate and talked about her made up life as a fashion model and designer. When the pasta and meatballs disappeared, the three adjourned to the living room. Tina and Ralph sat on the couch and Cindy took a chair facing them. A low table sat in between the couch and the chair. Ralph and Tina each had a cup of coffee in front of them. Ralph and Tina had watched his cup of coffee constantly. As with the meal, Tina had no opportunity to add anything to it. Tina with her body angled toward Ralph talked about a funny incident with one of the models.

"Rachel had put on some weight, enough so her skirt kept riding up her legs and ruining the fashion pictures. Cal, the photographer, kept complaining about the ruined shots he took and Rachel gave it back to him full measure. Finally, in exasperation, Rachel jumped onto a couch in the dressing room and ripped her skirt on the side. Rachel then smiled and said, "Well now the skirt won't run up anymore.""

As Tina finished telling the story, she pushed her arms out wide and knocked her coffee cup on the floor. She apologized.

"Oh I am such a klutz. Ralph could you get the cup, I can't reach it very well from here."

When Ralph reached down to pick up the cup, he kept one eye on Tina and placed his hand next to but not on the cup. One of the first things he learned in his trade concerned the value of distraction in overcoming an enemy. Tina's move looked staged to Ralph. He suspiciously watched Tina's right hand disappear into her purse on her right side out of his line of sight. Acting on pure instinct, Ralph pulled his 22 Beretta out of the special pocket in his pants as he slowly moved upward, keeping the gun below the table. Tina brought a gun to bear on Ralph as her hand moved toward him from the other side of the couch. With pure reflex, Ralph shot the handgun out of Tina's hand the moment it appeared, literally a split second before Tina could fire. Ralph followed up his first shot with two more shots, one to each of Tina's shoulders. Tina's shot, originally aimed at Ralph's head went wide when Ralph's bullet struck her hand. Tina's face became hard and mean as she struggled to deal with her injuries and the extreme pain she felt. Tina tried to access her poison stick and her river knife but her shoulders hurt too much. She cried out in frustration as much as in pain as she tried to defend herself. Ralph spoke calmly as he moved to place himself in front of Cindy.

"I wouldn't try to go for another weapon. I'll put a bullet in your forehead if you do. So now you show your true colors. As hard as I tried, I could never become comfortable with you Tina. Now I know why. You're an assassin, a monster wrapped in a nice package. Let's talk about your limited options here. The bullets in your left shoulder and right hand are no doubt painful and may require some surgery but they're not life threatening. The bullet in you right shoulder from the way it's bleeding seems to have severed or at least cut your brachial artery. This is serious. If I'm right, you have about five minutes before you lose consciousness. After that, death from a loss of blood will follow soon afterward. I have a first aid kit in the bathroom, which I will ask Cindy to bring here. I can use the tools in the kit to stop the bleeding in your shoulder. I have done so many times as a Seal in the field. I'll do so only if you honestly answer the questions I'm going to ask."

"I 'll give you nothing," Tina snarled.

"Then you will die. The choice is yours." Ralph calmly responded.

For three long minutes no one moved. Then the expression on Tina's face began to change to one of fear. Her right shoulder wound had already soaked her shirt. She applied pressure to the wound with her left hand but the bleeding hadn't slowed very much. Finally looking in Ralph's eyes, Tina said with more than a little concern.

"Okay what do you want to know. I don't seem to have much choice."

"Who gave you the contract to kill me?"

"CIA Black Ops. I work for them."

"Why?"

"They never said but I heard some things."

"What?"

"The Afghan President Karzam wants you dead. You killed his son on a Seal mission. Maybe the US government wants to appease him. I don't really know. My job is to kill not to make policy. Now please hurry. I feel faint. I'm going to pass out at any moment. I don't have anything more for you."

"Okay, that information is useful and is reinforced by some of my suspicions. It sounds like the truth even though there is really no way for me to know. If you're an agent and what you told me is true, it's dangerous to give that information. You're employer won't be pleased. Cindy, bring my first aid kit."

Despite the fear on her face, Cindy quickly responded, walking to the bathroom and retrieving the kit. As she did so, Tina continued. Her eyes already showed signs of fatigue.

'As you have already said what my employer does or does not do is of secondary importance. If I don't stop this bleeding, I'll be dead. The information is accurate."

"Tina even though you're bleeding out, you're making some sense." Ralph said as he began taking items out of his first aid kit.

After repairing Tina's shoulder, he helped the nearly comatose assassin to her car. He took her keys and drove to a place about a mile away. After arriving there, Ralph left her in the front seat of the car with the window down and called an ambulance. Whether she lived or died meant very little to Ralph. She would never get close to him or Cindy again. Ralph hurried back to his house. He needed to comfort Cindy. Another monster had appeared. From now on, he would find his women on dating sites.

Tina woke up in a hospital bed with an IV in her arm and monitoring equipment. She lost consciousness soon after Ralph dug into her shoulder. She felt weaker than she had in her entire life. Tina couldn't even see clearly. A doctor in the room noticed she woke and walked over to her.

"I don't know how well you can hear me but I'm Doctor Stevenson. You're a strong woman. You flat lined twice from a loss of blood but both times you made it back. Whoever took care of your wound before the EMT's arrived on the scene did an excellent job. He or she kept you alive. We were able to sew up your brachial artery, so it should heal pretty well. Both of your shoulders will be stiff as the wounds heal but I don't see why you can't regain use of them with a little physical therapy. The same is true with your hand, but I'm not sure if you will ever have full use of it again. Time will tell. Surgery will be needed. You only had one bullet remaining in your left shoulder. We got that rather easily. You must rest. You're not out of the woods yet. Losing the amount of blood you did would have killed most people. It still could cost you your life. Oh and there're people here to see you: several police officers and FBI agents and your brother Peter. You can see one person for a few short minutes but that's all. You must rest."

In a soft whisper Tina responded.

"I'll see Peter but I feel like falling asleep again."

Peter came running into the room and pulled up close to Tina. He whispered to her.

"Tina, I'm so sorry for asking you to take out Tager. I couldn't bear to lose you. You're the only thing I love on this planet."

"Peter it doesn't matter. I had to do it for my employer anyway. As this was so, I kept your name out of my negotiations with Ralph Tager for my life. I don't want him going after you. He is the most deadly person I've ever met. You have to promise me you will get rid of this Seal for me: one way or another. I don't like to fail. Also, my black ops employers will not like the fact that he is still alive. Although I must say Tager could have killed me but didn't. He had every reason to do so. But that is his weakness not mine. If you don't or can't kill Tager, I'll gladly kill him when I'm well. I'm fading. My injuries have really taken a lot out of me."

"Tina, don't worry. I'll get him as well as his new daughter. Now please sleep. Your life is still at risk."

"Okay bye Peter. I love you. Tell all those law enforcement folks that they will have to see me some other time."

"Will do," Peter said as he quickly walked away from the already sleeping Tina.

An hour later Tina forced herself awake. She felt threatened. Something didn't feel right. Tina depended on these instincts to stay alive. A strange woman dressed like a nurse who somehow seemed familiar advanced on her. Tina knew this person didn't work here. She reached for the call button but the woman's hand caught hers. Tina didn't have enough strength to fight the woman's strong grip. Tina tried to cry out but could only manage a loud croak. The woman shoved a cloth in Tina's mouth and bound both of her hands together. She then produced some duck tape, which she used to close Tina's mouth as she pulled out the cloth. The strange woman then spoke.

"You have been an excellent agent, one of our best, but this time you failed. Your intended victim shot you then ended up saving you. You must have given him something that could jeopardize our group in return for him saving your life. This is the only conclusion we can reach."

"I didn't give him anything." Tina tried to say but the tape made her response difficult to understand.

"Okay I will remove the tape. You should have the ability to speak. But it is going back on if you start to make a fuss. I think you are trying to say that you didn't give us up but we can't really believe that. Tager is a dangerous man. The more he knows the more dangerous he becomes. Also, other law enforcement people are waiting to talk to you. They could offer you something that will persuade you to talk. They don't like us and are constantly looking for ways to shut us down, particularly when it involves domestic operations. I'm sorry. You had no choice but neither do we. Also, you already had a black mark on your file for killing so many of your lovers. Before any of this occurred, some of the higher ups wanted to eliminate you, fearing your habits would compromise the group. I think this strongly influenced their decision to kill you. By the way, we do the same job but like so many black ops assassins we had no knowledge of each other. We have to operate in complete anonymity."

"If you are like me, you understood what I was trying to say. I didn't give my target anything of value and of course I won't talk with anyone else. They have no leverage on me. No one kills as efficiently as I do. Killing me is a waste and harmful to our mission. My dead lovers have no bearing on this."

"Maybe that is true and maybe it isn't but the decision has been made. If we're caught trying to assassinate a Seal hero on American soil, our entire program will be in jeopardy. Heads will roll. The assassination of Ralph has to be done discreetly. Your failure makes this much harder to do. If this Seal talks, we'll have plenty of explaining to do. Even if he doesn't talk, he will be much more on his guard and harder to approach. With you out of the picture, we can deny you ever had anything to do with us. You know the drill. It could just as easily be me lying on this bed and you standing over me."

With that, the woman put the tape back on Tina's mouth; removed a syringe from her pocket and shot an air bubble in Tina's IV. Tiny tried to pull or knock the IV out of her arm, but the strange woman easily blocked her moves. Tina simply didn't have the strength to fight the woman. Tina tried to get up but the woman pushed her back down on the bed. Meanwhile the air bubble entered Tina's arm. The strange woman smiled and said.

"Goodbye Tina. I'll take the cloth binding off your hands and remove the tape from your mouth. We wouldn't want the authorities to think you ran into foul play. I expect one day the same fate will befall me. I'll see you on the other side."

"Some of my friends will make sure you go there sooner rather than later." Tina snarled.

The woman only laughed as she walked out of the room. Now free, Tina hit her call button and screamed as loud as she could, but seconds later, Tina felt a sharp pain in her chest. Then her world turned completely black.

Task Force

Bob Prandini sat somewhat uncomfortably in a conference room at the very busy Chicago FBI office. On a 6-month assignment with an FBI task force dubbed Seal Hunt, Bob could think of very little else other than Hilda his girlfriend. Bob missed her terribly and texted and e-mailed her several times a day. Finally, she would visit him this weekend at his very small temporary apartment. He hoped this would satisfy his longing for the woman he intended marrying. Why they chose Chicago as the base of operations for the task force he did not know, but the vibrant city began to grow a little on him despite his great love of his home Seattle. Six other detectives from six other cities with reported Pay Back killings also participated on the task force along with FBI agents Sarah Thelon and Malcolm Rodgers and NCIS agent Cynthia Whitcomb. Malcolm began the morning brief.

"Once again we have no reported Pay Back killings for the month, but a mysterious death here is worthy of our attention. We received the file because of the mention of Ralph Tager's name in the police report. Our computer captures any such reports on law enforcement databases and sends them to us. A very beautiful woman with documents showing her to be Sally Richter showed up at Northwestern hospital with bullet wounds to both her shoulders and her hand. Sally Richter, we soon found to be a fake name. When we did a search of our databases, Sally Richter didn't exist. When we searched the database with a picture of the woman, a notation came back saying that the wounded woman worked for the government but her identity had been concealed for national security reasons. In our experience this usually means the person works for the CIA black ops group or some other clandestine federal task force or group. When we ran her fingerprints through an old computer database we sometimes use when we encounter this type of national security blockage, we identified her as Tina Ramirez. She had a long list of juvenile offenses, which had been wiped clean in the main government database but remained in this old database. Tina carried a permitted Beretta, which had been recently fired, a river knife and a very deadly poison stick. When Tina briefly spoke to the police as she was being taken into the OR, she refused to identify who shot her or whether she shot anyone with her gun. Medical personnel prevented any further conversation with the woman. One of the bullets in Tina cut her Brachial Artery but the wound had been expertly treated allowing her to survive an otherwise certain death.

"After carefully reconstructing Tina's movements over the last several weeks, the police found that she visited Ralph's office building on several occasions. When the police searched the database for persons of interest that might work in the building, Ralph's name appeared. The police then showed Tina's picture to a security guard at Ralph's building. According to the security guard, Tina showed up at the building every day for the last three weeks. They saw her with Peter on several occasions but they never saw the couple leaving the building together. The police also checked the house in Lake Bluff where Ralph lives with his daughter but no sign of the woman being there could be found. Also, no one in the neighborhood saw the woman coming our going. With some further digging, we identified Tina as the sister of Peter Ramirez. The FBI interviewed Peter as the possible host of the pervert website Hunters Fantasy but no evidence of his involvement could be found. Earlier in his life, Peter served time for a number of child molestation offenses.

"While ostensibly a model and fashion designer, we think Tina served as a black ops CIA assassin. The arms she carried support this theory, particularly the poison stick, as does the confidential file. She might have worked for another clandestine agency but the pattern here suggests the black ops group. What happened to her also supports this theory. Just a few hours ago after apparently surviving her wounds in good shape, Tina died of a heart attack. A nurse no one at the hospital recognized as ever having worked or officially visited there had been seen near Tina's room just prior to her death. The hospital cameras identify her entering the hospital, going into Tina's room past law enforcement officers waiting to see Tina and then leaving the hospital. She did not interact with anyone else at the hospital while there. Our facial recognition analysis of the strange nurse revealed she too had an inaccessible federal employment file. Unfortunately we do not know this woman's identity or how to obtain it. We couldn't access her file. She didn't turn up on our old database. We are doing an autopsy on Tina but I don't expect to find much of interest. So what do we make of all this?"

"I think it is pretty obvious to a point. The black ops group leaders told Tina to kill Ralph Tager. She used her feminine wiles to get close to Tager but failed to kill him. He instead found out what and who she was and shot her. For reasons unknown, after Tager shot Tina, he saved her life by binding her wounds and getting her to a hospital. The CIA"s Black OPs didn't like Tina's failure and decided to kill her. This analysis of course leaves a lot of questions. Why did the CIA want to kill a highly decorated Navy Seal? What information did Tina give Tager or what information did the CIA think she gave Tager? It must have been explosive for them to kill one of their own agents?" Bob Prandini said.

"Yeah that sounds right but there might be more to it. Just before a pervert killed Tager's wife and daughter, Tager's entire Seal Team fell in an ambush in Afghanistan. Twenty heavily armed Taliban waited for the team to land in their parachutes at the prearranged site. There is little doubt someone gave the Taliban the landing location. The Seals fought bravely but never had a chance. Tager had been promoted to a position where he no longer led his former team. Otherwise he too would have died in the ambush. They never found who betrayed the Seals but rumors persisted that someone within our government did so. Needless to say morale suffered after that. The death of Tager's wife and daughter and his subsequent forced resignation made matters much worse. The Seal ranks revered Ralph. Twenty percent of the Seals in the Great Lakes Command put in papers to leave the service shortly after Tager left." Cynthia said.

"Something really stinks here. Could Tina Ramirez have involved her brother in a CIA operation to kill Tager's wife and brutally rape and kill his daughter? According to the briefing books, Wiggle the pervert killer credited with killing Tager's family frequented the Hunter Fantasy website. Maybe killing Tager along with his men wasn't enough. The CIA had to make him suffer first. I can't imagine what this hero could have done to deserve this." Strom Roberts from Louisiana said.

"I don't know either. Ralph Tager's record in the Navy aside from him allegedly killing Ted Wiggle the pervert, which no one proved, was absolutely spotless. To the contrary, Tager received several medals for valor and would have received more except for the sensitive nature of many of his missions." Cynthia responded.

"I'm trying to sort this out in my head. If all this is true, the federal government actually created Pay Back by destroying Tager's life. We're supposed to find enough evidence against Tager so the federal government can arrest and prosecute him. But while they have us chasing around in our task force, they send killers to short circuit the process. If we arrest Tager I wonder how long he would stay alive in federal custody. I know what my job is but this somehow doesn't feel right. I seem to be helping the bad guy." Tom Madigan from the NYPD said.

"We're getting way off track here. Based on some random facts we're jumping to conclusions. The CIA Black Ops group doesn't share information with other people inside or outside of the government. They may or may not have had a contract out on Ralph Tager. If they did, we have no clue as to why. They wouldn't have gone after a decorated Seal lightly. As you have said our job is to find evidence against Tager, which is pretty hard to do when he has ceased operations against violent perverts. Our stings just got too close to him and his Pay Back teams. We missed one of his teams last time by no more than

5 minutes. What we don't know is whether this stoppage is permanent or temporary." Sarah Thelon said.

"We're focusing too much on Tager. Sid Worth is the real player here. It's his money that keeps the Pay Back killings going. Still, I'm sure Tager told him to back off for a while to let the heat die down. The question is whether Worth will start again without Tager, who now must be focused on our government's attempt to assassinate him for some unknown reason." Bridgette Rasputin from Bridgeport, Connecticut said.

"Yeah we need to increase our surveillance of Worth. He may try to meet with his teams. The problem is he uses doubles to throw us off the track. He isn't easy to find or track." Malcolm Rodgers said.

"Okay some of us can focus on that activity while the rest of us need to interview all the Seals Tager knew who have left the military. I'm convinced he recruited some of the members of the Pay Back teams from this group. So far, we have identified eight possible Pay Back team members for this group." Sarah said.

"What are we going to do about Tager?" Bob Prandini asked.

"Nothing. I think the CIA will take care of him for us." Sarah said.

"I don't know. Tager isn't easy to kill. He will try to remove the government's reason for killing him. He will be very aggressive about it. We should find out what his next step is." Bob responded.

"You can do that Bob. Tager is still involved with these vigilante killings somehow. He could still help us stop them. Meanwhile we'll focus on Sid Worth and the Pay Back teams we still haven't identified." Malcolm said.

The Luncheon

ॐ

Ralph walked cautiously toward the small table in the North Chicago restaurant just off the Great Lakes Naval Base. He examined every person in the room and all possible shooting angles before finally sitting down next to his long time friend and former superior Butch. Butch eyed Ralph for several seconds before saying.

"You should still be a Seal. None of this should have happened, but unfortunately it did. I haven't heard from you in a long time. Now you suddenly ask for a meeting. What's up?"

"Butch congratulations on getting your command back. You should never have lost it in the first place. Putting a non-Seal in your job really hurt the service. Like you Butch I'm direct. I have a request. I want to temporarily be returned to active duty and go on a Seal mission to Afghanistan."

"Why do you want to do that?"

"I'm going to trust you Butch. I don't know what else I can do. CIA Black Ops sent an assassin to kill me named Tina. She tried but I managed to wound her in both shoulders. The bullet I put in her right shoulder cut her brachial artery. Facing death from loss of blood, she spilled the beans. Tina said that Afghan President Karzam wanted me dead because I killed his son on a Seal mission. So Tina's employers ordered the hit on me. I remember the mission well. You're orders were very specific: kill Karzam's son. Our team did exactly as ordered. Given this information I think it is very odd that my entire ex Seal Team were ambushed and killed on a mission soon afterwards. Even my wife's killing and the rape and torture of my daughter are suspicious. Tina's brother is head of the violent pervert website Hunter's Fantasy. The abductor and killer of my daughter Ted Wiggle frequented that site. Finally, Tina, after recovering in the hospital mysteriously died when a nurse no one recognized visited her room. The medical examiner although he could not prove it believed someone put an air bubble in her IV. Butch there are too many coincidences and facts here to ignore. Karzam wanted revenge for his son's death and our government gave it to him by sacrificing the Seals who participated in the mission."

"Whoa Ralph that is a lot to take in all at once. You are making some pretty serious and explosive allegations here. I can't give any credibility to any of them and expect to keep my job. But if you're right it may help explain my transfer and the brass's hounding you out of the service. The brass never gave me a reason why they did this or why they reinstated me."

"Butch, I wish all of this couldn't be true but I suspect it is. This is why I'm making the request. I need to somehow remove the reason for the Afghans to target me. I must somehow convince Karzam to stop targeting me. I can't do that here. I must do it there."

"You don't know how you will do this?"

"No. I don't really know but I will find a way." Ralph responded.

"Okay, say we send you to Afghanistan. You will want to split off the main Seal force when you land? It is what I would do. Ordinarily I would say absolutely no. Once you leave the Seals, there is no coming back, but because of the mess caused by the brass's actions, I have now been given the right to bring back retired Seals for specific jobs. We simply don't have enough Seals to do the work otherwise. I'm not promising anything but I will try to get you attached to a mission. But beyond that I can't help you once you are there. You are on your own. I don't give you very good odds of ever returning from there."

"Whatever the odds, I'll take them. Thanks Butch, you won't regret it."

"Ralph thank me when I have you on a mission."

A half hour later, Ralph sat in his home with his head in his hands. The talk with Butch had gone very well, too well in fact. As a Seal, Ralph learned how to detect lying. He used the training in countless high-risk situations and it had saved his life and those of his men many times. Butch almost certainly lied. Ralph suspected Butch knew about the CIA operation or at least strongly suspected that such an operation took place. Why else would he suggest that his transfer and Ralph's forced leaving of the service had anything to do with it? Also, the Butch he knew would never make a statement about the political situation in Afghanistan. He never engaged in speculation about the reasons his Seals were sent into combat. Butch hated politics and politicians. If Butch put him on an operation, he would be placed there to die as his Seal team comrades already had. Butch and his superiors would assume he traveled to Afghanistan to kill their President Karzam. He really had no other play. Ralph also doubted the Navy had any new policy allowing the reinstatement of retired Seals. Butch might have been involved in the whole mess from the beginning. At that moment, Ralph lost all faith in the man he regarded as his mentor. Still, if Butch allowed him to go on a Seal mission to Afghanistan he would go. Ralph had no other choice. If at all possible, this very dangerous mission just became more dangerous.

The Mission

Butch called Ralph a week later with the good news. The Navy granted Ralph permission to accompany a Seal Team on a mission to Afghanistan. Ralph quickly absorbed the mission profile and dressed carefully to look as much like an Afghan as possible. He already spoke both major Afghan languages Pashto and Dari but not particularly well. As a legend in the service, the rest of the Seals on the mission quickly accepted him into their ranks. Ralph as always carefully selected the equipment he would take on the mission.

Before he left the service, Ralph placed some of the Seals most highly effective new weapons in a secret storage area in his house. While not a legal or ethical act, Ralph felt very uneasy about the circumstances that forced his resignation from the Seals. Ralph also felt that he had earned the weapons from the many sacrifices he made while serving as a Seal. Two of the weapons held particular interest: the first, a colorless odorless gas that rendered people unconscious for a half hour then effectively wiped their short-term memory. This allowed the user the ability to place weapons or poison in an area without the guards recognizing it. The second, a very advanced poison that gradually disrupted the victim's heart rhythms until he had a fatal heart attack, Ralph also took. This poison killed at different rates, the weaker the targets heart the faster he would succumb. This allowed the killing of several subjects without too much suspicion. Also, the poison could not be detected with normal blood tests. It degraded in the target's blood stream after being ingested. These two highly classified weapons would be the tools he needed to implement his assassination plan. They slipped rather easily into the pack he would carry on his back.

Ralph also focused on his parachute, the easiest way to kill him, if the government decided to do so. As a precaution, Ralph packed his own parachute and tied very thin almost invisible strands of plastic to the zipper and Velcro areas allowing access to the parachute. He used a very specific pattern in tying the plastic threads. Several hours later, as the Seals lined up at the transport bound for Afghanistan, Ralph discreetly traded his parachute for one of the spares in the storage area. The strands once fastened to his parachute bag had been broken then reattached differently in the short time between his packing of the parachute and this moment. Butch or someone else in on the CIA operation tampered with his parachute. As Ralph performed this simple switch, Ralph had to focus all his energy on placing a neutral look on his face to avoid suspicion. He felt like an angry rattlesnake ready to strike at anything that came close to him. Ralph easily faced danger but he hated betrayal. A Seal could not survive without trust in his teammates.

The night jump near the Afghan capital of Kabul went smoothly. Per his orders, Ralph separated from the rest of the jumpers as he descended to his own designated landing area. He would after landing join up with them at a later time. After his former team died in an ambush, the Seals liked to separate at least one man from the body of the team to look for ambushes. When the other team members fell out of his sight, Ralph made further adjustments in his descent to another landing site of his own choosing about a half-mile away from his designated site. He no longer trusted anyone and remembered very well the ambush that waited for his Seal team.

The ground came up quickly in the darkness, but his parachute performed well. With uncommon speed, Ralph retrieved and folded his parachute. Then he hid along with his parachute in some thick bushes. Ralph carefully controlled his breathing as he patiently waited for what came next. As expected, two troop transports roared by in the darkness on their way to Ralph's designated landing site. After they passed, Ralph quickly moved through the woods to the hidden road and walked the other direction. He needed to put as much distance as possible between him and those troops. When they didn't find him at the landing site, they would expand their search. Fortunately, the leaders of this mission would not be concerned about his absence from the landing site. They expected his parachute to fail, which would put his body in a large area outside of the landing site. Ralph hoped that this would give him the time he needed to get away.

Once Ralph reached the main road, he tried to secure a ride into Kabul on the odd assortment of vehicles that roared past him in the early morning. He sweated heavily as he did so. Ralph lay exposed to the two troop trucks should they return this way. Finally, he received a break. Two loud diesel trucks belching black smoke hit each other bringing both of them to a stop. As the two drivers argued, Ralph slipped into the back of one of the trucks. He barely had enough room to fit among the boxes stored there. As he settled in and closed the truck rear-loading door, Ralph noticed the two troop transports roaring past. For now, fortune favored him. The drivers of the troop trucks would have noticed him walking along the road.

An hour and a half later, the truck driver who had started again only minutes after Ralph entered the truck, entered the area in Kabul near the Presidential Palace. Ralph knew this because his portable GPS device indicated as much. When the truck began to turn away from the area, Ralph exited the truck at a stop sign. By walking and using buses, Ralph reached the expected banana truck route to the palace, which he had carefully identified before going on the mission. He arrived in plenty of time to meet the truck. According to Ralph's intelligence, President Karzam loved bananas. Once a day, a truck with thirty or more bananas along with other fresh fruit and vegetables would be driven to the palace. Ralph saw the truck on video taken by some local army personnel. Ralph planned to drug the two guards in the back of the truck with his sleeping gas and inject each banana with a small amount of the special CIA poison through its skin. He would use a hypodermic needle to do so.

The plan had many holes and Ralph knew it. What if he couldn't gain access to the back of the vehicle? He possessed various lock picking tools, which he knew how to use but picking locks always carried the risk of encountering one you couldn't open. Also, picking a lock on a moving truck presented a particular challenge. Further, what if people reported him entering the truck? He had no answer for this but Afghans did many strange things with vehicles including riding on the backs of them. What if he ran into Afghan or American soldiers? He had no specific plan for this problem. How many people would die from the poison? If too many died, the whole operation would raise suspicions. The list went on and on. Ralph would have much preferred to shoot the Afghan President and blame it on the Taliban but he would need logistical support for this approach, which he did not have. Finally, Ralph cast all these worries aside. He had a plan and he intended to implement it.

As Ralph waited, he thought of his original plan to inject the bananas at the depot before the truck went on the road. He rejected the plan for several reasons. First, at least ten heavily armed Afghan soldiers patrolled the site. He could get passed them but if he committed any mistakes even small ones, he would be dead. Second, the delivery service frequently changed the trucks it used for this delivery. Ralph would have a very hard time determining which truck carried the bananas. He knew this would be the right truck because of the route and the banana delivery schedule. Third, if he luckily reached the right truck, he would not know how much time he had before the guards entered the truck. Ralph had no intelligence giving him this information. Is short, while the plan he now pursued had many holes and risks, the depot attack had even more.

Twenty minutes later, right on schedule, the banana truck stopped at the light where Ralph waited. Quickly and adroitly he grabbed the back door, pulled himself upright and picked the door lock with a tool he had at the ready. Fortunately for Ralph, the old lock presented no challenge. Cracking the rear loading door open, he threw in the small gas canister. Several bullets whizzed past his head and others impacted his bulletproof vest but the fast acting gas stopped the firing in less than a minute. Ralph opened the rear door of the truck, put on his gas mask and rolled inside. The two guards lay fast asleep next to the banana clusters. They had positioned the boxes carrying the fruits around them. They still gripped their AK-47's. Ralph expected the truck driver to stop and investigate the firing but he didn't. The Kabul streets produced huge amounts of noise and backfiring trucks. Even gunshots occurred fairly often. Ralph breathed a sigh of relief, removed his syringe and began injecting the poison into each banana. In the space of five minutes, he injected all thirty bananas in the truck. Without a moment's hesitation, he placed the needle back in his pack, removed his gas mask and quickly moved out of the truck, locking the rear padlock as he clung to the outside. When the truck slowed down for a bicycle, Ralph rolled off onto the sidewalk area. He kept walking until he put as much distance as possible between him and the truck. Ralph shed the bulletproof vest in a trash receptacle along the road. His use of the vest would create suspicions on his journey to come. Also, the vest had the bullets fired by the men in it. Ralph also inspected the deep bruises caused by the bullet impacts. They hurt but provided no impediment to his movements. He could easily tolerate the pain. Ralph apparently suffered no rib breaks this time. Such breaks could impede his movements.

Ralph's work, now done, he headed on a local bus to the main bus station where he would take a cross-country bus to Islamabad in an hour. Ralph didn't consider a flight from Kabul an option. He would be spotted and detained if he tried to leave the country this way. Going through the old soviet republics up north or Iran to the East also seemed like poor options. They would be very suspicious of him. In an hour and a half, Ralph hunkered down in the crowded cross-country bus as it left Kabul. The local bus trip presented no problems. He looked like a bored Afghan and as a result received no attention. Ralph had no idea whether his assassination would be successful. The guards would wake up disoriented, minutes after he left the truck. They wouldn't remember shooting their guns or falling asleep for that matter. They might see the new bullet holes but the truck already had bullet holes in it. People occasionally shot at the truck as it sped by. The guards had only added three. The rest exited the truck out of the open door. They might not notice that anything had happened. The bananas and the crates had been returned to their original positions. Even if one of them noticed some changes, like the firing of their weapons, telling the authorities carried risk. They would have a lot of questions asked of them, which could lead to their firing or even detention. They would likely claim that some random shots found the truck. At least, Ralph hoped they would.

The Crossing

R alph, who could bear almost any discomfort, still intensely disliked the crowded hot bus. He retained his backpack but had removed all other traces of western civilization. Ralph threw away all the materials he brought for the assassination. All he had was his identification and some dirty Afghan clothes and some Pakistani money. His challenge lay at the Pakistan border. Although he had identification claiming him to be an Afghan citizen and looked the part, he could not survive a long interrogation. He had a poor command of the Pashto and Dari languages and his accent would puzzle anyone who spoke with him for any length of time. He survived by being a man of very few words. The less he spoke the greater chance he had of passing as an Afghan.

Ralph suffered several hours of discomfort, which kept him focused on his surroundings. Nonetheless, the sudden appearance of the border surprised him. Some very hardened and mean looking soldiers on both sides eyed the bus and its occupants suspiciously. Ralph had no way of knowing whether his efforts in Kabul or his failure to show up at the landing site had somehow made him a wanted man. They might have pictures of him at the crossing. After examining each of the occupants, the Afghan sentries waved the bus forward but the Pakistan soldiers on the other side of the border brought the bus to a halt. They then ordered everyone off of the bus. Lining up with the rest, Ralph reviewed his options. He only possessed a small sharp knife in his shoe, which a normal search would not reveal. He bore no gun. The Pakistani soldier with a 50-caliber machine gun trained on the passengers would not react well to anyone bearing a firearm. His now discarded vest would have received the same reaction.

After checking everyone's papers, the guards looked for valuables and money. After relieving the passengers of everything they had of value, they finally concentrated on Ralph. When they found no valuables when they patted him down other than the Pakistani currency, which they pocketed, the guards took his backpack. After a brief conversation they asked him in Dari where he obtained it. Already expecting the question, Ralph replied in Dari, a dead American soldier. The guards laughed and then threw the backpack on the ground next to Ralph. The dirty clothes inside had convinced them that they didn't really need the otherwise empty backpack. Ralph wisely did not move. Making any move with these guards would likely provoke a response. When the guards finally waved everyone back on board, Ralph picked up his backpack and re-boarded the bus very slowly. When the guards returned to their booth, an alert informed them of a dangerous American named Ralph Tager, who might try to sneak through the border. The guards had not seen any Americans for several days, so they disregarded the alert.

Twenty minutes later with the bus once again on the road to Islamabad, Ralph reflected on what took place. For a moment, when the guard asked him a question, Ralph worried that he would have to take action. If they detained him and carefully searched his clothes they would not only find the knife but his other set of fake English Identification, which he intended to use to exit Pakistan. The guards would then know that he was not who he pretended to be. They wouldn't react well to this information. Ralph had already analyzed what he would have to do. The plan, which involved stabbing the nearest solider and using his gun to kill the remaining guards only had about a 30% chance of success. Nonetheless, these greedy guards presented Ralph with a serious problem. With his money gone, Ralph would not be able to buy a ticket out of Pakistan or purchase an English suit. He could not use a CIA site. Before leaving the U.S., Ralph studied the various CIA and Defense clandestine sights as well as the stashes of money, identification cards, passports, and contacts located in various parts of the capital. Ralph decided not to use any of these resources. The CIA and Defense could easily find him this way and decide to make his life very difficult. Even if his assassination had been successful, Karzam wouldn't die for another week at the earliest, but his American comrades would still be hunting him. He had, however, another option. On a mission to Islamabad five years ago a British Secret Service agent gave him an address and a code to enter an apartment the British kept in Islamabad. Ralph wrote the code down and slipped the tiny piece of paper in a hidden place in his wallet. If the British site still existed, he could obtain money and clothing there. Ralph would have to be lucky again.

An hour after they left the border, when Ralph finally began to relax, he saw a small pick up truck filled with heavily armed soldiers approach at high speed. Robbers or Taliban soldiers, they would not treat the bus passengers well, particularly when they discovered that the Pakistani guards had already taken everything of value from them. Ralph quickly scanned the bus for other possible warriors. Ralph found two tough looking men with whom he locked eyes but aside from them, the bus contained people with no apparent military skills. They would be easy prey. Ralph, needing to take some chances in the few minutes he had before the truck pulled alongside, continued to look at the two tough men while he pointed to his boot. They nodded and pointed to areas within their clothes where they apparently had something hidden. Ralph made a gesture with his arm as if he grabbed someone and the two men mimicked the move.

The pickup truck cut off the bus bringing it to a screeching stop. Six armed soldiers ordered the passengers to line up outside the bus. When they did so, the soldier, who seemed to be in charge, shot an old man in the line to death. He made some comment that Ralph understood to mean that the old man was worthless and needed to go to Allah sooner rather than later. Ralph recognized the tactic. The soldiers wanted to instill terror in the passengers to gain better control of them. He noted with some relief that the two hard men didn't react with any kind of fear to the killing. Their eyes just became harder. The situation rapidly grew worse as the robbers found nothing to steal. They shot a middle age woman in the head when they found no jewelry on her. Finally, the robbers moved far enough down the line, so Ralph and the two hard men each had a robber opposite them. With a simple nod, Ralph removed the knife from his shoe by slowly moving his leg upward, slit the robber's throat in front of him and grabbed his Ak-47. The two hard men did likewise but on the way down, a robber managed to shoot one of the hard men in the chest. Seconds later, the other hard man and Ralph mowed the rest of the robbers down with concentrated fire from their stolen rifles. In less than a minute all six robbers apparently lay dead but before they succumbed, the robbers fired some rounds at the line. In addition to the hard man, two other people died, bringing the passenger losses to five and the robber losses to six. When the firing stopped, the hard man calmly walked up to each fallen robber and shot him in the head. Indeed one of the robbers faked his death and tried to reach for a gun before the hard man shot him again. This part of the world left little room for compassion.

To Ralph's surprise, the passengers after taking whatever they could of value from the dead robbers, re-boarded the bus and calmly took their seats. Ralph replenished his supply of money from the dead robbers, but doubted he had enough money to buy a suit and purchase a plane ticket. He only had enough money for the ticket. Ralph might still have to visit the British site. Ralph had no need for anything else the dead men had. Moments later, the bus driver started the bus again and they resumed their trip to Islamabad. As the bus headed down the road, Ralph realized almost nonstop warfare had made all these people very hard. Not one person cried out in fear or panicked.

Before leaving on his trip, Ralph memorized the location of the clandestine British site. His bus route to downtown Islamabad would take him about a half mile from the location. He also studied the likely bus route he would use. Ralph asked the bus driver to drop him on a street closest to the site. The bus driver after what Ralph had done readily agreed to do so. The bus driver realized he would probably be dead if Ralph and the other two warriors had not acted when they did. Ralph had another reason for leaving the bus early. After the incident on the road, the authorities might very well decide to interview the bus passengers when they docked at their destination. Ralph in his disguise would almost certainly be detained for further questioning when his interviewers ascertained the hollowness of his story and his poor command of the Dari and Pashtun languages.

When Ralph left the bus, he waved at the bus passengers. Many waved back at him. They like the bus driver owed their lives to Ralph. Ralph walked quickly toward his destination becoming more anxious by the moment. He had no back up plan if the site had been abandoned or way of explaining his presence to anyone using the site. The apartment lay in a non-descript building. When Ralph approached the door he noticed a keypad. Without a moment's hesitation, Ralph removed the piece of paper from his wallet and keyed in the code his British friend had provided to him long ago. The door clicked open. Ralph entered a plain apartment with a small kitchen, a bath with a shower and two small bedrooms. The apartment had big closets. When Ralph opened them, he saw a large collection of different types of outfits, male and female, which included some very nice British suits. Ralph found one that fit and carried it to the bathroom. Ralph, after removing his underwear, took a quick shower. Ralph followed this with a shave. He also took care of his bathroom needs.

After dressing, Ralph walked casually toward the laptop on the kitchen table. The laptop quickly came to life as Ralph booked a ticket to London. For whatever reason, the laptop contained the same code he used to gain entry to the apartment. Ralph arranged to pick up the ticket at the airport. Ralph would pay cash. Credit of any kind would be traceable to him. After printing out his receipt, Ralph erased any trace of his booking. Then Ralph quickly wiped down any surface he touched. Ralph did not search for or take any money. He didn't need it. Also, the money would be missed. People using the apartment would be less likely to notice the missing suit. Ralph placed his Afghan outfit in a bag and walked out of the apartment with it. As he left the building, a man dressed in a suit like his passed him. Ralph merely waved, said Cheerio and kept walking. The man said nothing in return but did look a little puzzled. After walking several blocks, Ralph placed his bag in a trash container. He then hailed a cab for the airport.

On the way to the airport, Ralph practiced his English accent. During his Seal days, he worked with British soldiers and frequently mimicked their accents. A half hour later as he stood in front of a Pakistani soldier on the security line, Ralph used his forced relaxation training. While he felt like a bomb ready to explode, Ralph on the outside looked completely relaxed. Finally, Ralph stood in front of the guard checking people and ID's. To release the tension, Ralph joked about a recent Manchester United Football game with the guard. His accent sounded pretty good at least to his ears. The Pakistani soldier relaxed and waived Ralph through the line after making some comments about the prowess of the Pakistani national team. After Ralph settled on the British Airways plane, he finally began to unwind.

Still, his route took him through London and Toronto, Canada. He would then cross the border at Windsor, pretending to be a day commuter. When he finally gained admission to the U.S., he would once again become Ralph Tager. While his plan could still put him in a difficult position, Ralph felt fairly confident of success. The hard part had already passed. Ralph faced death many times but somehow, someway over the last several days he avoided it.

Butch

Butch, who never drank during the day, nursed a Jack Daniels on the rocks in his office. He betrayed his friend and the Seals who worked under him but he did it to protect the Seals, an institution he loved. At least Butch felt that this is what he did. Admiral Templeton, a very mysterious person indeed, wanted Tager and his men dead and Tager to suffer before he died to satisfy the Afghan President. Otherwise, this President would expel the U.S. military from his country and make the sacrifice of thousands of soldier lives and the expenditure of hundreds of billion of dollars meaningless. When Butch didn't play ball with the Admiral, the Admiral stuck him in a windowless room with nothing to do in the Pentagon and gave a non-Seal his command. The Seals suffered with a bureaucrat as a leader. Almost to a man they wanted a transfer. Some just quit. Admiral Templeton seemed content to leave it this way until an angry President, a former Army Ranger, wanted to know why so many Seal teams seemed to be unavailable for missions. The Admiral's bureaucratic responses resulted in Presidential threats to replace him and many of his comrades. As a result, Admiral Templeton offered to re-instate Butch but only if he finished the original mission: eliminate Tager. The Admiral needed closure on this mission. President Karzam seemed satisfied with what had taken place so far but wanted Tager dead. Also, the Admiral and his allies in the CIA began to realize that as each day passed with Tager still alive, concealing this dirty mission from the press and the administration became more and more difficult. This secret if made public would bury them all.

As a result, a Butch, Butch did not know, arranged for Ralph to be re-instated for a mission that no one intended he complete. Then Butch cut all the parachute cords fastening the parachute to the harness in Ralph's parachute bag and replaced the thin plastic threads Ralph placed in the bag to reveal any tampering. Ralph would fall to his death from an accident that was in fact a murder. After Ralph left on the mission, Butch searched for the tampered parachute but did not find it. Ralph certainly used it on the mission assuring his death. Yet, after the mission took place, no one could find Ralph's body or parachute or any other sign of the former Seal. He seemed to have disappeared. Ralph had not landed at his designated landing site where an ambush awaited him should he somehow have avoided the parachute trap.

While these signs seemed positive, Butch still worried. His gut told him that Ralph still lived and probably hid somewhere inside Afghanistan. While Ralph had no resources in that country to use, Butch knew that his best Seal always found a way to get the job done. Still, the Afghan President appeared to be in good health even though he reputedly had some heart problems. If Ralph pursued the Afghan President he should already be dead. Ralph must be dead. Still, as a precaution, Butch notified the Afghans of Ralph's possible attempt to exit the country. If all else failed, the Afghans would capture Ralph and remove him as a threat.

As the Navy Captain drained another glass of whiskey his private cell phone jarred him. With a sigh, Butch answered the phone. Only people he knew well had this cell number, which made this call important enough to answer.

"Butch", he growled into the phone.

"You are a Judas, a betrayer and coward, not fit to wear the Seal uniform. Did you really think I wouldn't notice your awkward retying of the thin plastic threads? A man would have faced me rather than trying to make my death look like an accident. You disgust me. You are just a paper-pushing coward. I don't want to ever see you again. If I do, I will spit in your face and blow your head off."

Before Butch could answer the line went dead. Butch recognized Ralph's voice on the other end. Butch grabbed the fifth and drained the rest of it in one gulp. Butch needed to dull the pain in his heart. Ralph had been absolutely right. He no longer deserved to wear the uniform that was like another skin to him. Seals did not betray other Seals. Still, an alive Ralph presented a major problem for Butch. Where did the call originate? What had Ralph done about his mission? How would Butch explain this call to his superiors? Butch mulled these questions until he suddenly passed out behind his desk. He found no answers to his questions before sleep overtook him.

Back to Normal

Two weeks after Ralph returned from Afghanistan, Ralph read this news report in the international section of his newspaper.

"President Karzam died of a sudden heart attack on September 19th. One week later an aide to the President died of a heart attack; three days after that a kitchen worker in the palace died of a heart attack. According to Afghan sources, an autopsy of the three men did not reveal drugs or poison in the men's systems. Their hearts just seemed to stop. All foods in the palace were carefully examined for toxins but none were found. The three men did not come in contact with each other or appear in the same room together these same Afghan sources claim. The strange coincidence of three men, who occupied the palace, dying of the same cause close to one another in time, could not be explained. Some Taliban leaders are blaming the CIA but without any evidence their claims are not receiving much support. American officials vigorously deny any involvement in Karzam's death. They claim the Afghan President who had a history of heart problems simply died of natural causes."

The news report cheered Ralph. He heard about Karzam's death but worried about what other deaths might follow. Two additional Afghan deaths seemed to be quite minimal considering the amount of poison in the bananas. He suspected the Afghan investigation to suddenly turn toward assassination and the U.S. Ralph could easily become entwined in the investigation. Yet this had not happened, perhaps because the Afghan President and the US seemed to be working so closely together.

For whatever reason, the Afghan government seemed satisfied to leave the President's death a natural occurrence, following this conclusion being reached in all three autopsies. According to another detailed report on the dead President, talking of his rise to power, personal relationships and other unique things about the fallen leader, President Karzam ate two bananas a day but did not like other people in the palace eating his bananas. Apparently all but a few complied with his wishes.

Meanwhile, Butch sat in a conference room with several angry admirals.

"Butch what the hell happened? Tager should be dead. Instead Karzam is dead. We trusted you to get the job done and you failed. State is having a fit. Karzam's VP Saddam, the idiot thinks he is the real Saddam Hussein, will take over for a while. He is okay but weak. Karzam's second son, Rashid is expected to run in the next election scheduled in 6 months and win. We know nothing about this son. He speaks to no one. He takes no political positions. Rashid received his education in the US and Britain, but even these sources reveal nothing about what the man thinks. He may like his father hold us responsible for killing his brother and maybe now his father as well. We just don't know. With Saddam in power, the Taliban may be emboldened just as we are trying to pull back our commitment. It is obvious to us Tager used KZ 80 to poison Karzam. The additional deaths of two young healthy people confirm it. We know you had some of the poison at your facility. Tager apparently inserted the poison into Karzam's bananas but no one has any record of Tager being anywhere near the bananas taken to Karzam. The body count would have been much higher if Karzam hadn't prohibited his staff from eating his bananas. What the hell do we do about this bloody mess?" Admiral Templeton said.

"Retaliating against Tager doesn't make any sense at this point. No one in Afghanistan is asking for his death anymore. We have no proof that he had anything to do with Karzam's death. Even if we did, it doesn't serve our national interest to have one of our heroes linked to the assassination of Karzam and of course his son at an earlier time.

In any case, Tager isn't stupid. If we go after him or anyone he loves, Tager will release information he does have on our orders to eliminate Karzam's son. He may also be able to link the death of his Seal team to officials within our government. If we leave Tager alone, he is unlikely to mention these incidents again. He still loves the Seals and wouldn't want to do anything to hurt them." Butch said.

"I'm not so sure. He is vulnerable through his daughter. Using her we can kill him. Dead men don't talk. If Tager arranges the release of papers after his death we can challenge their authenticity. At least that way, we won't have a war hero testifying against us. I'll consult with the CIA and State and see what they say." Admiral Templeton said once again while the other two admirals in attendance staid quiet.

"Admiral I think you're making a mistake. Killing people won't make this problem go away, but I am so deeply in this whole mess I'll do whatever you want." Butch said.

"Stay in touch Captain. If we need you, we will let you know." Admiral Templeton said dismissing Butch.

On the way back to base, Butch decided he would do the right thing for once. He dialed Ralph's number and when the voice mail came on as expected he said.

"The death of Karzam didn't put an end to it. For you and your daughter to be safe Admiral Templeton will need to go. He is determined to kill you and may use your daughter to accomplish this goal."

Butch didn't care what happened now. He had played Admiral Templeton's game long enough. Butch wanted out. Ralph would give that to him.

Personal Crisis

Ralph couldn't believe the message he just received from Butch. Ralph had to kill an admiral, what he called the lethal force option, to insure his and his daughter's safety. What kind of insanity could this be? Could he believe Butch after the man tried to kill him? Strangely, he felt that he could. Butch had nothing to gain from telling him this information and much to lose. It was his way of making amends. The other scenario that Butch laid a trap for him didn't make any sense. This bureaucratic admiral would never set himself up as bait. He ordered other people to take risks. He didn't personally take them.

Two nights after listening to Butch's voicemail, Ralph for the first time in his life had a nightmare about his profession. First the faces of all those he killed and recognized appeared. Each one looked at him with hollow eyes and asked a simple question. "Why?" In some cases, he had the answer. When Tina appeared whom he had not really killed, he could simply say in response that she had tried to kill him. In other cases, they fell in the murkier area of collateral damage. The two Afghans who ate the poison bananas fell in this area. Butch saw their faces as they had been printed in the newspaper. They had been particularly loud in his dream, yelling in Dari about their abrupt trip to see Allah. Then blank faces of men and women appeared, people who died because of the war Ralph constantly waged. In truth, Ralph did not know how many people died by his hand. On numerous occasions, he fired explosive shells, as well as machine guns into dense concentrations of the enemy. Sometimes he saw bodies; sometimes he did not. Even if he saw the bodies, he had no way of knowing whether he killed them or not. On more than one occasion, bodies of noncombatants such as women and children, lay next to the bodies of the soldiers who had fought him. Ralph knew that at least some of them must have died at his hand. Their deaths haunted him the most. Modern wars caused terrible messes. Innocents died. As a warrior he had to accept this truth but he could not easily do so.

When the nightmares appeared night after night, Ralph became very concerned about his physical and mental condition. The nightmares made it difficult for him to concentrate on the daily tasks he had to perform and robbed Ralph of the sleep he needed. Although a businessman now, Ralph remained a soldier until those waging war on him stopped doing so. To be an effective soldier, Ralph had to think of the mission and only the mission and be in the best possible physical and mental condition. This much he knew. If he became distracted during battle, death would come for him and not his enemies. When Cindy started asking him about his exhaustion, Ralph decided to visit Father O'Brien again.

As before Ralph slipped into the confessional when he knew the father sat there.

"Bless me father for I have sinned. It has been several months since my last confession." Ralph told Father O'Brien somewhat automatically.

"Ralph my son I remember our previous conversation very well. What has changed in your life that brings you here today?"

"Father for the first time in my life I have begun to have dreams of the many people I have killed. They all ask me why. In some cases, I know the answer in others I do not. Why are these spirits coming to me now after all these years? I have never seen them before. "

"Some spirits are at peace when they die; others are not. Those who are not often die unexpectedly or violently. The feel that they have been cheated out of life and in some respects they have. Those spirits attach themselves to the person or persons they feel responsible for their untimely death. Sensitive people see them right away. Non-sensitive people generally don't see them unless so many spirits attach to them that the spirits break through into a person's subconscious. This is what has happened to you."

"What can I do to stop them? They are robbing me of sleep and disturbing my mental concentration which I depend upon to survive."

"You can talk to them through your thoughts. You can explain that you are a warrior and thus called upon by others to take lives. Some of them may already know this; others may not. You can apologize for what you felt you had to do. This sometimes helps. Still, the spirits may never truly forgive you. The best you can hope to do is to lessen their anguish enough for them to move on to our heavenly father. When they are there, they will no longer haunt you. With so many people involved, this is a difficult task but one you must pursue to preserve your own sanity."

"I could have used you in my Seal days. Many Seals under my command developed severe cases of PTSD when they returned to civilian life. Some have even taken their own lives. They asked me for help but beyond recommending them for care at the VA I didn't really know what to say to them. My condition is mild compared to theirs but disturbing nonetheless. Anyway, Father how do you know all this?"

"Son I have spent a lifetime studying these matters. It is part of my faith and yours too."

"What about new deaths I might cause?"

"Yes I almost forgot. Warriors don't stop being warriors just because the dead visit them. All I can recommend is that you kill only when absolutely necessary. Now that the old spirits have broken through, the spirits of your new kills will be able to access your subconscious as easily as those who you killed long ago. Actually, the anger of the newly deceased is even stronger than the anger of your earlier victims. One thing I would strongly recommend is to personally talk with each of the spirits and identify them if you can. This will help you to reason with these tormented souls and show them that moving on to our heavenly father's grace is the right course for them."

"Father I am very tired. I have fought others my whole life. Now I have to fight their spirits too. I don't know if I have the strength."

"Ralph you will find the strength as long as you maintain your faith in God and his only son Jesus Christ."

"Father no matter how many of these people I kill, they're will always be more of them and more of their spirits. I don't see this every ending for me or my daughter."

"So it is with warriors. You live and fight each day. Only God will decide when to call you and your daughter to him." The priest responded.

"You mean I can actually go to heaven with what I have done?"

"Yes. God set up the conflict in this world. He can hardly punish those who must participate in it. As long as your heart is pure and your motives true and justified you can go to him after you ask for his forgiveness."

"I will father. I will."

A Target Again

Ralph in a hurry to reach his car parked two blocks away in downtown Chicago did not see the woman trailing him at first. With the help of some technical friends, Ralph devised a rearview mirror system he wore on his corrective glasses that gave him an excellent view of the world behind him. When he looked as he instinctively did every few minutes in his rearview mirror, he immediately recognized the woman trailing him. Although she had obscured her face in the videos taken of her in the hospital, Ralph knew this woman assassin trailed him undoubtedly with the purpose of killing him. For Ralph did not solely rely on a face to identify a person. He also carefully noted the height, weight and other personal characteristics of a person and above all the way they walked. If you studied people carefully you could tell who they were by the way they walked. Ralph also recognized the dead eyes of the woman, the look of a killer. When on a mission, his own eyes looked this way.

Ralph studied the woman behind him to derive clues as to how the woman would attack and what weapons she would use. Woman assassins liked to use poison or silenced small caliber pistols. Ralph did not see the bulge of a weapon but he thought he saw the slight bulge of a poison stick that the CIA Black Ops like to use. One prick from this weapon and he would be dead in minutes. Even though adrenaline poured through his system, Ralph slowed his breathing as best he could and continued to walk as if he had not noticed the woman. He held an advantage if the woman believed she approached him unobserved. She would be less cautious. With the parking lot not too far away, the woman would make her move soon, assuming that she had done her homework and knew where he headed. Ralph had his deadly hands, throwing knife and silenced pistol to defend against the woman's likely attack. The throwing knife would be the best weapon. If the woman drew near enough for him to use his hands, she could easily prick him with the stick. If he drew the pistol, the woman would immediately notice, as would any bystanders nearby. The throwing knife fit in his hand and could be concealed until thrown.

Suddenly the woman picked up her pace, quickly closing the distance between them. The poison stick appeared with its retractable needle and as soon as she did, Ralph whirled toward the woman throwing his knife in the same motion. As the knife entered the woman's throat, Ralph moved quickly to one side as the woman thrust the poison stick forward. The stick missed and the woman gurgling and choking on her own blood fell forward before she could bring the stick back toward Ralph. The woman died moments after she hit the ground. Ralph removed the knife from the woman's neck, cleaned the blade with a cloth he carried and returned it to its hidden position. Then he continued walking toward his car as if nothing had happened. The whole incident from the time the woman thrust the stick until Ralph walked away took place in less than a minute. The crowd stunned and frozen at first finally reacted as Ralph disappeared into the parking garage. They gathered around the dead woman. The crowd, which grew quite large, bumped one man into the poison stick still held by the assassin. The sharp point of the stick struck him in the ankle. To the horror of the crowd, seconds later the man collapsed on the sidewalk clutching his chest. While the crowd concentrated on the dead woman and the dying man, Ralph drove out of the parking lot on the opposite side of where the deaths took place.

Three hours later, Admiral Templeton stared at CIA agent, Sergio Sanchez, with contempt. His face turned a bright red as his blood pressure skyrocketed.

"What a damn mess! What have you done about the death of the innocent civilian?"

"We leaked through some sources that the agent who died was in fact a foreign double agent from a country on our terror list. She worked for us at the CIA but on the orders of her foreign government tried to kill one of our other agents. This other agent, who for security reasons must remain hidden, killed the double agent. We didn't identify the country due to national security concerns. Since we wiped our agents history from all databases, the press won't be able to confirm or deny our story. The innocent bystander just happened to get tangled up in the fight between the two agents. He is like the pedestrian who is run over in a cop chase. The price of keeping us all safe sometimes involves the death of innocents."

"And that is going to hold up? It is untruthful, vague and full of holes. The media will be on this story like a bunch of bloodhounds. Your people better keep their mouths shut." The Admiral challenged.

"We will Admiral. Make sure yours do as well."

"They will but that still leaves us with the problem of what to do with Tager. Do you actually have someone who can kill the guy without dragging us all into it?" Admiral Templeton said.

"We have contractors, of course. They are the best assassins in the world. They are expensive which is why we tried to do it in house but in this situation I guess we will have to bite the bullet and hire one. These contractors do not fail."

"They better not fail. If Tager keeps dodging us like this he will eventually bring us all down. I hope you realize that."

"We do. If necessary we will bring Tager's adopted daughter into it. It is not as clean that way but failure is not an option this time."

"Do whatever you have to do, but bring me Tager's dead body." Admiral Templeton said as he waved the agent out of his office.

The New Target

Ralph read everything he could about Admiral Templeton. Then he visited a client in Washington. When done with his local business, he began following the admiral from his home to the Pentagon and then from the Pentagon to wherever else he went. Ralph looked for the aberration in his behavior that would make an attack not only successful but also as stealthy as possible. He didn't want to be identified. Ralph soon became frustrated. Admiral Templeton, a widower, went directly to the Pentagon in the morning and returned in the evening to his home. On Tuesdays, he visited a grocery store. Most of the time the Admiral ordered takeout food, which he had delivered from three or four restaurants he liked. The Admiral spent most of his time at the Pentagon.

Ralph did not like having to stay in Washington watching the Admiral. He worried about Cindy constantly. For this reason, Ralph finally concluded that a home invasion left him the only opportunity for success in his mission. Ralph would have preferred to kill the Admiral in a crowd but the Admiral avoided crowds. Also, his staff often drove him places, making an approach more difficult.

Donning the clothes of an employee of the local electric company and using a carefully crafted fake electric company ID, Ralph knocked on the Admiral's brownstone door on a typical warm hazy Washington day. Ralph wore a disguise, changing his hair and eye color and placing some padding in his stomach area. Ralph also changed his walk from one of a powerful predator to a slightly bent over middle age man. As expected, the guards in the home challenged Ralph when he presented the ID. Prior to coming, Ralph altered the duty roster at the electric company to cover his short inspection. When the guards checked with the company, the employee reached examined the duty roster and confirmed Ralph's visit. After the guard's nodded to Ralph, he quickly moved into the house. Ralph needed to modify the admiral's alarm system a task his recent work made him more than qualified to perform. He placed very small explosive charges in the main alarm box, which could be triggered by his cell phone. Then he inspected the house very quickly and left. Ralph allowed twenty minutes to complete the task. He required only fifteen.

That evening after taking a flight back to Chicago, Ralph talked seriously with Cindy.

"Cindy, I'm doing everything I can to make us safe, but unfortunately we have serious and determined enemies that won't allow this to happen. They are powerful people trying to cover mistakes they made by making us go away. I won't let that happen but I'm up against some difficult odds. I'm not superman but just a highly trained warrior. My greatest fear is that they will try to use you to get to me. This is why I'm asking you to go with my mother to our safe house. I will join you there as soon as it is safe. Oh and by the way I'm calling in a big favor from an old military friend. He will guard you and mom at the safe house. "

"Of course I will and don't worry. You do what you must. Grandma and I will be alright." Cindy said.

"My friend will be here in an hour. His name is Bill Bradley. Here is his picture. Don't go with anyone else."

"I know the drill dad. Safety always comes first." Cindy said coming to Ralph and putting her arms around him.

Another Mission

&

A week later at one in the morning, Ralph approached the admiral's house in Washington. His doubts about carrying out this mission against a high-ranking naval officer disappeared when his security cameras detected a well-armed team of agents penetrating his home after Cindy left with Bill for the safe house. They trashed the house and of course presented no search warrant. These agents intended to abduct and perhaps kill Cindy, the most precious thing in his life. Their puppet master would pay tonight for this attack. They crossed the line before he did. You never went after someone's family. After he completed his mission and returned to Lake Bluff, the video would be sent to a wide list of people. He doubted anything would ever come of it, but at least the local authorities would have a video of his pursuers. He needed to appear to the extent possible as the victim not the aggressor.

As he usually did on covert missions, Ralph dressed in all black with a black mask and black sneakers. Ralph once again changed his appearance by donning a long blond wig and putting green contacts in his eyes. He moved soundlessly. Ralph instinctively knew where the guards would be. They patrolled the exterior of the building paying special attention to the front and back door. The guards held their automatic rifles loosely scanning every movement near the brownstone. Ralph pulled his blowgun out of his pocket and slipped in a drug-laced dart. Trained by experts, he could hit targets at up to thirty yards. Ralph came up behind the first guard from the shadows near the garage as the guard walked passed the rear of the brownstone. At ten yards,

Ralph blew a dart into the guard's throat. The guard wheeled toward Ralph and swung his gun in Ralph's direction but Ralph slipped into the shadows. The guard quickly removed the dart and started to walk toward the garage, assuming the dart had come from there but after only a few steps fell into a heap. Without a target the guard never fired. Ralph moved forward out of the shadows and as he did so loaded his blowgun with another dart. Ralph lay on the ground in the dark waiting for the other guard. He would be moving in the opposite direction to Ralph's left to his right. Ralph could not let the guard see his downed partner. As Ralph looked around the corner of the house, he saw the other guard moving toward him. The guard already appeared wary as he expected to see his friend at about this moment. Ralph needed to take a risk. At a distance in the dark, he would look like the other guard. So he moved casually around the corner firing his dart as he did so. A difficult shot, Ralph breathed a sigh of relief when his dart entered the second guard's throat. The stunned guard reacted slowly. By the time he brought his gun up, the drug had already begun to claim him. Still, he sprayed the air with bullets as he fell to the ground. Even if he had fired straight from the hip, Ralph would not have been there to shoot. Ralph had hit the ground and rolled after taking his shot. These shots came nowhere near Ralph.

Ralph checked his watch. The guards would be out for a half hour at least but Ralph needed to do the job in far less time. Others would be checking the guards on their cell phones. If they didn't respond units would be dispatched immediately. Also, the shots fired would draw attention. As Ralph ran toward the back door, he set off the charges in the alarm system. It immediately became inactive while admitting only a faint sound. Ralph picked the back door lock with his tool set; then used a thin metal strip to pull back the bolt. To be on the safe side, Ralph opened the door and hit the deck in a roll. A deadly crossbow arrow flew over his head. When Ralph checked the house as an electrician, no such cross bow set up appeared. Without a moment's hesitation, Ralph gained his feet and walked quickly to the second floor. Ralph paid little attention to his surroundings, which he knew fairly well from this earlier visit as an electrician. Because of his training, Ralph could memorize a layout in great detail with a quick examination. As he passed the front door, Ralph noticed another crossbow pointed at it. Ralph wondered why the admiral used such a primitive weapon. A shotgun would be a much better weapon.

When Ralph reached the second floor, bounding up the stairs near the entrance, he heard a slight noise from down the hall, followed by the sudden appearance of an armed guard. Already reacting to the noise, Ralph whipped out his silenced Berretta and dropped the guard with a shot to the forehead. Ralph didn't have time to use his blowgun. Ralph also could not afford to just wound the guard in the shoulders and legs. The man might still be able to bring a weapon to bear. Ralph hated collateral damage but in this case he had no choice. The guard fired several shots but they went wild when he took the bullet from Ralph. Ralph won the exchange by only seconds. Having already identified the room the guard emerged from as the Admiral's room when he worked on the house a week ago, Ralph silently moved toward it. Based on the guard's movements, Ralph decided to assume that the Admiral lay in ambush inside his room. He didn't have time to verify this assumption. Too many shots had already been fired. The Admiral's backup would be on the way. He had to move now. Praying that he made the right assumption, Ralph kicked the door in, tossed a stun grenade inside and leaped backward, falling to the ground as he did so. A long burst of submachine gun fire followed, ripping apart the wall opposite the door and the area near the door on both sides. The bullets missed Ralph by inches and traced the area where he would have been had he remained on his feet. When the grenade went off, Ralph rolled on the ground in front of the door and shot the disoriented Admiral in both hands. His submachine gun fell to the floor. Ralph spoke but masked his voice through a device he brought.

"Admiral you crossed the line this time."

As Ralph spoke, he fired a bullet into the admiral's forehead. The admiral had a look of surprise on his face. Paper pushers only thought they understood the realities of armed conflict.

Not wasting a moment to check on the Admiral, Ralph ran downstairs and exited the house the way he came. Ralph had been lucky and he knew it. As Ralph disappeared into the night, he heard the approaching sirens. If Ralph spent another minute in that house, he would have been caught.

Inquisition

After returning home, Ralph answered his door two days after the Admiral's murder. Some stiff looking navy officers greeted him. They did not hesitate.

"Are you Ralph Tager a former navy officer and seal?" Terry Peters said.

"Yes. What is this about and who are you?"

"Admiral Templeton, the head of Naval Intelligence died two nights ago from an assassin's bullet. Did you know the Admiral?" Cynthia Whitcomb said.

"Before I answer, please identify yourself.

"I'm Terry Peters and this is Cynthia Whitcomb. We are NCIS agents investigating the Admiral's death."

"Okay. I'm not sure of your jurisdiction here but I'll answer you. I never met or spoke with Admiral Templeton but he became my boss's boss as I left the Seals here in North Chicago. Whatever I know of the man comes from others."

"Did you have reason to believe Admiral Templeton wanted you dead?" Terry asked.

"No. Why would he want me dead?"

"This reason is classified. I cannot really say but I think you know the reason." Cynthia said.

"All I can say is that I disagree with you."

"Where were you two nights ago when the Admiral died?" Terry asked.

"Here at home. I put my daughter Cindy to bed early. She fell fast asleep. Cindy has finally started to sleep through the night after her terrible ordeal, which I believe as early investigators in the incidents around her abduction and attack you know well."

"Can anyone else verify your story?" Cynthia said.

"Other than my daughter no one. We like to spend time together at home when I am not on the road for my job. We ordered food early in the evening, but that is it." Ralph said.

"Did you kill Admiral Templeton?" Terry asked.

"Obviously not. I had no motive and no opportunity."

"Commander Tager we are just starting our investigation. You will see us again. Thank you for your cooperation." Cynthia said formally as she and Terry turned on their heals and left.

In fact, Terry and Cynthia interviewed him three more times, bringing him down to the local police station the last time. They also talked to his daughter. Yet, in the end, they had absolutely nothing to tie Ralph to the murder. As best they could tell, he spent the time of the assassination in Chicago not Washington. When Ralph traveled to Washington, he used one of his best disguises, that of an old man and identification that he had obtained from one of the best forgers in the Middle East. He paid for his tickets with cash. Seals at his level always had some of these non-government sourced identities that insulated them from possible betrayal by their own government or by spies within their government. Finally, after almost a month of constant scrutiny, the NCIS halted their investigation. One of their biggest problems proved to be lack of cooperation within the Navy. Classified information on the Afghanistan problems that brought the Admiral and Ralph into conflict lay beyond the NCIS's reach.

Black Ops

"So our so called admiral leader is dead." A hard looking man said as he stared at similar looking but older man across from him?

The older man looked around the plain room buried deep in the CIA Headquarters before answering.

"Yes, and if I had to guess Tager is the one who did it. The guy is really good. He closely examined the house several days before the hit with a fake ID. He changed his appearance so much the guards could not identify him as Tager when we showed them his picture but it had to be him. Then Tager invaded the house in the evening several days later and took out the admiral. The two guards he drugged that night could not identify Tager. He looked different than the real Tager and different than the fake electrical employee. The hit was absolutely clean. We should have hired this guy."

"Did our dead admiral take out the contract on Tager?" The younger man said.

"We gave him four of our best contractors, but then washed our hands of it. I'll tell you we've had a lot of messed up ops but this has to be the worst. Killing off a heroes' wife and pushing a pervert to torture and kill his child is low even for this group. Then they invade his house without a warrant looking to kidnap his daughter. Those idiots at State and the Navy should stop crawling on their hands and knees to every tin pot dictator with a turban on his head. And what did we get for it? We lost two of our best assassins one of which we had to take out. I have no idea how we are going to replace these valuable assets."

"In my opinion, Tager has earned the right to live. He never deserved to be targeted in the first place. Every action he has taken, Tager did to protect himself and his family; the same kind of actions anyone of us would take. The Navy may need to cover its butt but we don't. The problem is we have no idea if the admiral took out a contract on Tager with any of these assassins. His replacement, a newly minted admiral who actually likes the Special Forces, doesn't' either. If he knew how, he would call off the hit. But they're a hundred places our dead admiral could have buried the expense and no records, phone, digital or written on the hit have been discovered. All I know is that the Admiral told me he intended to do it. I just hope his desire to kill everyone doesn't open up this whole mess to the public. Tager has threatened to go public if he or his adopted daughter is harmed. He has an envelope out of our reach ready to be mailed to the media in such a case. At least that is what Tager claimed in an untraceable note that showed up on our door. The deceased admiral felt his PR guys could deny and stonewall the claims but I'm not so sure. His truthful version of events will answer a lot of questions we haven't. The public tends to believe a decorated Seal like him." The older man said.

"I'm with you, the envelope worries me. The story is so good the media will pursue it like a pack of bloodhounds. We ought to put our resources into finding the envelope."

"We're looking for it right now, but I'm not very confidant we can find it. Maybe we ought to protect Tager instead of trying to kill him. He might give us the envelope then."

"I don't know about that but we can at least find out if the Admiral hired an assassin and if so who he is. If we send Tager this information, this will help Tager fight the guy. Also, we can try to cancel the guy's hit. If we help him he may help us. But from what I hear, these guys aren't easy to cancel once they start."

"Make it so. I think our safest play now is to have a happy and alive Tager. Anyway, the new President of Afghanistan, the youngest son, is proving to be the most pro western ruler we have had there. The father really hated us and wanted us out of his country. He was just using us long enough to stabilize his grip on power. His eldest son hated us even more and wanted us out of his country immediately. He had very close ties to the Taliban and was definitely a death to America kind of guy, just like the middle son Tager and his team killed. The youngest son is completely different. He really believes that an alliance with us is the best thing for his country. This young son is the best we will ever get in that godforsaken country."

"Yeah we owe Tager. We need to make things right with him not only for how he has helped us in Afghanistan but also to fix our image with the Special Forces. Because of what happened to Tager's family and his Seal Team, the Special Forces guys don't want to work with us. They don't trust us. It makes our job a lot harder. If Tager puts in a good word for the CIA, it may help us a little with these guys. They might be more willing to believe that this mess is the dead admiral's fault. They never liked this paper pusher and any version with him as the villain may work."

"Yeah blame it on the dead guy. He can't defend himself."

"Funny. Let's get working on this. We need to put this bad op to bed before it stinks up our whole operation."

"Wait a minute. We should pass this up the chain. This op is so bad we have to make sure we cover our butts. There is a real danger that if this goes south they will be looking for scapegoats. I'm not volunteering."

"Neither am I."

White House

President Taylor fumed after reading the complete brief of Ralph's activities. His chief of Staff, Blaine Wing, absorbed much of the abuse. The President gritted his teeth as he spat out the words.

"When you, State, the Joint Chiefs and the CIA sold me on this super secret task force, which could draw freely on the resources of several of our security and police agencies and departments, you convinced me that this task force could do things the other agencies could not do in a compressed time frame that would serve the national interest. I'm paraphrasing your own words. You said nothing about killing off our own Special Forces troops or targeting a hero's wife and daughter with a sexual pervert. What kind of moron would authorize that? On top of this, we have bodies of our assassins or ones we hired all over the place. If this got out, I would be impeached in a matter of weeks.

"Worse still, our Special Forces operations are in shambles. The soldiers applying for and making it through the training have dropped almost 30% while many in these services are looking for a way out. What do you expect, when you torture one of our most respected Seals' daughter, kill his wife and betray a whole Special Operations Team? You point headed bureaucrats don't know what it means to be a soldier, let alone an elite Special Forces soldier. I'm almost glad this Admiral Templeton got taken out. He had no clue what its like to be a warrior. Templeton was nothing more than a glorified nasty paper pusher. He made one bad decision after the next. Let me tell you this, if I start to go down, I'm firing everyone who had anything to do with this mess starting with you."

"Mr. President I know there have been problems. We should have just taken out the Seal Team, the leader Ralph Tager included, and told Karzam we couldn't follow through on using the pervert. Karzam would have complained but he still would have received the revenge he sought. Templeton didn't want to take the risk. Our entire Afghanistan policy depended on satisfying Karzam. We killed his middle son after all. We had no idea what these killings would do to Tager. Even though we can't prove it, he seems to have killed half the dangerous sexual predators in the country. They're dropping like flies. Recently, these killings have stopped but there is no telling when they will start again. We have a FBI Task Force, including some local personnel with sexual predator death cases, working on the problem but they don't have enough evidence to arrest anyone. Finally, Tager probably killed Admiral Templeton and his personal guard. We have no proof but don't know who else could have done it. Templeton wanted to take Tager out so he beat him to the punch. The question is now what do we do with Tager?" Blaine responded.

"Leave him alone. If he took out Karzam as we expect, Tager made a significant contribution to our foreign policy. All of his kills if we have them right seem justified to me. As a former Special Forces guy he merely killed those who tried to kill him. This is how we trained him. Admiral Templeton should have known that. As to the perverts, the world is better off without them. If someone came after my daughter, they would regret it." The President, a former Army Ranger, said.

"Okay we can live with that but we think Templeton hired another assassin to go after Tager. We can't seem to find where the money came from or the name of this guy. Even if we did, I'm not sure we can stop him. Most of these assassins go dark after they start their hunt."

"If this assassin kills Tager so be it. We want to stay as far away from this mess as we can. Oh and by the way, disband this Special Task force. They're more trouble than they're worth. Let the CIA Black Ops handle missions like this in the future."

"Yes Mr. President."

A Vacation

Feeling a little safe at least for the moment, Ralph picked up Cindy at his safe house and the two of them flew to Colorado, where Ralph booked a cabin near Vail. Just before the ski season, the fall weather in the mountain town proved to be spectacular, a combination of warm sunny days and cool cloudless nights. Cindy and Ralph spent their days hiking in the mountains, riding the chair lifts and gondolas to start off high above the valley floor. On one day, the clouds rolled in and a few flakes of snow fell but not enough to accumulate much. The clouds soon cleared leaving some shimmering snow covering the pines and the aspen. The beauty of this place soothed Ralph's troubled soul. He had his fill of death. Ralph hadn't been this happy since his beloved wife and daughter lived. Cindy's beauty, energy and smile lighted his dark world. If he had the choice, he would spend the rest of his days doing what he did on precious days like this.

While walking along the spectacular bowl on the backside of Vail Mountain, Ralph turned to Cindy and said.

"It's so beautiful here. I wish I could stay here forever. I've been in the darkness too long. All I can see is death and murder. Only with you can I actually see any light. I have to leave my warrior world but I don't know how."

"No one is letting us leave. I'm in the same world with you even though you go on all the missions. When you first came to adopt me, I thought I might be better off if I lived with a regular family. All the people at the orphanage and everyone else that came to see me told me this. But I realized that only with you would I be safe. The dark forces would find me with a regular family and they wouldn't be able to protect me. This is what happened to me at my home and with my parents. That man who came for me at the school would have come for me whether I lived with you or not. The perverts have decided to take and abuse me. The police can't protect me. Only you can."

"I wish you were wrong Cindy but I'm afraid you're right. I'll have to stay engaged to protect you but I'm going to tell Sid that I can't hunt the sexual perverts anymore. I don't need any more enemies. You don't need any more enemies that I've made. We have enough already." Ralph said.

"It's okay. You've done enough. The police and the FBI are supposed to arrest these bad guys. Let them do it instead of wasting their time chasing you."

"You're pretty wise for a twelve year old. Okay now this is resolved I feel better. I just wish we could spend the rest of our lives together here, soaking in the beauty of the world."

"So do I." Cindy said happily as she skipped off down the trail.

Two hours later when they returned to the top of the Gondola for a ride back down to Vail Village, the warning voice echoed in Ralph's head. On the way up the mountain, Ralph had no such concerns. He held Cindy back from the Gondola line.

"Cindy as a warrior I've developed what I call my inner voice. It warns me of danger. This voice has saved my life more times than I can count. Right now in this beautiful place, my inner voice is warning me not to go down the gondola. I know you're tired. I'm a little tired too but I'd be foolish to ignore this warning."

"Dad I rely on you to keep my safe. If you feel there is danger, I won't ride the Gondola down. I'm strong enough to walk." Cindy replied.

"Okay let's go. Follow me carefully. I'm going to walk in a random unpredictable way. If there is someone out there, this kind of approach works best."

Cindy and Ralph said little as they worked their way down the mountain in the zigzag way Ralph mentioned. Ralph and Cindy used a trail parallel to the gondola to descend giving him a view of the gondola through the trees, but providing a poor target for a sniper. About half way down, Ralph began to wonder if his recent experiences made him too cautious. No one knew Cindy and he journeyed here. If the CIA or the Navy wanted to kill him after the death of the admiral, they would need time to set up the operation correctly. They had failed too many times up until now. The CIA and the Navy would be careful. Then Ralph saw the glint hidden in the trees on the other side of the gondola open space. This glint might as well been a neon sign saying assassin's rifle here. Ralph's body tensed as he motioned Cindy to bend over as he did to make a less visible target. Ralph hoped the sniper studied the gondolas descending as opposed to Cindy and his descent on the other side of a stand of trees. As the two of them walked out of sight of the glint, Ralph thought he saw the glint move but couldn't be sure. He turned to Cindy.

"A sniper in the woods waited for us to descend on the gondola. I could see the reflection off his scope. He intended to shoot us in the gondola car, where we had nowhere to go or hide. I have no idea how he found us. I thought I saw him move just now, but I couldn't be sure. He'll eventually abandon his sniper spot and look for us in Vail. We need to get back to our room as fast as possible."

"Okay Dad. I'll keep up. Sometimes I think I'm in a movie."

"You are but not one you want to see."

Moving at a fast pace, Ralph and Cindy descended into Vail Village and walked to their room. Ralph turned to Cindy and said.

"We have to pack and move. Just throw your clothes into the suitcase. Time is important to us. The assassin probably knows where we're staying. We have a head start on him. We must keep it."

In a matter of minutes, Ralph and Cindy left the hotel. Ralph explained to the hotel clerk he had been called back home and paid the bill. With the new fast checking in and out procedure, Ralph encountered very little delay. Ralph piled the suitcases in front of the car. Then he removed a small electronic device, which he carefully moved over every square inch of the exterior, including the bottom of the car.

Ralph received a weak beep under the front right door. Ralph put his hand under the door and removed a little transmitter. The assassin had placed a tracking device under the car but according to Ralph's device not a bomb. Ralph then looked carefully at the parking lot to see if any cars might be leaving. Ralph finally noticed a SUV with luggage piled on a rack at the end of the lot. He saw a man come down and put luggage in the back, then walk back inside presumably to find more luggage. Seeing his chance Ralph ran to the SUV placed the device under it turned and casually walked back to his rental car. The man saw Ralph walk back toward his car but paid little attention to him. Ralph unlocked his rental car and filled the back with the luggage.

With Cindy firmly in her seatbelt, Ralph left Vail as quickly as he could without drawing attention to his driving, but stopped along the road within site of the Vail entrance. Ralph hid the car in some trees making him almost invisible from the road in case the assassin came before the SUV driver. If as expected the SUV headed toward Denver, Ralph would head the opposite way working his way back through the mountains to Colorado Springs. If the SUV headed the other way, Ralph would travel to Denver, his original destination. Exactly ten minutes later, the SUV headed toward Denver. Ralph headed the opposite direction. The assassin emerged from Vail a half hour later following his tracking device on the road to Denver.

The Hideaway

R alph bought the cabin years ago as his personal safe house. Deep in the woods but nestled against a very rough shallow cave with poor access above and a meadow in front, the cabin could be well defended from snipers and a frontal assault while making access from the rear difficult. Radio activated mines that could be armed in danger situations but otherwise stayed inactive also lay along the front path to the cabin and in random locations across the meadow. Despite the dangers, Cindy liked this retreat in the Northern Wisconsin woods. She knew where the mines lay and easily avoided them. Ralph taught her to think like a soldier and she did so. Her life depended upon it.

Bill Bradley, for the second time in the last two months, took up residence in Ralph's remote cabin with Ralph's mother and Cindy. Per Ralph's instructions, he activated all the mines in front of the cabin. Bill adored Cindy. He had never met another little girl like her. Beautiful, nice, smart and talented, Cindy could light up any room she entered but at the same time, Cindy seemed old beyond her twelve years. She could be a regular little girl one moment and a deliberate cool little soldier the next. Until this moment in his life, Bill, who spent his early years in orphanages, cared very little for anyone other than his Seal buddies. Cindy began to change these feelings of remoteness and isolation. He turned down a lucrative assignment to be here. Ralph needed to spend time at work taking care of several large customers. He told Bill and Cindy that he would join them as soon as he could.

The first bullet came while Bill and Cindy sat on the floor playing checkers. Cindy said.

"Ha, King me. You paid so much attention to your attack you didn't see me coming."

"Yeah. I'm a Seal after all just like your dad. We attack first and ask questions later." Bill laughed. At the time, Ralph's mother worked in the kitchen preparing dinner. The first bullet penetrated the bulletproof glass front window but the bullet didn't travel very far once through the window. The second bullet hit the side of the house but didn't pass through the steel inner wall. Ralph spoke quickly as he stood up while signaling Cindy to stay put.

"The assassin is probably using full metal jacket ammunition. He wanted to test our windows and walls to see what kind of penetration his bullets had. The assassin also wanted to announce his presence. As you know, Ralph buried heavy steel in the walls of the cabin. Even the snipers metal jacket bullets couldn't penetrate them. The window is another story. The bulletproof glass he used isn't designed to stop metal jacket bullets."

"This is probably the same guy that tried to attack us at Vail. Ralph hoped the assassin tracked him after he sent me here. Apparently, the assassin decided to come after me instead. I already texted Ralph. I'm waiting for him to respond." Cindy said.

"Ralph may not get here in time but if I know him he'll try. Meanwhile, I think I'll send this assassin a little message. I'll scan the woods with Ralph's telescope hidden in the walls. If I see a glint, I'll try to take a shot at our shooter through the special hole in the wall designed for a sniper rifle. It's supposed to clear this afternoon. If I am patient the sun will reveal our foe." Bill said as he looked through the carefully concealed gun scope at the place from where the bullet likely came. Meanwhile, Ralph's mother sat beside Cindy and held her.

After ten minutes, Bill finally spoke again.

"The sun just came out. I see him. He is buried in the woods. I don't have a very good shot but I'll take it anyway. If I don't he'll try to assault us by circling to the left or right. He is probably too good to catch one of our hidden mines in doing so but the mines should slow him down as will my sniper shot." Bill said.

Bill quickly lined up his shot, making all the necessary adjustments on his sniper rifle for the wind, and then Bill calmly fired. Bill re-loaded his rifle but by the time he lined up for his second shot, the glint of the assassin's rifle disappeared. Cindy who watched carefully anxiously asked.

"Bill did you get him?"

"Either the bullet came very close or it killed him. I can't tell. We'll have to go on the assumption that the bullet missed. The assassin will soon come to realize he has no way to assault our cabin. He faces mines on a side or frontal assault and an almost impossible repel on the cliff behind us. If he does try to approach us from behind, the moment he starts to repel, our infrared alarm will go off and I will pick him off him with my sniper rifle as he descends the cliff. As long as we remain in here, we're safe. Meanwhile, Ralph will make his way to the cabin, putting the assassin between two Seals. He won't want that." Bill said.

"What will he do then?" Cindy asked.

"If he is smart, the assassin will leave and try to find Ralph on more favorable ground." Bill said.

"He may not go far. The assassin may retreat a little into the woods and wait for Ralph." Ralph's mother said.

"Yeah he could do that. So we will have to warn Ralph to not come charging in here. But he has the advantage. Ralph knows these woods well." Bill said.

The Master Assassin

The big powerful man carefully arranged the photographs spread out before him. All of their eyes save one no longer took in or reflected light. These men and some women lay in cold graves dug in many countries. The photographs made to look like trading cards lay in a very specific order. The hardest to kill lay on top, the easiest on the bottom of the pile. Each of the cards had a place on his large wall mural, once again the most challenging kill at the top of the pyramid while the least challenging took up the bottom. The man also used a bright red color for the important men who fell by his hand. They did not gain any slots toward the top by being important but only the color to celebrate their important lives. The man fingered his latest card of Ralph Tager very carefully. He currently occupied the third slot on his wall mural but depending on how his death came about could easily rise to the very top now occupied by the fierce, fearless enforcer for a drug cartel. Enrique had taken the big man to the very limit of his endurance and skill in finally succumbing to the man's throwing knife in his throat. The big man had a hunch that Ralph would compete for this top spot before he too finally died at his master assassin's hands.

Theodore Rasputin emigrated to the U.S. after serving in the Spetnaz or Russian Special Services. Various U.S. police and secret agencies watched Ted very closely after he arrived in the U.S. but after a time discovered him not to be a spy. Rather they soon utilized his unique skills as an assassin. In fact, Ted excelled in every facet of the assassin business including planning, surveillance, tactics and weapon use, including of course the use of his hands. As a Russian he acquired language skills early in life and continued to add language skills, as he grew older. As a result, Ted could speak six languages fluently and several more adequately. He could assume almost any identity through superb acting and makeup and kill almost everyway that had ever been designed to kill. Others might be slightly better in any one area, such as the use of a sniper rifle, but no one could come close to his ability in all the areas of assassination. The reason he excelled to this degree presented no mystery. When not on assignment, Ted spent at least nine hours a day practicing his craft. He had no other hobbies or interests. Ted just wanted to become better at what he did, the very best in history.

Ted became enormously wealthy from the use of his skills. So much so, he began to carefully select his clients based on not only the fee but also the difficulty of terminating the target. He wanted the greatest challenges to improve his skills. He also had an almost obsessive need to replace the cards at the top of his mural. He wanted the very best on top, which might take a lifetime to find. For this reason, he quickly accepted the Navy Intelligence assignment to kill Ralph Tager who had gained a reputation as one of the most difficult targets to kill in the world. Ted performed many assignments for US federal agencies and departments over the years, but this one presented the most difficulties. Although not an assassin per se, Ralph held many of the same skills Ted did. Ted would in fact be hunting himself.

Since taking the assignment, Ted's regard for Ralph actually grew. He set what seemed to be the perfect trap for Ralph in Vail. First, Ralph did not know he had been targeted so soon after he killed the admiral. What he could not know is that the admiral had hired Ted almost a month earlier. Second, Ralph had no idea who hunted him. Third, Ralph would be handicapped by his need to protect his young daughter. Ted had no such distractions. Fourth, Ralph and his daughter had used the chairlifts and gondolas for several days before Ted arrived and targeted the gondola. Yet, somehow some way, Ralph had discerned that Ted lay in wait for the gondola. Something Ted did alerted Ralph but what it happened to be he did not now. Ted, a very meticulous planner, did not like this one bit.

As a result, Ted decided to use Ralph's adopted daughter against him. Ted didn't like to use leverage like this, being the very best he did not need the advantage and it made him look petty and weak, but this time Ralph's considerable talents made this approach necessary. At the end of the day, there would be someone dead and someone alive. Ted needed to be the live one. With the extensive file the Navy sent him, Ted located Ralph's summer home in Wisconsin with only a little legwork. A friendly grocer in a small town near the house provided the final information. He would kidnap the girl and force Ralph to come to him on his terms.

What took place in the meadow in front of the log cabin nestled in front of the small cave shocked Ted. Almost every approach to the cabin exposed the intruder to withering fire. Also, buried mines made even a crouched attack very problematic. Ted knew from the moment he approached that his presence would be detected. So he hid in the trees and looked for a long distance sniper shot. Ted in frustration tried to shoot out the main window but the metal jacket bullet barely made it through the bulletproof glass. A second bullet shot into the wall went nowhere. There must be steel or something else embedded in the walls. Ted needed a rocket-propelled grenade to make any progress against this heavily fortified house, but he didn't have one with him. He could, of course, obtain one but these military weapons were bulky and difficult to conceal when travelling. Authorities could also trace them more easily. Finally, Ted did not want to waste the time needed to procure one.

Then as Ted pondered what to do next, the sun suddenly emerged from behind thick clouds. Ted immediately hit the dirt but barely in enough time. A sniper bullet grazed his head, leaving a painful path across the side of his skull and taking a piece of his ear. Pure instinct saved his life. Ted immediately realized the sun would throw a reflection off his scope that a sniper in the house could see and use. If he had fallen to the ground one second later, his brains would be all over the tree behind him. Still, he bled very heavily from the wound. Ted after applying a thick layer of anti bacterial lotion on the wound, held a cloth to his head waiting for the blood to coagulate and the bleeding to stop. When it did, he wrapped his head with the cloth.

Now ready, Ted moved quickly out of the area near the cabin to recollect his thoughts and better bandage his wounds. The wound hurt a great deal and began to unleash the rage inside him. Rage tended to get one killed. Ted needed to refocus and concentrate on completing his hit. In the last ten years, he avoided close calls like this one.

After a moments' reflection, Ted realized he had an advantage. Because Ted threatened his daughter, Ralph would come to the cabin to help. Ted knew Ralph had not journeyed to the cabin as yet. A friend must be staying at the cabin to protect his daughter. Ted would simply scout the best place to ambush the man and do so. The sniper would in all likelihood stay where he was. As soon as he walked into the clearing in front of the house, he would become a target. His job would be to protect the girl, not to expose himself this way. Ted wouldn't be there to take a shot, but the sniper in the house wouldn't know this.

Ted worked his way back up the trail to where he left his rental car in a small lot near the trailhead. He found some dense bushes near the entrance and carefully worked his way inside. Ted had a perfect view of the lot. Better yet, a large tree stood near the bushes allowing Ralph to seek cover in case he needed it. As soon as Ralph parked his car, Ted would have a clean shot at him. Ralph wouldn't have the chance to fight back. He would be dead.

Ted took care of his bathroom needs in the port a potty at the trailhead. Then he ate a sandwich and waited a few hours before moving to his hiding place in the bushes.

Hours later, Ralph, who had already been on his way to the cabin when he received Cindy's text, didn't go to the parking lot where he ordinarily parked. If the assassin survived Bill's bullet, which he probably did, the assassin would wait for him there. Bill's cell phone call, following the assassin's attack, gave Ralph some important intelligence he could use. Rather, Ralph parked in a small, concealed turnout area where a rough path led back to the main path. He checked all his weapons and bullet proof vest and walked quickly into the woods. Ten minutes later, Ralph approached the trailhead. He knew where the sniper would be positioned, the bushes next to the large oak tree. Drawing his 15 shot magazine 9mm pistol, Ralph rapidly fired all of the bullets in his magazine into the bushes, going from left to right on an upper level where a crouched man's head would be then on a lower level where a crouched figure's legs would be located. Then he rolled into the woods while replacing his spent magazine with a new one. Less than a minute later, bullets came out of the bushes toward his former position on the trail but missed him. Silence followed. Ralph did not move.

The fury of the sudden attack stunned Ted. His bullet proof vest plus the especially designed bullet proof leg coverings he wore caught most of the bullets, but one bullet managed to pierce the top part of his shoulder and another struck the top part of his foot. His chest and leg coverings barely stopped three more bullets, but the bullets left bad bruises and in once case a half-inch deep hole in his leg. Despite the hail of bullets, Ted instinctively rolled toward the large oak tree after he heard the first shot. The move saved his life. From a more protected spot, Ted quickly poured anti bacterial lotion on his wounds and swallowed a strong morphine pill. None of the bullets struck an artery but the three wounds bled heavily and produced extreme pain. He bandaged the wounds tightly to stop the bleeding. When the morphine took effect, Ted searched for Ralph in the bushes next to the trail.

Protected from Ted's likely line of fire, Ralph poured bullets into Ted's rental car, leaving two tires flat and the gas tank penetrated. When a puddle began forming under the car, Ralph shot a bullet into the puddle. Moments later the car exploded. Ted wouldn't be going anywhere soon. Ralph's actions drew some fire from Ted but Ralph's position prevented any of the bullets from striking him. Ralph heard Ted moving deeper into the woods. Ralph took a few shots at the retreating Ted but this time failed to hit him. When Ted disappeared into the woods, Ralph examined the bushes and nearby tree to ascertain what he could about Ted's condition. The large amount of blood there encouraged Ralph. He would have a slight advantage. The loss of blood weakened men physically and more importantly slowed their thinking.

When Ralph heard a rustle in the bushes in the direction Ted fled, Ralph leaped toward the safety of the tree but a bullet still grazed his shoulder. Ralph felt lucky. He should have waited longer to examine the bushes. After Ralph bandaged his wound and put antibacterial lotion on it, he struck out in a different direction. Ted fired a few shots toward Ralph but as he presented a poor target the shots missed.

For the next half hour, the two highly trained men shot at each other from varying distances. Ralph received another graze on his leg as did Ted on his left arm but the bullets largely missed their mark. Both men attained the rank of marksman but the distances, moving targets and dense woods made the shots very hard. Ralph did everything he could to move Ted toward the cabin. He wanted to wedge the assassin against the heavily fortified cabin. Ralph found that his knowledge of these woods gave him a distinct advantage. By making certain calculated moves, Ralph pushed the assassin closer and closer to the cabin.

Suddenly, the woods went silent. Ralph could no longer hear his adversary. The assassin lay in ambush, but where. Ralph stopped moving and concentrated on listening. The slight movement in front of him immediately forced Ralph to the ground. As he hit the ground, Ralph emptied both of his 15 capacity pistols at the disturbance, intentionally keeping his fire low. He had drawn the extra gun to put more bullets into his opponent's location. On the way down a bullet pierced Ralph's hip below his bulletproof vest. Distracted by his own attack, Ralph didn't even hear the shot. The extreme pain caught Ralph by surprise. As his opponent had done, Ralph quickly bandaged and applied anti-bacterial lotion to the area. Then he took a morphine pill. Ralph would more thoroughly address the wound later when he had the opportunity. As best he could tell, the bullet missed his femoral artery.

As the drug took affect, Ralph began to reevaluate his strategy. Obviously, the assassin lay out there behind some cover evaluating his next move. The assassins' loss of blood and the open field at his back left Ted with only one good option: an aggressive charge with guns blazing. If one of his recently fired bullets caught the assassin this would only make the charge more necessary, provided of course that the assassin could still charge. The charge could come at any moment. Ralph reloaded both his pistols and trained them straight ahead. Rolling to a position behind a fallen tree from his position behind a standing tree, Ralph waited. Sweat rolled down his face and drenched his shirt. His hip bled but not too badly. Time seemed to slow down.

When the attack came, the ferocity of it surprised Ralph. With a feral scream, Ted charged directly at Ralph firing both of his handguns at the same time. Ralph responded in kind, noticing that his recent fire had further wounded his opponent in the other shoulder and the base of the neck. The wounds thoroughly soaked his opponent's shirt. A bullet caught Ralph in the left shoulder again but he kept firing. Ted ran toward Ralph and with only ten feet remaining, the heavily blooded Ted leaped into Ralph. They exchanged fire but hit each other's vests. As before, both men felt the impact of the bullets but ignored the pain. They now fought hand to hand with knives as the guns they had held no more ammunition. Ted seemed to be on some very special drugs. He fought without fear or restraint despite his many injuries. Finally, Ralph could feel Ted weakening. Seizing on the temporary advantage, Ralph hit Ted's temple with the butt of his knife when Ted wouldn't allow him to turn the knife toward his throat. Ted fell backward from the blow but produced a third gun aimed at Ralph's head as he did so. Ted motioned Ralph to throw his guns and knives into the bushes and then stand. Ralph immediately complied. For the first time, the assassin spoke.

"You fell for my fall away trick. I've practiced it a hundred times. You nearly killed me and your friend messed up my head. I'll have to spend months rehabilitating and suffering through plastic surgery, but in the end I won. Toss your keys to me. I don't suppose you will tell me where your car is. I'm afraid my rental car is a little worse for wear. "

"Why should I? You will kill me anyway."

"True. It's my job. But you haven't any need for it where you're going." Ted laughed.

"Ted you know this whole thing is very ironic. The assassin who killed my wife and daughter also had the name Ted. What is it about this name?" Ralph wanted to keep Ted talking as long as he could. Ted bled heavily. He might yet gain an advantage.

"Nothing. It is merely a coincidence. Anyway the last Ted while he had some military training, acted like the brutish pervert he was. He did not have my skills or yours for that matter. Now I need to finish our business here. Time is not on my side. I've lost a lot of blood. Goodbye Ralph. You were a great adversary."

Ted said as he suddenly began to wobble. The long fight had finally taken too much of his blood. Panicking, Ted immediately fired his gun but his blurred vision caused Ted to miss Ralph's head, as Ralph instinctively moved out of the way. Ralph, regaining his balance leaped for the assassin and pushed his gun hand away before Ted could fire a second time. Ted fought back but his strength failed him. Ted's world began to spin. In a desperate attempt, the assassin grabbed the knife he produced earlier with his free hand but Ralph intercepted it and turned the weapon toward the weakened assassin. With all his remaining strength, Ralph buried the nine-inch blade in the assassin's neck. The assassin fell backward dying before he hit the ground.

Ralph called his Seal buddy Bill, gave him his GPS coordinates and collapsed on the ground next to his dead foe. Bill came quickly, his medical kit along with the one Ralph kept in the house with him. With Bill's extensive training he removed the bullet from Ralph's hip and bandaged this and the rest of his wounds. Bill then started an IV with a bag of Ralph's blood he kept in the refrigerator for such emergencies. Ralph immediately began to look better. He woke up the next day at the cabin with Cindy, Bill and his mother at this side.

Meanwhile Bill buried the assassin about five miles from where he fell in woods as dense as those near Ralph's cabin. Bill removed all of Ted's identification, pulled the bullets from his body, and then carefully carved up the dead man's face. Finally, Bill cut off the man's fingertips and buried them elsewhere to prevent fingerprint recognition. In the unlikely event someone discovered Ted, the greatly altered body of this foreign assassin would be very difficult for anyone to identify.

Recovery

Ralph slowly recovered from his injuries, but his physical suffering and rehabilitation didn't occupy his thoughts. As a Seal, he had experienced this routine before. Pain had always been part of his world. This might change if he suffered a serious disability but at least this time he would eventually return to normal. Rather Cindy's safety and whether the government still sought him dominated his thinking. Bill stepped forward and took care of Cindy along with his mother, but this only partially relieved his anxiety. Then three months into his recovery, when Ralph began to assume his normal duties and responsibilities, Ralph received this unsigned note in his mailbox.

The government is no longer hunting you. Thank you for your service.

Ralph carefully examined the note, looking for fingerprints and other markers but found nothing. This information gave the note more authenticity in Ralph's mind. The government had received the benefit from him they wanted and no longer would pursue him. The government called off their dogs. Of course, the note could be a fake even though it did not appear to be so. Also, the Hunters Fantasy and its members probably still sought him as did the FBI and many local law enforcement agencies for his activities as Pay Back but after he withdrew from this activity, Ralph heard very little from them. Also, Ralph left some tracks and enemies in Afghanistan. Still, Ralph believed that this change in government strategy might in time offer him and Cindy some measure of security and safety. Ralph had to be vigilant but he would hopefully not have to face death everyday as he had.

After receiving the note, Ralph concentrated on completing his recovery. With Sydney's blessing, he reassumed the Presidency of Sydney's security firm from the temporary head appointed while he recovered. Ralph worked hard and enjoyed a good measure of financial success. Cindy also prospered. Attending Lake Forest High School in the fall, she had a number of friends including several boys who had shown an interest in her. She also spent time with her best friend Priscilla, who Ralph sometimes referred to as his second daughter. Bill had become Uncle Bill to Cindy. He often visited between his various jobs and like Ralph schooled Cindy in the art of self defense. Between Bill and Ralph, they made sure one of them watched Cindy when the other had to travel.

Cindy's Routine

indy woke up as she always did with acute awareness of her surroundings. At first, she listened very carefully to every sound in the house: the tick of the clock downstairs, the slight wind noise on the windows, and the soft purr of her cat Terminator. Everything seemed to be within the normal range. Satisfied, Cindy opened her eyes and scanned her room. She had a defined place for everything. Nothing moved overnight. Her guitar lay against the music stand where she placed it last night. Her many Judo, Tae Kwan Do and Karate trophies starred at her from the bookcase. Cindy began to relax and sleepily put her feet on the floor. After she used the bathroom, Cindy would systematically go through all her Karate, Judo and Tae Kwan Do routines and stretching exercises. She would be fully warm and loose before she hit the showers and prepared herself for school.

Cindy as always keenly felt Ralph's absence from her bed. Upon reaching puberty, Cindy decided to remove herself from Ralph's bed but she never slept as well without his powerful figure beside her. Cindy only felt safe when he stood or lay near to her. In Cindy's mind, the outside world contained many demons looking to harm or kill her. Safety meant everything to Cindy. She could not exist without it.

Sighing Cindy dressed for school, ate a quick breakfast and jumped in Ralph's car. Ralph always took her to school when he did not travel.

Cindy missed Priscilla. She often wondered how she would have survived those first years after coming to live with Ralph and his mother without Priscilla. When Priscilla and her mother finally moved out of their house in Lake Bluff when they could no longer handle Priscilla's father, they found a place to rent in Mundelein. Priscilla had to leave their Lake Bluff School at the end of the 7ᵗʰ grade. Still, Priscilla and Cindy called and texted each other several times a week. They helped each other navigate the tricky world of puberty, boys and friends.

Later that day, Brad flirted with Cindy. Every girl in her 8ᵗʰ grade class desired and flirted with Brad. Handsome, smart and athletic, Brad stood atop her school's social world. Unfortunately, Brad displayed a compulsive desire to conquer all the attractive girls in his class. All of them succumbed to his charms except Cindy. If a psychopathic pervert not entered her world, Cindy might have become one of his girls, but the Cindy she had become had a difficult time dating a boy her age, particularly one that looked at women as conquests. Although Cindy never said so to anyone, Brad looked like a foolish but attractive child to her. Ironically, the more Cindy rejected Brad, the harder he tried to attract her attention. Cindy knew Brad would never stop trying, but she could never say yes to anyone who treated relationships so casually. Brad interrupted her thoughts as she descended the stairs in her school.

"Hi Cindy. You look beautiful as usual. Are you coming to the Highland Park football game and the Dance afterwards? I have a whole cheering section but it wouldn't be complete without you. I promise I will dedicate the victory to you." Brad said hopefully.

"Sorry Brad, I have a full plate tomorrow including play practice followed by a test for my Second Degree Karate Black Belt. On top of that, as the lead singer in the school musical, I'm supposed to carry the production but my male lead and I are having trouble working together. He sings well but his timing is terrible. We are supposed to have our first performance in a month but we are very far away from being able to do it right. Also, my Karate teacher really pushes me. He will fail me if I make the slightest mistake. Because my dad Ralph is such an incredible fighter, he expects the same from me. But I'm not my father. I'm a girl." Cindy replied somewhat automatically but with a little rebellion in her tone.

"Yeah I have seen your step father. He is one tough looking dude. If Saturday doesn't work out, I will find another time we can get together. Hey, I have an idea. Are you going on the field trip to the Field Museum? I used to like to go to this place as a kid. On a whim I signed up so I could hang with some of my friends outside school. I heard you signed up too." Brad said.

"Brad I'm not really going with anyone, so I'd be happy to talk with you while we are there." Cindy said.

"Yeah okay let's do that. See ya, beautiful." Brad looked back toward Cindy as he walked away.

Fateful Day

After some persuasion, Cindy convinced Ralph to allow her to go on the school field trip to Chicago's Field Museum. Cindy tried very hard to fit in with her classmates. She just began the teenage ritual of hanging out with her girl friends. Dating boys represented a greater challenge for Cindy. When boys touched her, Cindy automatically flinched even when she didn't want to do so. Only Ralph could touch her without Cindy feeling this way. A man or boy would have to be extremely patient with her to overcome these feelings. So for now, Cindy began to develop friends who happened to be boys. Brad became the latest and most interesting of these boy friends. While struggling with her school relationships, a part of Cindy remained the child warrior trained mostly by Ralph with a little added by Bill.

When Cindy entered a room, she continued the vigilance she displayed in her wake up routine. Cindy immediately scanned the area for potential threats. She closely examined each person in the room to see if any of them could turn into aggressors. Cindy also noted any weapon or item that could be used as a weapon, its location and whether someone there could use it. Cindy also avoided secluded areas and developed an escape plan should a bad situation develop. Cindy often looked distracted when she entered a room for this reason. She needed to conduct her threat assessment before she could socialize with her friends.

As a compromise with her father, Cindy decided to take the bus with her other classmates to the museum but to return with Ralph. Some of the other kids on the trip also followed this plan, so Cindy felt comfortable with it. Cindy also wondered whether Brad's casual inquiry contributed to her desire to take the bus. Whatever her motivation, Cindy closely scrutinized everyone who boarded the bus, including her classmates. She only took her seat after looking everyone in the eye and not finding anything of concern there. Cindy also spent some time with the bus driver to make sure he didn't participate in some kind of plot. Satisfied, Cindy had a great time on the bus, giggling and laughing with her friends on the way to the museum. She sat near Brad and his friends exchanging a few glances with Brad while making some casual remarks aimed in his direction.

Once in the museum, Cindy scrutinized everyone she could. As taught, Cindy looked for someone not interested in the museum and its displays but someone interested in her and her classmates. In particular, Cindy looked for Peter the head of Hunter's Fantasy. He had the greatest issues with Ralph and with her. Ralph obtained a blurry picture of the man and made sure Cindy memorized it. Ralph kept emphasizing that if and when Peter struck he would be disguised. Cindy had to be able to see through the disguise and identify the man in the fuzzy picture.

For the first hour of the two-hour visit everything went very well. Cindy liked the dinosaur and ancient mammal displays, the Egyptian section and the gemstones. Her teachers for the last several days reviewed the exhibits during class so the students could better understand them in person. Cindy marveled at the huge ornate building. She spent a few minutes walking with Brad but Brad suddenly rejoined his friends and Cindy did not bother to chase after him. When it came time to go to the restroom, Cindy talked several of her friends into going with her. As she left the restroom on the basement floor to join her classmates for lunch in the cafeteria, Cindy noticed a man staring at her. He had a beard, moustache and blond died hair. The man quickly disappeared before Cindy could identify him but clearly the man wore a disguise. Following her protocol with Ralph, she texted him with this message. "Suspicious looking man watching me come out of the bathroom with my friends." Ralph immediately texted her back: "Could present a threat. I'm on my way to the museum, 20-30 minutes depending on traffic." Cindy now considered how she would act in the next half hour to prevent an attack from this man. She learned to expect the worst and acted accordingly.

Careful to position herself in the middle of her class, Cindy accompanied her fellow students to the special exhibit on the Maori Indians in New Zealand. Cindy didn't like the dark areas of the exhibit so she moved to the front of the line near the teachers. Having adults nearby made her feel more comfortable. Still, for the first time on this trip, Cindy could feel cold sweat work its way down her neck and arms. Time passed slowly. Half way through the exhibit, Brad walked up next to her. The distraction helped. Cindy could focus on something other than the disturbing looking man near the bathroom. Brad talked almost nonstop. He even made her laugh a little despite her combat ready state. Just as Cindy began to relax a little, the disguised man suddenly materialized several yards in front of her near the exhibit exit. Three of her friends, Brad and one teacher stood nearby. The teacher looked annoyed and said.

"Let us pass."

"I think not. I want the blond girl behind you. She and her father killed my sister. They have to pay. The rest of you are free to go."

After saying that, the man opened his coat to reveal a Nylon CIA type Knife and a plastic gun. Cindy knew that plastic guns had yet to prove themselves, often misfiring as many times as they fired correctly but Ralph had just told her that some new hand made ammunition made plastic guns more reliable. So Cindy could not say whether the plastic gun represented a threat or not. It might even be a fake. She spoke quietly in response, taking as much time as she could. Time would be her friend. She needed this time for a museum guard, policeman or Ralph if he had reached the museum to respond. Cindy noticed that her friends, Brad and her teacher froze when they saw the man's weapons. Finally, Cindy said.

"Mr. Jones, Brad and the rest of you need to leave. The knife is a serious weapon. The plastic gun maybe an even more serious weapon. It could be a fake. Even if it is real, plastic guns tend to misfire hurting the shooter as many times as the person they intend to shoot. Still, the danger it presents cannot be dismissed. I don't want any of you to be hurt on my account. The man wants me. I think it is Peter the head of the Hunter's Fantasy Website, a known pedophile, who supported my abduction and rape by another of his kind several years ago."

After Cindy's little speech, the man looked uncomfortable and indecisive. She exposed him. Then the man's expression suddenly changed to one of rage. No one moved. Cindy lay out of his reach. With lightning speed, Peter pulled out his knife and stabbed Mr. Jones in the side. Mr. Jones stood nearest to him. As Mr. Jones hit the floor, the rest of the students, including Brad, started running back the other way, screaming as they did so. Cindy stood her ground. Peter walked up to her with the bloody knife in his right hand. He quickly withdrew the plastic gun with his left hand.

"Cindy you have become so much like Ralph. You aren't the helpless little girl you once were. But no matter how well trained you are, you can't fight two weapons trained at you. Oh and by the way, this gun is something new, it's plastic with a ceramic lining inside the gun barrel. I also have special ammunition inside of it designed to avoid the problems other plastic guns have. Now come along we are leaving this museum. One false move and I will kill you."

"You will kill me anyway." Cindy challenged.

"True but you have no reason to hurry your death. I need you as a shield to get out of here and as a lure for your father. I need to meet your father on my terms not his." Peter replied.

Peter stuck the CIA knife in Cindy's back and pushed her out the exhibit exit. Peter placed the gun back inside his coat. Cindy made careful note of this move. Apparently, Peter, despite his earlier boasts, did not have total confidence in the gun. Cindy had a better chance against the predator now. Guns provided more defensive problems than the knife. If he released the pressure of the knife on her back, she could make a move. When Cindy and Peter emerged from the exhibit, the museum guards stood at the entrance to the exhibit with their guns drawn. A crowd gathered. Peter made an announcement.

"Anyone makes a move on me I will gut this girl like a fish. So stay back. We are leaving this building."

The museum guards did not have the training to handle this situation, so they stood their ground and allowed Cindy pushed by Peter to move toward the elevator. Peter drew Cindy toward the wall. He wanted the wall at his back not the guards. Peter inched along the wall until he reached the elevator. Then he pushed Cindy inside and they both descended to the first floor. Upon exiting the elevator, Peter moved Cindy along the first floor wall. He paused at the intersecting corridor and the stairs coming down from the second floor but seeing no one he pushed Cindy quickly into the area.

Cindy saw no opportunity to make a move on Peter. She could fall backwards but in this position she could not fight Peter moving after her. So Cindy waited and watched. As instructed by her many martial art teachers and her dad, Cindy focused on the task and did not allow her mind to be terrified or to think what might happen if Peter successfully removed her from the museum. Then Cindy heard a distinctive tap, tap on the wall of the intersecting hall behind her. She knew what this meant. Ralph and she used this tap as a secret signal between them. Ralph stood somewhere in the intersecting corridor. Since Peter held the knife a little more loosely than before, Cindy immediately fell to the floor, cushioning her fall with her hands as she had been trained to do. As Cindy did so, she could hear Ralph's knife enter the back of Peter's head where it intersected with his neck. Unfortunately, because Peter moved at the last second, the blade became blocked by a neck vertebra and only partially entered Peter's neck rather than penetrating it deeply. As a result, the knife did not immediately kill or paralyze Peter. But Peter, who felt the knife enter his neck, panicked, and forgot about Cindy in his efforts to pull the knife from his neck and to stop the bleeding. Just as Peter pulled the knife out, Cindy stood and punched Peter in the Adams Apple with all her strength and then kneed him in the groin. Peter lost his breath for several seconds and winced in pain, but as soon as he regained his breath, Peter cursed, mumbled and increased his grip on his knife, which he brought to bear once again on Cindy.

"I'll kill you, b----"

Still a little disoriented, Peter made a somewhat clumsy effort to stab Cindy, missing her as she deftly moved away. Before Peter could bring the knife forward for another try, powerful hands tore the knife from Peter's hand. Those same hands then grabbed Peter's head and snapped his neck like a twig with a violent twisting motion. A loud cracking sound echoed in the marble corridor. Peter died before he hit the floor. Ralph stood over Peter, rage suffusing his face.

Only seconds later, Cindy jumped into Ralph's arms, tears pouring down her face.

"My knight you protected me again. I tried to do everything you said. Still, he almost stabbed and killed me. He wanted to use me to kill you."

"Cindy, you saved your own life as much as I did. If this pervert had moved you out of the museum, he would have killed you. You also saved the people with you. As to me, I would have gladly sacrificed my life to save yours. Fortunately. It didn't come to that."

"Yeah all of those bad things could have happened but I can't think about that now. I need to settle my nerves before I have a panic attack. I am not the warrior you are quite yet. Let's go home."

At just this moment, Brad appeared. He just starred at Cindy. Finally, he said.

"That was amazing. You're amazing. You attacked that armed maniac twice your size even though he had a knife and gun on you."

"Brad I've been attacked twice and almost killed before today. That is why I train in all these self-defense disciplines. I've been forced to act like an adult not the 8th grader I would like to be. My life has depended on it. As I just told my dad, I need to get out of here and spend some time at home. By the way this is my dad Ralph." Cindy responded.

"Nice to meet you sir. You have one incredible daughter."

"Yeah I know. Just treat her well. She needs friends her age, but as you can see she doesn't react very well when people threaten her. Now we really do need to get going. I'll tell the police to interview us later. That is the best way to handle this, the same way we did at your concert."

"Yes let's go please."

At this moment, the police came storming into the museum with their guns drawn. Paramedics followed in their wake. Brad backed away. Ralph arms in the air calmly explained to the police what took place, while the other students took the paramedics to their fallen teacher. Cindy confirmed Ralph's story. Twenty minutes later, the police, after carefully verifying Ralph's and Cindy's story with what eyewitnesses said, including Brad and the other kids, allowed Cindy and Ralph to leave after making them promise to come down to the station the following day. Cindy waving goodbye to Brad said.

"Dad can we finally leave? I can still feel that pervert's knife in my back. I need some time with you at home sorting this attack out in my head. Just when I begin to feel safe something like this happens."

"Cindy I'm doing everything I can to defend against these attacks but they seem to keep coming. I guess there is no real way to stop them completely. We just have to fight the bad men together."

"Each time this happens I become a little less afraid. The danger is the same but with your training I feel I have a chance to survive. For now, this will have to do. But tonight I may have to sleep in your arms like I used to do. I won't be able to sleep otherwise. My hands are still trembling."

"Truthfully, I miss having you fall asleep in my arms. I didn't think you would do so ever again. You are getting too old."

"I'll never be too old. Ralph I love you with all my heart and will always feel this way about you. Mentally I had already died when you rescued me in that warehouse. You've slowly brought me back to life. Without you, there would be no me. Still, I need to find you a girlfriend It shouldn't be too hard. The first time I put your picture and history on line, hundreds of girls responded."

"Did any of them work for the CIA Black Ops?"

"Very funny dad. No they just look like nice accomplished women. We are striving for normality here something we both need."

"Cindy I don't know if I could ever offer another woman a normal life but I'm willing to try." Ralph said as he led Cindy out the door.

Aftermath

Six months after the Field Museum incident, Cindy and Ralph's lives returned to normal. The police never charged Ralph with a crime. He clearly acted in self-defense to protect the life of his daughter. The teacher, knifed by Peter, thanks to some excellent EMT's survived. Cindy received honors and accolades for her courage from the school but largely ignored the praise. She instead focused on her music and the company of her male and female friends. Although they did not date, Brad and Cindy became good friends. Ralph prospered as the President of Sydney's security firm. Ralph doubled the firm's business and Sydney compensated him well for it. For the first time since the murder of his wife and daughter, Ralph began to relax, as did Cindy. They started enjoying the life that they always wanted to have. Ralph seemed to have been in a terrible storm for several years and only now saw some light in the distance. Still a phone call inviting Ralph to lunch brought him back to his recent past.

Ralph Tager settled into a nice remote street side table in a Lincoln Park café. A fine late spring day, Ralph allowed the warmth and sweet smells of spring to wash over him. Bob Prandini seemed to appear out of nowhere. Ralph rose, shook the big man's hand and casually said.

"What can I do for you Bob? If I remember correctly, our last meeting seemed a little strained. Your phone call took me by surprise."

"Our Special FBI task Force on the Pay Back killings is being disbanded. I'm going back to Seattle. We never collected enough evidence to prosecute anyone but the so-called Pay Back killings stopped. So I guess by some standards we succeeded. We have no real purpose anymore, but justice has not been served. We have a number of unsolved murders across the country, including the one in Seattle which involved me in this mess in the first place."

"I have never been a detective or a policeman. You must be very frustrated, but I don't see how I can help you."

"You and Sydney Worth planned and executed these murders to satisfy your need for revenge. I can't prove it. The task force could not prove it. Still, I want you to know that I will never forget. In the little free time I have, I will continue to pursue the investigation. I will ask others to help me. And if you ever decide to start killing again, we will nail you."

"Let me correct you. Some violent sadistic perverts died. Their community of like-minded felons will be glad to know that they have you as their champion. Now that these pervert killings will start again, your city SVU units can resume their normal business operations of trying to catch these perverts after they have done their damage. The victimized little girls and boys that these monsters abuse can be your nightmares. They won't be mine." Ralph responded with a little anger in his voice.

"That's the irony isn't it? We stop the murders of despicable human beings so they can torture and murder children. Yet, that is our job. The laws apply to everyone. Someone has to enforce them." Bob said.

"That is true but in the Special Forces world where I operated, we killed who needed killing in the national interest. Our criminal laws sometimes took a backseat to getting the job done. We come from two very different places. I don't fully understand your world and I don't think you will ever fully understand mine. If we clash again which we really didn't do this time, I hope both of us come out of the experience in a good way."

"We won't. One of us will die or go to prison. These two different ways of doing things can't be reconciled here at home. Only our way works."

"Then good luck to you. I'm retired from my Seal world. I'm a businessman now. We won't have any reason to see each other again."

"You can't admit to anything you did?"

"I fought for my country and protected my family. That is all I ever did. Now have a good day and enjoy our city before you return to your fog and rain." Ralph laughed as he got up to leave.

"Remember Ralph I will always be watching you. There is no statute of limitations on murder. You will pay for your crimes."

"Bob I've paid my dues in ways you will never understand. Now I intend to just live. God alone will ultimately judge me not you."

"Then regard me as your God because I will hold you accountable."

"Bob I won't debate religion with you. I have my priest for that. I really have nothing more to say. I'm leaving. Thanks for the coffee."

At just this moment, Ralph noticed a slight change in Bob's eyes. Ralph immediately realized that a man accustomed to danger saw something. Looking in his special rear view mirror on his glasses, Ralph saw a small dark man clutching a copy of what looked like the Koran advancing toward them. He wore a very bulky jacket on what had turned out to be an increasingly warm day. A policeman about a hundred yards away also seemed to take notice of the man as he began to draw his gun. He also yelled at the man. Ralph didn't need any more information than this. A suicide bomber would detonate his bomb within seconds. His entire world slowed to his next movements. Ralph leaped across the table tackling Bob and as he did so pulling the lunch table on its side as a shield. Instinctively Ralph placed his hands over his ears. He drove both of them to the ground. The powerful explosion came moments afterwards. The explosion pushed the table up against them but stopped most of the nails in the bomb. Still, the table fell on them with some of the sharp nails having pushed through the heavy plastic table. Both Ralph and Bob had some small puncture wounds from these nails but they had not penetrated too deeply or into a sensitive area of their bodies. Simple band aides and disinfectant would treat them. Otherwise, they lay unharmed from the blast with the exception of Bob whose eardrums ruptured. Unlike Ralph he did not instinctively place his hands over his ears. As they both clambered to their feet, Ralph and Bob witnessed a scene of mayhem, death and smoke. Many bystanders lay dying or dead around them, including the policeman Ralph saw earlier. Many people wailed and screamed. Both Bob and Ralph began the slow process of trying to pull themselves together in the chaos as sirens wailed in the distance. Bob suddenly turned to Ralph and said in a very loud voice.

"I suppose I ought to thank you for saving my life, but this is your world not mine. This mad man came for you not me or these other poor people. He stared at you and you alone. You and others like you have brought your wars and its deaths to our country."

"Bob, I don't think you can hear me but in our modern world war is everywhere. This is the new reality. People like me fight these wars wherever we are. This is a day in my life. I lived today but I may not tomorrow. I will keep fighting to the end of my life, as you must against the criminals you face. I'm leaving now to check on my daughter. If the police or FBI want to speak with me they know where to find me." Bob said as he quietly left.

Ralph walked away from the carnage as he had so many times before. They only difference this time is that none of his brothers in arms left with him. He watched the shock on people's faces from the terrible scene but as horrible as it was to Ralph it also seemed like another day at the office.

The Talk

A week after the incident, Ralph and Cindy sat at the dining room table examining all the women looking for men Cindy took from several dating websites. She had updated her search. They hadn't done this since the black ops woman attacked them. After many hours, Cindy and Ralph narrowed the list to two. Per their agreement, Ralph communicated with the two women placing his profile in front of them. He would now wait to see if they agreed to meet for a date. Cindy smiled at Ralph and then finally said what had been bothering her since they re-started this project.

"Dad I'm already jealous of these two women. I can't help it. I suppose if I had a boyfriend it would help, but I'm not quite ready for that. I promise I will be nice to these women but I'll probably have to go downstairs and hit the punching bag for an hour or so to calm myself. I guess I don't know how to share you yet. I wish I could put all my problems behind me but it isn't easy to do."

"I'm so proud of you Cindy. You're almost normal. Considering where you came from, this is quite an accomplishment. As to boyfriends how about Brad? If I have to court a girl, you should be spending time with a boy." Ralph answered.

"I like Brad but I don't trust him. I can't afford to become another trophy on his wall. If I did, I think I would lose some of the gains I've made. I'm not ready for heartache."

"Guys like Brad do that with girls but when they fall for a girl they fall as hard as any other guy. I've noticed how he looks at you. You're an amazing girl, beautiful, smart, courageous and talented. At some point in your life, you have to open your heart and let someone in. If things don't work out with Brad, I'll be here to catch you."

"And I you dad if this dating thing doesn't work out. At the end of the day, we are here for each other. Nothing else matters. But I'm worried. The attacks on you don't seem to stop. This suicide bomber is one of the most serious. I still can't figure out how you could survive the bombing when some many other people didn't. I don't know how I could survive without you." Cindy said.

"I wouldn't have had it not been for the Chicago cop. He drew his gun and forced the bomber to detonate his bomb before he could draw closer to me. Of course, I feel the same way about you, you are my world, but I'm a warrior and need a purpose in my life. Making money by providing security programs and equipment doesn't do it for me. I wanted to be just a normal father so I could protect you but it hasn't worked vey well. The attacks keep coming. I have to be proactive not reactive. The Pay Back project gave me a purpose. I need to get this purpose back. I'm going to meet with Sydney to see if he wants to fund a return of the Pay Back in some form. I have a new way of eliminating targets that should throw off the authorities. I have successfully used it before. I know I have been all over the place on this. One moment I want to have a simple life and protect you; the next I want to be a warrior again. This time I think I have it right. I guess what I'm asking is whether this will be okay for you."

"I'll worry but I feel the same way you do. You have to live your life not spend all your time worrying about death. I assumed you would eventually go back to being Pay Back. Part of me really wanted you to do that. No child male or female should have to go through what I did. I want to fight for them. So I guess what I'm saying is that it is okay with me if you become Pay Back again. It is one of the reasons I love you so much. Every time you go out there you fight for me. I know that when a sexual pervert attacks some child you and others like you will make them pay. In fact, whatever I do with my life will center on some purpose like yours. I should have died in that warehouse. Every day I have on this Earth is time given me to right some of the wrongs I suffered."

"I understand you my daughter and agree with everything you say. In the mean time we will find some people to share our lives but they may not like what we do and who we are."

"If they don't, we will find someone else. They can't see our purpose they can't see us."

"You really are my daughter." Ralph laughed.

After a minute pause, Cindy spoke again.

'Dad, do you want to know what I really think? I've been scared to say it before. I didn't think you would accept it. Some people might think I'm weird for saying it."

"Sure. I'm willing to listen to anything you say."

"The truth is I don't think any kind of relationship you or I have is going to work out. Who will accept what we are doing? Most women would be scared to death if they realized you are Pay Back. Worse yet, they might go to the authorities and have you arrested. I don't know how you could ever trust any woman you found. The woman we eventually choose might not be an assassin but she could ruin our world anyway. I am in the same boat. I will never feel safe with any man or boy but you. It isn't just your fighting skills. I might find a man with your fighting skills however unlikely that might be. But I would never find a man with your most important skill. You have some kind of 6th sense about danger and how to combat it. You do things no one else could do. When we were at Vail you demonstrated that. I still haven't figured out how you knew the assassin would target us on the Gondola. We rode it all day until you suddenly sensed it was unsafe. So I have come up with this solution. It is the only one that makes sense to me. Until I am 18 I remain your daughter. At 18, I become your lover and at 21 your wife. I know how strange this sounds but you and I are connected for life. No one could ever become a part of what we have even though both of us have pretended another woman or man could."

"Wow Cindy I don't know how to respond to what you just said. You are many years younger than me and still a child but oddly what you just said makes sense. I could never marry and live with someone else and have you marry someone else and live separately with this other person. I would worry that someone would harm you and I would not be in a position to help. This is where a traditional approach to our future would lead. I suggest we date other people until you turn 18 and if we feel the same way then, we see if what you suggest is going to work. Time and circumstances could change my mind and yours. One thing, however, will never change. I will love you forever."

"And I you."

Sydney

In another one of his warehouses, Sydney sat in a dimly lighted area at a small table. Sean Lafferty, the world knew as the Director of the CIA, sat opposite him. Sydney spoke.

"Our plan has worked very well. Hundreds of violent sex offenders are dead. Karzam's younger son is in power as he should be, but I don't feel very good about it. When I asked you to find me the best Special Forces soldier and motivate him to take up my cause, I had no idea you would murder his wife and daughter to provide him that motivation."

"Karzam's demands to kill and torture Ralph and his family had to be met. He needed to have his revenge. We would have a Taliban state in Afghanistan if we had not provided this to him. Our two objectives came together nicely. Ted Wiggle proved to be the perfect sadistic sex offender. Although until his attack on Ralph's wife and daughter Wiggle had not committed any violent acts we could pin on him, his psych profile said he was a time bomb ready to detonate. Making the abduction of Tager's little girl and the murder of his wife a military objective gave him the excuse he needed to indulge his fantasies. What we didn't know is that once Wiggle started he couldn't stop. Cindy and her parents quickly became his second victims. We created a monster. Fortunately, Tager put him down as we expected he would before he could continue his rampage. As to Tager's wife and daughter, they simply became collateral damage in a larger war. There is nothing pretty about what we do at the CIA but it is necessary and in the national interest."

"Should I fund Tager and his Seals to kill more violent sexual offenders? The more I kill the better I will feel about what was done to Tager's wife and child."

"Yeah, we should allow him to continue, but despite our note to him that the government no longer pursued him, Tager is still a potential threat. He just knows too much. If he were ever to learn that you had a role in the killing of his wife and daughter you would be in danger. In such a case, we would have to go back on our word and kill him. Yet, we might not have to kill him. The Afghans may do it for us. Some of the confidential information we have ties the suicide bomber back to the Afghan government. This bombing is an act of war against the U.S. and could never be disclosed to anyone. Otherwise public opinion and the congress might force us to take action against Sharif and his government even though he is still the best and most pro western President we are likely to get in Afghanistan. If our confidential information on Afghani involvement is accurate, I'm sure Sharif or someone else in the Afghan government will continue to seek Ralph's death. In Afghan culture Sharif would be duty bound to seek revenge. Sharif or someone else in his government could succeed and save us all the stress and risk of eliminating Tager."

"Yes but I will be sad when Ralph dies. He is a great soldier and the instrument of my revenge. I will need someone to take his place. I will keep killing these violent sexual offenders until the day I die."

"A noble cause my friend. I would be happy if you killed them all. In my book, these perverts have no right to live. And I will find you another Ralph Tager even if I have to make another one like I made Ralph." Lafferty said as he rose to shake Sydney's hand.

Sharif's Thoughts

harif, the new President of Afghanistan mourned his brother's and now his father's deaths in his own way: silently and without any outward indication. Nonetheless, he carefully set up Abdul's trip to Chicago to kill the man responsible, Ralph Tager. While Abdul, who had expressed a desire to martyr himself to kill the infidels for many years now, failed in his attempt on Tager's life, he had killed many innocent Americans. The Americans just another invading nation needed to know what it felt like to experience terror on their own soil. Afghans experienced this on a weekly basis. Although not his primary motive, Sharif's actions had gained him support among the many Afghan Tribes. They expected him to strike back and he had done so in a spectacular way. This support would almost certainly allow him to stay in power longer than he would have had he not acted. Still, Sharif had not avenged the deaths of his father and brother as yet. The job remained unfinished. He would need to try again, but in a more subtle way this time. An assassin would have to be utilized. The Americans, who he depended upon to stay in power, had started asking questions about Abdul. They suspected high-level involvement from his government in the attack. Yet, Sharif covered his tracks well. He had even persuaded a close follower to assume the blame if necessary.

Sharif reflected on Ralph Tager for a moment. What an extraordinary soldier. Sharif had absolutely no proof the highly decorated Seal caused his father's death. All Sharif knew is that Tager parachuted into the Kabul area a month before his father's death and weeks later reappeared in the U.S. What he did and how long he stayed in Sharif's country remained a mystery. Yet, Tager did kill his brother albeit on orders from his superiors. This had to be enough along with Sharif's suspicions that Tager killed his father as well. Someone had to pay. Ralph Tager would be that man so long as Sharif drew breath.

A Year Later

The next year flew by quickly. The bomb attack slowly disappeared from the news cycle when the identity of the killer never became known to the public. The CIA and FBI did a great job of hiding the man's identity. Ralph worked diligently at his security job and continued to do well but his pledge to renew his efforts to kill sexual predators went unfulfilled. Sydney unlike before did not respond to his requests to meet and start a new campaign. In fact, Ralph heard from his many contacts that another effort to kill these perverts had begun but without his knowledge or involvement. Then last week in an unmitigated disaster, law enforcement caught four ex Green Beret soldiers in the act of carrying out an assassination on a new and particularly vicious sexual predator. The predator died from a rifle shot to his head but according to the papers the four soldiers had been arrested and charged with his murder. Sydney as of yet had not been charged but faced an enormous risk of arrest should any of the soldiers identify Sydney as the funder of the assassination. Ralph wanted more details about this disaster but he feared becoming involved in any way. Someone else failed. They would have to pay the price of that failure. He needed to lay low.

Still, Ralph puzzled over the hiring of a new team. He had been very successful in his assassination efforts. So why did Sydney replace him? Ralph needed to know why. He still carried some risk from his earlier operations. If a problem unknown to him caused Sydney to seek the help of someone else, Ralph wanted to know all about it. A phone call from Bob Prandini heightened his concerns.

"Ralph this is Bob Prandini. We finally caught you guys in the act, but I can't tie it back to you. The four soldiers tell me that they don't even know you. If this is true, your employer went a different direction. It doesn't make any sense. I'm calling to verify what they said."

"Bob I don't know who these guys are but as Green Berets at least the paper says there are I wouldn't have any reason to know them. Seals don't work with berets very often. They have different mission profiles. So I can't really help you."

"I don't think you are involved in this but Sydney Worth the billionaire hired this group like he hired you. With the leverage we now have, we can get him to offer you up on a platter. You would be better off negotiating a deal with us now. Your terms will be better now than they will be after we interrogate Sydney."

"No deal. I have nothing to do with this. Investigate and prosecute the people in front of you. You don't need to come after me."

"I can and I will even though you saved my life. You'll regret the day you saved me."

"I am a soldier. I save colleagues on the battlefield. This is what I do. You are no different."

"But I am and you will soon find that out." Bob said as he disconnected the call.

Ralph doubted that Sydney would confess to involvement in this operation or as a part of a deal on his previous operations. Sydney as a billionaire would have the finest defense counsel available to him. He wouldn't admit to anything. Still, Ralph worried. His renewed effort to bring sexual predators to justice seemed to be going nowhere.

Despite Ralph's issues, Cindy seemed to be doing well. Now at high school, she hung out with a group of friends while continuing her active martial arts schedule. She tried out for the high school musical and to her great surprise won the lead singing role. She still refused to date a boy individually but enjoyed their company in groups. Brad still tried to date her but Cindy stubbornly refused his advances. She knew her girl friends actively dated boys but the torture she endured as a young girl stayed with her. One thing, however, did change. The two of them took frequent walks with each other. Ralph insisted they both wear thin bullet-proof vests, but they took some risk nonetheless in this new activity. Ralph used the walks as teaching experiences, carefully pointing out how to assess potential human threats and how to evaluate the terrain they walked. Ralph's training proved to be critical on one of their walks. They walked in a local Lake County forest preserve on a fine fall Saturday. Cindy addressed Ralph in a low whisper.

"On our 9 o'clock, an ordinary looking middle age woman is keeping pace with us. I saw her on my way to school yesterday. You would not have seen her from the driver's position in our car. This woman is wearing a coat with big pockets that looks very warm for a day like today. She never glances at us and looks like a typical middle age housewife. She blends in nicely with what one would expect to see. This is why she makes me nervous. What should we do?"

"Good pick up Cindy. I am looking at her now. I think I see a slight bulge in her jacket. There is a stand of bushes and trees just ahead that will block our view of her. When we emerge from these bushes and trees she will have a good shot at us before we can respond. If she is what we think she is, this woman assassin will hit us there. So we will stop just as we disappear from her view in the bushes and wait. If we see her walking into the clearing after the bushes, we will know that she is probably not after us. If she does not appear, we will know that she is waiting for us."

The woman did not appear in the clearing ahead of them. Ralph spoke again.

"We have to assume this woman wants to kill us. She has three choices once she has waited for us to appear a little longer and we don't. She can appear in front of us, work her way through the bushes to come at us from there or appear behind us. I don't think she will come at us through the bushes. She will make noise no matter how careful she is. We can easily see her if she tries to come at us from behind. Nonetheless, I want you to face backwards and move close to me. I can feel you tense if she comes from there. I think she will approach from the front firing as we come into view. Both of us need to drop toward the ground as I fire back at her. I want you to fall to the earth now but keep your eyes on our rear. Nudge me if you see her. If she comes from the front, our assassin lady will focus on me as I want her to do. She will assume I have a bullet-proof vest on and try to hit me in the neck or head area. If I take a bullet, take my gun and fire on her. This all comes down to reaction time."

"Got it dad.' Cindy said with more bravado than she felt.

Time slowed. Minutes passed. Cindy and Ralph heard nothing. Then with lighting quickness the woman appeared firing a silenced 25 caliber extended magazine as she did so. Ralph retuned fire from his silenced 9mm as he fell toward the ground. Ralph could feel a bullet graze the top of his head. Cindy lay beneath him and out of the line of fire. Ralph quickly glanced toward the woman who lay on her back with a bullet to the middle of her throat. She coughed some blood and then lay still. Ralph spoke hurriedly,

"Cindy, are you okay."

"Yeah, but I could feel bullets pass over me. If we had stood when she appeared both of us would be dead. Is she dead?"

"Yes my bullet caught her in the throat. I thought she would bend or drop like us but she didn't. I wonder who she is. The Afghans or the sexual predators hired her, probably the former. There is nobody here at the moment. I have a spare barrel for my gun. I will put it on and bury the other barrel. If the police seize my gun the bullet will not match the one in the woman. I have a permit to carry this gun. We will leave the woman where she is but we have to leave the park as fast as we can. It is self-defense but I don't want to struggle with the police over that. I am on their radar. They will make this incident as difficult for me as they can."

Cindy and Ralph quickly left the forest preserve, found their car and left the scene. No policeman followed them, but they did hear sirens as they entered their house. Ralph treated the bullet scratch on his head. Some antiseptic, a thorough cleaning of the shallow gash and a little gauze took care of the problem. Ralph immediately placed a hat on his head to hide the wound. After treating himself, Ralph sat Cindy on the couch.

"The woman assassin got off two shots, one as she rounded the corner and the second as she faced us. My shot reached her as she fired the second time. I think my bullet ruined her second shot and the first sailed above my head. She was an excellent shot as she walked turned and fired and still shot straight. My dropping caused her to be a little high. As I thought, she assumed I had on a vest. Cindy you saved us both. You noticed her the first time while I didn't. If we hadn't been prepared, she would have killed us. After a year with no problems, I though we were in the clear. We are obviously not. I don't know what to say."

"It's okay Dad. This is the third threat I have faced. Each time I am a little less afraid. You have enemies who have included me in their attacks. We just have to be ready for them. The two of us together are now better than one. We will survive."

"Yes we will."

Two days later in the early evening, Ralph answered the door. As always, he carefully checked his visitor. Ralph recognized detective Earl Williams of the Lake Bluff Police Department. He had spoken with him before. Another office accompanied him with Lake County Sheriff badges. Ralph opened the door.

"Hi detective Williams. How can I help you?"

"HI Mr. Tager. This is Sheriff's Deputy Walt Corzine. May we come in?"

"No, let's talk outside."

"Okay here goes. A middle age woman died in the Lake County Forest Preserve not far from here. She had a bullet in her throat. We thought it was a murder at first but she had a very expensive custom assassin's gun clutched in her hand that had been fired. After a little research by the detective bureau and the medical examiner, we determined the woman's body exactly matched the description of the Plain Jane Killer wanted for assassinations in jurisdictions throughout the world. She is considered by some in the law enforcement community as the best assassin in the world. She blends in so well with her ordinary looks and manner her victims don't see her coming. We know that you and your daughter walk in this forest preserve. Do you know anything about this killing?" Earl said.

"No we don't. She sounds like a scary person, but in her line of work the day eventually comes when someone shoots back." Ralph said without emotion.

"Yeah I suppose that is true but whoever killed this woman had to be a very good with a gun and tactics, someone like you Ralph." Walt added.

"Gentlemen we live near a large navy base with some Seal Teams in residence. There are many people living in this area that fit this description." Ralph responded.

"Mr. Tager before we came here I received a call from a man named Bob Prandini. He is a detective in the Seattle PD. He knows you well. He is convinced you are the shooter in this death. Bob called you Pay Back. Do you mind if I and my partner here have a look around your house?"

"I do mind very much. I am in the security business. I never let anyone search my house without a warrant. I preach this gospel to my clients. I have to practice it as well. Now if there isn't anything more I will wish you a good day gentlemen."

"Where were you last Saturday at approximately 3 pm?" Walt pressed.

"My daughter and I were in my car going for a drive."

"Were you in the Forest Preserve on Route 22?"

"Yes we were headed there. But we didn't see any assassins."

"I think you are lying. We will obtain a warrant and won't be gentle when we return." Walt said in a threatening way.

"Then we will talk again, but I must say I am unhappy with your hostile attitude." Ralph said as he slipped inside the door and closed it in the officers' face.

As Ralph returned to the living room, Cindy came into to join him.

"Dad that was a little scary. I heard everything they said through an open window. Do you think they will come back with a search warrant?"

"No. If they had some witnesses or anything else specific to us, they would have showed up with a search warrant. They need probable cause. Obviously, they don't have it. I have a defense attorney who practices in Lake County. I will have him monitor the issuance of search warrants. If the officers file for one, I will have him challenge it. We will be okay." Ralph said.

"We were lucky no one saw us. If the officers come to my school and try to talk to me alone, I will insist you be present as you have taught me to do." Cindy said.

"Cindy I am afraid they will try this. This is the biggest case the Lake Bluff Police Department and the Lake County Sheriff's Office have ever had. They don't have a dead international assassin everyday. They won't stop with this visit."

"The hardest part of all these threats dad is the uneasy relationship we have with law enforcement. A lot of people die around and near you. They always turn to you before anyone else."

"Yes this is a problem, but a problem that will never go away as long as people try to kill me or you. Law enforcement doesn't approve of some of the techniques used by Special Forces in pursuit of their missions."

Afghan Talk

The Assistant Afghan Ambassador to the U.S, Randy Pashar, who to those in the know actually ran the embassy in D,C., settled uncomfortably in front of Ralph at a small café close to the Afghan Embassy. His security guards eyed Ralph suspiciously. Ralph came to the meeting well armed. He would not go quietly if they chose to come after him. Ralph spoke into the silence.

"You came here today to see what evidence I have against your President, who has twice tried to assassinate me. The bombing in particular creates problems for you. If the American people knew you set up the bombing, we would withdraw our support for you. The Taliban would assume power within months. I do have some documents and intercepts that implicate your government in the plot. If by some strange chance, I should be murdered they would be mailed to every news outlet in this country. Your President believes he has reason to target me. Allegedly, a Seal Team killed his brother. Former President Karzam believed my team did the job. Karzam then pressured our government to eliminate my team by placing us in jeopardy on an assignment. My fellow Seals were killed but since I was not on the mission, I did not die. My wife and daughter were instead killed and then after a suitable length of time for me to suffer after their deaths, attempts were made on my life. I did go to Afghanistan in the hopes of killing Karzam. I needed the assassination attempts to stop. But because of a lack of support from my government, I failed to do so. As fate would have it, Karzam died weeks after I returned to the U.S. of a heart attack.

"I am highly motivated to reveal what I have against your government and also the U.S. who was complicit in this messy affair, but I will give you the chance to voluntarily stop these assassination attempts on my daughter and I. If I have your assurances, I will not reveal this information. Of course, I have no reason to believe any assurances you might give me, but your assurances are better than nothing."

After a long pause, Randy finally spoke.

"I cannot give you those assurances, but I will contact the President and see what he says. You and your daughter Cindy will remain vulnerable. You have no friends or allies in this. All you have is your threats, but I am here so obviously we have not dismissed them. I do have sympathy for your predicament but my sympathies mean very little. You acted in accordance with your orders. I have done the same. I spent many years as a soldier before entering the Foreign Service."

"This is all I can ask of you. But whatever decision you make, I will not go easily should you come after me again."

"We are aware of this. You may be the best soldier we have ever encountered but at the end of the day you are just one man. Good day to you Ralph Tager."

Ralph's Latest Plan

As a long time Seal, assigned to many hotspots around the world, Ralph had access to special people the rest of us do not know exist. Terry Schiller, a bespectacled, pudgy middle age man, occupied this space. A brilliant engineer, Terry developed self -propelled drones for many purposes. When Ralph last spoke to him three years ago, Terry worked on very small insect size drones for surveillance and assassination purposes. Terry in particular liked men and women fighting in the field. An ardent patriot, he only sold his products to Americans. He did not care for noncombatants who he regarded as paper pushers pretending to be soldiers. Ralph had an idea on what to do with his new Afghan opponent. After his meeting with Randy Pashar, Ralph knew that he must eliminate the new President of Afghanistan.

When Terry peered at Ralph through his surveillance system, he happily opened the door and let the former Seal inside. Ralph had always been one of Terry's favorite warriors.

"Ralph you have had a busy time since you lost your family and Seal Team. A lot of people have died presumably at your hand. The Seals lost one of their best when they forced you out. If as rumored, you eliminated all those sexual perverts, you have done society a great service. I wish I could kill each one of them with my bare hands. How can I help?"

"Since I left the Seals, I have had a number of assassins try to end my life and the life of my adopted daughter. They have all failed but I have an enemy who will keep sending these assassins until my daughter and I are dead. I possess a classified slow acting poison that will kill this man in about three weeks time but I need a remote controlled delivery system. I know you worked on some the last time we spoke. I expect this man will be in Washington at the end of next month."

"The bee is perfect for this type of mission, provided the amount of the poison is small. The bee looks exactly like a real bee but is in fact a remote controlled drone. When I met you last, I had developed the bee but had not yet devised a self-destruct mechanism. I have now developed this crucial part. I cannot afford to have anyone identify me as the manufacturer of the delivery device. I will sell you a bee and the controller for $5000 dollars. Just so you know, I would not sell the bee to just anyone. Only a warrior and patriot like you could ever buy one of these from me. Since I trust you, I will not ask you who you intend to kill."

"You have a deal Terry. How do I operate it?"

"I will send you an encrypted email with the instructions. Good hunting. Oh and by the way, none of this is recorded. I sweep this place everyday."

"I assumed you did. Thanks for everything Terry. I hope my hunting will be as good as you say. Here is a cash envelope with $6000 in it. You can have it all." Ralph replied.

Fateful Day

Two weeks before the President of Afghanistan would give a speech on a stage near the Potomac River in Washington, Ralph, dressed in his old man disguise, walked the area. Fortunately, an apartment complex of four stories lay within the bee drones' range to the stage. By claiming to be a relative of one of the residents, Ralph gained access to the roof. He found a shelf near the rooftop air conditioner that lay in the shade. He nodded with approval when a sweep of this gloved hand revealed a heavy layer of dust on the remote shelf. Ralph placed the drone as far back from the edge as he could and quickly left the roof and minutes later the building. Minutes more after leaving the building, Ralph drove his rental car back to Reagan airport to catch a flight back to Chicago. Ralph had spent hours studying Google maps of the entire area and knew exactly how he would fly the drone when the day of the speech came. Ralph had also spent days practicing how to fly the drone in a remote piece of land in a rural area that he knew the US Government owned but did not use. If a certificate would be handed out to operators for proficiency on the use of the bee drone, Ralph felt that he would easily earn it.

Ralph knew that his plan held many risks of failure. His Internet connection to the drone might fail even though he had tested it many times in the Chicago area. Also, his timing would have to be excellent. The drone had limited battery life. It would have to fly to the target and inject the KZ 80 poison without hovering or taking too indirect a route. Of course, the drone might also fail to inject the subject as expected or run into unforeseen obstacles. Finally, the small amount of

KZ 80 might not kill the healthy young Afghan President Sharif even though the poison in all the research he read seemingly would do so. Ralph placed his chances of success at no better than 40% but if he did not kill the Afghan President he had no clue as to how he could keep his daughter safe. The assassins the President hired would eventually find him and his daughter and do what others had failed to do, kill them both.

The day of the speech finally came. Ralph sat in his downstairs office in Des Plaines with the best computer and Internet equipment he could buy. His drone controller sat in front of him hooked up to his computer, which had been set to the Internet connection he would need to operate the drone. Fortunately for Ralph a minor cable network decided to carry the speech live. Watching the broadcast with one eye while he established his Internet connection with the drone, Ralph patiently waited for the President to arrive. Sharif came about twenty minutes late but after lengthy introductions strode slowly and confidently to the stage. Now the test came. Ralph activated the bee drone and obtained a reasonably good picture of the apartment roof. Not surprisingly, a local police officer stood guard at the edge of the roof, studying the distant stage and area around it carefully with a high-powered set of binoculars. The officer also had a high-powered sniper's rifle set up on a tripod in case it should be needed. Ralph lifted the small drone quietly from its resting place and at an altitude of about 50 feet above the rooftop began his slow journey to the stage. The officer did not hear the tiny drone, which made a faint whirring sound, and thus did not look for it as it made its way to the Potomac. By the time the drone came within the policeman's view, the tiny drone could not be seen very easily. The officer missed it entirely and even if he had seen it would have thought it to be a bee, which of course the drone looked like.

After reaching the Potomac, Ralph steered the bee along the river until it lined up with the platform. Taking an abrupt left turn the drone under Ralph's capable hands flew directly for the back of Sharif's head. He had spoken for about ten minutes when the drone arrived. The bee operated flawlessly, pushing its tiny needle into the President's neck and then immediately removing it as the bee drone fell toward the ground. At almost ground level, the bee flew back to an area filled with empty boxes used for the audio equipment and fell lightly behind one of them. Immediately a highly concentrated form of Hydrochloric acid surrounded the bee and quickly devoured it, leaving some dark ash behind. The moment the bee fell to the earth, the battery level on Ralph's monitor showed less than 1% life remaining. Ralph shook his head in disbelief. He expected a higher battery level at the end of the operation but did not take into account a stiff headwind the bee encountered flying down the Potomac. As the bee disappeared in the acid, Sharif made a joke about the aggressive mosquitoes in Washington. He assured the audience, however, that the ones in his home country were far more dangerous as indeed everything in his country was.

Done with his task, Ralph took the controller to his burial site in a Lake County Forest Preserve where it joined weapons, vials and other items Ralph used in his profession. Deciding the buried items presented too much of a risk, Ralph tossed Hydrochloric acid on them. After eliminating this last shred of evidence connecting him to the assassination attempt on the President, Ralph drive home to spend time with his daughter. The next two to three weeks would be anxious ones as Ralph waited to see the result of his attack. He expected law enforcement to come looking for him.

Meanwhile Peter Ramos, who had been assigned to the Afghan President's protection detail by the Secret Service viewed the tape of the Afghan President's speech a 5th time. The president's remark about the mosquito puzzled Peter. No one else at the event, at least as far as he knew, experienced any kind of bite or sting. Such a bite could have occurred but in Peter's eyes it appeared to be highly unlikely. Rather Peter believed in another possibility, a new insect size drone that could be used for remote controlled assassinations. Peter had seen an article on them in one of his security magazines. Unfortunately, he had no evidence of one being at this event. As proof of this, the President of Afghanistan Sharif had returned to his country and by all accounts remained healthy. Still, slow acting poisons existed that would not have acted as yet. Also, in walking the site after the event, Peter found a patch of grass that had recently been patched in the area behind where the stage had been. After interviewing the groundskeepers for the area, one mentioned that he remotely remembers replacing soil in a burn area there but he couldn't be sure. He constantly made patches and they all began to merge together after a while in his mind. Peter also examined the possible areas for the launch of a drone including the apartment roof where the drone actually departed. Peter easily found the shelf but found no trace of a drone having been there. What he did find, however, is a shelf, which saw little use, wiped mostly clean. This further aroused his suspicions but once again provided him with little in the way of proof. Finally, Peter interviewed every person he could who attended the speech. Only one person remembered seeing an insect. This young lady thought she saw a bee, but didn't remember where she saw it.

Based on this evidence, Peter surmised that a drone took off from the apartment rooftop, injected the Afghan President with poison and then self-destructed, but of course his weak and circumstantial evidence could not support such a conclusion in any forum. Peter nonetheless submitted a memo to his superior with these conclusions who quickly dismissed Peter's findings because of a lack of credible evidence. Peter's memo would go no further than his boss's desk.

Then three weeks to the day after the speech, reports from Kabul stated that the Afghan President had suddenly collapsed from heart problems and lay in the ICU at a local hospital. The young president had no history of heart problems. Two days later he died. Peter's memo gained new life. He and a FBI agent, Rachel Minnow, received orders to work together on finding out more facts about Peter's memo. The probe would be conducted in the utmost secrecy. The Afghan government experienced great disruption following the death of the young President and our government feared a takeover by forces allied with the Taliban. As in the father's death, many prominent Afghans blamed the U.S. for the death but as before had absolutely no evidence of US involvement.

After some hard work and investigation, Peter and Rachel made their way to Terry's home and workshop. If a drone had been used,

Terry would be the likely creator of the drone. At first Terry refused them admittance, questioning their credentials and claiming that he did not know them. Finally, they talked their way inside but Rachel in particular took too hard a line with the very experienced Terry.

"Terry we can shut you down if we chose and seize all your plans and prototypes. You made an off the books sale to a spy or warrior of a miniaturized drone and now it has resulted in the death of a foreign leader close to the U.S. You are in big trouble unless you cooperate."

"Listen young lady. I make devices for the military, the CIA, other law enforcement agencies and your own agency the FBI. I have many friends in these services most of whom outrank you. You can't just walk in here and make wild accusations and threats without any proof. My catalogue has many drones of different types offered for sale. Miniaturized drones are for the most part still in testing phases and are not for sale. So, in short, I don't know what you are talking about." An angry Terry responded.

"Look Terry, all we need is the name of the person you sold the drone to. That is it. If you do that, you are in the clear." Peter said.

"Sorry as I said before, I can't help you. I have made no sales through my catalogue of any drones like the one you seek. If you want to subpoena my records, you are welcome to do so." Terry replied.

"We are not talking about a regular sale. People in our agency claim you make private sales of merchandise to maintain the secrecy surrounding some of your merchandise. This is what we are after." Rachel pressed.

"My answer is the same as before and will continue to be the same as many times as you ask it. I don't know anything. Now if you will excuse me, I have work to do." Terry responded.

With no further discussion possible with an uncooperative Terry, the two agents left his residence and shop. As they left, Peter took Rachel aside.

"Rachel you handled that very poorly. Terry is not some ignorant private person you can handle the way you did. No one in either one of our agencies is going to back us up if you go after Terry. He is considered a highly valuable asset to our community. Agents come to Terry because they know he will protect their secrets. He would be ruined if he started sharing information that you asked for and word got out that he did so. If we ever approach Terry again we had better have more information than we have now. If we did, we could appeal to his patriotism to help us. Threatening him just pissed Terry off." Peter said.

"I don't care. I know he is part of this. He needs to do what is right if he wants to keep us as clients. Now we have to find another way to get the information we need. I have sent a memo to all the agents in various agencies who deal with this type of operation. Let's see what comes back to us."

"Rachel I hope something does. Otherwise, we have nowhere to turn." Peter responded.

Two weeks later, Rachel came running into Peter's office. She had a typewritten page with no identification on it. The page read.

Ralph Tager, an ex Navy Seal, is the man you seek. There is much to his story. So do your research before you question him.

"Peter I have already started doing research on this man. I will leave with you a copy of what I have collected. We have many people we have to interview before we confront him."

"Sounds good to me. We will find out what happened to the Afghan President and hold those responsible for his death accountable." Peter said grabbing the materials from Rachel.

Final Interview

6 months after the Afghan President's death, Ralph answered a knock at his door. As his custom, he talked through the door before he would open it. The man and woman identified themselves.

"I am Peter from the US Secret Service and this is Rachel from the FBI. Can we come in and talk to you?"

"I will come outside with you. I don't let people in my house without a warrant." Ralph responded.

When Ralph walked outside, he shook hands with the two officers and said.

"Now how can I help you?"

"Six months ago, the President of Afghanistan, Sharif, a young and healthy man, visited Washington D.C. Three weeks later, at his home in Afghanistan he died. We suspect someone poisoned Sharif in DC with a slow acting poison, probably KZ 80. You're Seal Unit had some KZ 80 in inventory but no one can find the poison. It has simply disappeared with no accounting of where it went. At a speech Sharif made in Washington, he complained of a mosquito bite. No one can recall any insects being present at the speech. We believe the so-called bite came from a miniature drone injection of the KZ 80. We also believe the drone launched from the top of an apartment complex less than a mile from the speech site. A man named Terry made the drone and identified you as the person he sold it to. Also, you have history with Sharif's family. On a Seal mission, you killed on of the two brothers of the recently murdered Afghan President. Many people in Afghanistan believe you killed the recently deceased President's father Karzam, who preceded him in office with the same KZ 80 poison. In short, you are the man who killed Sharif and his father as well." Rachel said.

"You've created a nice fantasy Rachel, but it so full of holes you could drive a truck through it. I admit to none of your narrative. For starters, Seal Missions are classified as top secret. If you reveal any details of such a mission you can end up in jail not me. Also, if I am not mistaken, the papers said that Karzam died of natural causes."

"Where were you on March 17th the day of the Afghan President's speech." Rachel said as forcefully as she could.

"I was here and have a date stamped video to prove it. I went in and out of my house several times that day. My cameras record all activities that occur outside the house but none that occur inside the house. Now if you have no further questions, I will take my leave of you." Ralph replied.

"We will need that tape." Rachel demanded.

"I will search my archives, copy the relevant sections and deliver it to your office." Ralph replied.

"We want it now." Peter said.

"Then bring a warrant to search for it. I don't like my things disturbed. I should have the tape for you in a couple of days." Ralph replied.

"You won't admit to any of this?" Rachel said.

"No and I believe you are lying about any meeting I had with Terry as no such meeting took place to the best of my recollection. Now if you aren't going to arrest me, I have work to do in my house."

"What a minute before you go would you remove your hat? I think you are hiding something." Rachel said.

"I will not. What I choose to put on my head is none of your business." Ralph said.

"We will get you Ralph Tager if it is the last thing we do. " Rachel snarled back.

"Have a nice day agents," Ralph said as he disappeared behind his front door leaving the agents on the stoop.

Agent's Frustration

As Rachel and Peter drove away from Ralph's house, their frustration showed.

"All this information is very sensitive. My boss has made it very clear that he doesn't want any of what we have to be revealed to the public unless we actually have a case. The State Department has lied about American involvement in these assassinations and would like to keep it under wraps. I thought the lie about Terry would spring some information from Ralph." Rachel said.

"He knew we were lying. Terry probably told Ralph we were fishing for information. That is the problem with using a lie to flush out information. If it doesn't' succeed, you lose any amount of trust you had with a possible perpetrator. I for one am going to move on with my other business. This investigation has actually harmed my goal of protecting the President on his detail. I look like a failure fond of far out theories. I have informed my boss of everything we have discovered. He is satisfied even if I am not."

"I am in the same boat. My boss is closing this investigation and assigning me to another. The task force is being terminated. Whatever action is taken by your or my agency, however, will not stop me from continuing this investigation on my own time. Ralph is guilty. He needs to be held to account." Rachel said.

"I agree. As I find new information I will send it to you." Peter said.

"I will do the same. Oh and by the way, I think Ralph is hiding a wound on his head he probably received from his last encounter with an assassin. Remember the famous assassin that died near here. I think Ralph killed her." Rachel replied.

"What makes you think that?" Peter asked.

"He wore his hat indoors. Who does that if they don't have anything to hide? We should try to catch him without his hat."

"What would that prove even if he had a wound there?"

"That he lied about not being targeted by the assassin recently found dead in the woods near here."

"He will have an explanation if such a wound exists. It may be suggestive but nothing else. Still we should have grabbed his hat." Peter said.

"I don't think you can take anything from that man that he doesn't' want you to take, but it would have been worth a try." Rachel laughed.

"If there is a next time we talk to him, we will take his hat. You now have me very curious about how his head looks."

A New Day

"Ralph turned to Cindy with a sly smile on his face.

"I have several serious matters to discuss with you. I've been waiting for certain things to be resolved before I did. The assassination attempts on us may finally be coming to an end. All the people who wanted to kill us are dead. We may be truly safe but of course you can never be absolutely certain. I have left a lot of bodies in my wake and many police departments and police agencies would like to arrest me. They don't have cases now and as time goes on they will eventually lose interest but they are still out there. I have decided to leave Secure Networks for another firm Security International. They will allow me to live and work here. Their head office is in Cincinnati but as the their new CEO, I can eventually move their home office here. I need to leave Sydney and his company behind. He is still not communicating with me. Whatever our issues are it is better that I don't work for him anymore. I still think about my obligation to hunt sexual predators but at the moment I have no means to do so. Are you okay with that?"

"Yes. Sometimes you can't hurry things. You've taught me to be patient. I must ask you to be the same. But know this. You don't have to hunt sexual predators for me anymore. My anger toward these perverts declines every year. I just want to forget about this time in my life. I know this also has to do with your dead wife and daughter so I can't tell you not to go back on the hunt again."

"Yes but as you say their memories have faded a little with time. I am not as consumed with rage as I was. Still, if an opportunity comes along, I may engage again. Whether it is moral or immoral, I don't believe these violent sexual predators deserve to live any longer. I may never change my mind on this point. You are 14 1/2 now. We haven't talked about our arrangement of what would happen when you are 18 and 21. Have you forgotten about that?"

"No I think about it all the time. I'm still having problems dating high school students. I had to grow up too fast. They just aren't in the same place as me. Also, I still don't feel safe with them. This has not changed. I am not ready to make love to a man or boy but if I was it still would be you."

"As you know my dating has not been very successful. Like you I seem to be frozen until you make your decision. I just can't trust any woman I am dating not to betray me when they learn of my past. Even though I would try to keep my past from a girlfriend, in my experience when people are close to you, information is difficult to keep from them. When they learn of my secrets, they will think of me as a felon. Maybe there is a woman out there for me and there is a man out there for you. I just don't know. I do know that I love you just as much now as ever. Without you I would be very lonely. So I guess we keep the status quo."

"Yes that is good for me. I don't know what I would do without you. When my demons come calling on me often in my dreams, you are always there to anchor me and help me fight them. How can any other man understand these demons and how I must fight them? They could try to empathize but I just don't think they would in the right way. I think I am going to return to your bed like I did as a child and I did briefly after the museum attack. I don't sleep very well when you aren't beside me. I will be fully dressed of course, but at least I will be there."

"Cindy you are always welcome in my bed, but you are an absolutely gorgeous woman. Don't press up too close to me. I won't be able to control my feelings."

"I won't but as a woman I won't mind being near to that sculpted body of yours. I still get jealous when you bring home a date and she spends her whole time staring at you."

"I feel the same way when a man or boy stares at you. As you say, we need to be patient. When you are 18 we will decide."

"Yes we will." Cindy said as she suddenly kissed Ralph on the lips.

Two More Years.

Two more years slowly passed without any more incidents, but Cindy and Ralph did not change their behaviors. Sixteen and a half now, Cindy looked like a Sports Illustrated model but she still did not date an individual boy. Instead she would socialize with a group of friends just as she had done in junior high school. Now a second-degree black belt in many disciplines, she became even more lethal than she had been before. Cindy also sang in the talent shows and participated in the school plays. Her morning routines also remained the same. She seemed to be frozen into her routines.

Ralph also stayed the same. He moved his business to the Lake Bluff area and as before excelled in running his business. The investors in the business expressed their satisfaction by increasing his pay and bonuses. Ralph became a more and more wealthy man. His social life also remained frozen. He dated less and less frequently becoming frustrated in looking for the right woman. Cindy remained the one woman in his life and he seemed to be okay with that arrangement.

On a regular late fall day, Ralph first noticed the man near their house as he drove Cindy to school. He gestured toward the man with his head. Cindy responded the moment she saw him.

"He is watching us. The way he looks, walks and behaves looks to be military. The man could be a lot better at surveillance than he is."

"Cindy, you are correct. The man looks as if he is part of a military team. This team might be nearby. My enemies have changed tactics. They want to come at me with a military team, guns blazing. If I led this team, I would be looking for a place to attack. Our home is heavily fortified but they wouldn't necessarily know that. They could try a classic box in attack, blocking the roadway from both sides with trucks. Then they would merely open up on us with everything they have. Another option would be to capture you at the High School and force me to come to them to save your life. Finally, they could attack our house from all sides leaving us no escape. I think our best course of action is to drive toward school and then suddenly take our alternate route back home. If we immediately turn toward home they might intercept us. What do you think?"

"Yes, I can't go to school until this is resolved. The house is our best defensive position. Our escape tunnel leaves us the option of abandoning the house if they bring too much firepower but still gives us powerful weapons with which to fight them."

Without further comment, Ralph suddenly turned their armored 420 horsepower Mercedes down a side street and accelerated to the highest possible speed he could navigate. As Ralph did so, he heard diesel engines rev to high power. As Ralph drove around a barrier at the end of a dead end street, he quickly disappeared into his hidden garage behind his house. To anyone coming after him it would have looked if he had disappeared. Ralph quickly activated the cameras he had placed on the wall behind his house and the wall in front of his house. Within seconds, Ralph observed two heavily armored military vehicles roar down the street after him. They came to a screeching halt when the dead end offered no way forward. One vehicle remained at the dead end while the other drove to the front of their home. Ralph now knew that they had intended to box him and Cindy in somewhere on their way to Cindy's school.

Shortly after the vehicles stopped six heavily armored and equipped young men poured out each of the vehicles. Without hesitation, men at both locations shouldered a rocket-propelled grenade and fired at the wall surrounding the house. Two large holes appeared in the wall on each side of the house. Seconds after the blasts, Ralph activated a remote controlled 50 caliber gun on each side of the house that fired on the military vehicles, which had come into view through the holes in the wall. The first shells in both guns were made of spent uranium. These specialized shells tour apart the armored vehicles. The drivers of both vehicles who thought themselves protected were killed by the very heavy shells, which easily penetrated their military vehicles. The vehicles themselves because of the heavy fire erupted from within as ordinance inside the vehicles detonated. One man on the attack team at the rear of the house had his arm torn off by the gunfire and a man on the front of house lost part of his leg. The wounded men were carried to a safe place out of the line of fire, and given the best first aid possible.

The remainder of the experienced soldiers took cover outside the range of the dangerous 50 caliber gun. They began to throw grenades over the wall toward the guns. The detonations reverberated up and down the otherwise calm streets. A couple of small caliber guns embedded in the walls on both ends answered. A man in the rear of the house took a bullet to his face dying instantly, but otherwise the soldiers' vests handled the small caliber bullets well. Also, when the guns locations were identified the men easily avoided them. With concentrated fire the soldiers finally destroyed the remotely controlled small caliber guns but at the very last moment, one of the guns tore into the hand of one of the soldiers at the front of the house when he drew too close to the embedded gun. Bleeding badly and unable to handle his equipment he had to retreat to the same area where the first victims received care. When the injured men finally received the battlefield care needed to stabilize them, the remaining soldiers, four soldiers at the front of the house and four at the rear renewed their assault. By throwing every grenade they had, the teams at the front and rear were able to finally silence the two 50 caliber guns. Somewhat battered the four men crouched just outside the blast holes in the front and rear walls.

The leader of the assault team, Berry, positioned in the front spoke to the team assembled in front of him and the team assembled at the rear of the house through their walk talkie type communication devices.

"Three of our comrades are dead and two more could lose their lives unless they are admitted to a hospital very soon. Our final wounded comrade can't fight very well with his hand torn up by a bullet. We have only ten minutes remaining until every policeman and swat unit in this area descends on us. Both of our vehicles are out of commission, nothing more than charred ruins. We shouldn't have engaged our target at their home, but we are already committed. Our job is to kill the Seal and his daughter. The only way to accomplish this now is with a fast and furious front and rear assault. We can expect fire as we attack the house. We have two rocket-propelled grenades left. A team member will stay at the rear of the assault team and fire the grenade as soon as we isolate the place in the house where our two targets are firing at us. The grenade should open the house to us and if we are lucky injure or kill our adversaries. If you have a chance, throw a stun grenade and a tear gas canister inside the house. This may give us an advantage as we attack. Assemble your teams. We must go now."

Inside the house, Ralph peered onto the front lawn through a specially designed reinforced gun position while Cindy did the same at the rear of the house. With a communications device, Ralph spoke to Cindy.

"As soon as the last soldier enters the lawn area, I will activate the front and rear mine field. This should take care of several of the soldiers and make the rest vulnerable. They may have more rocket-propelled grenades. If they shoulder this weapon, move as far away from your gun position as possible unless you can drop the shooter. They will attack at a run in an attempt to overrun us. Cindy I love you with all my heart. We will get through this."

"Dad I know we will."

Seconds later, the two teams attacked firing their assault weapons and yelling. Ralph activated the mines. The lead man in the rear, the second in command, immediately hit a mine. The mine tore him into pieces. The rear attack team temporarily froze, but kept firing at the house. With the team frozen, Cindy quickly dropped the man in the rear with the RPG and wounded the other two men but had to back away from her gun placement to avoid the heavy fire directed there. As she did so, a bullet grazed her shoulder creating a painful but not debilitating injury. The two wounded men at the rear of the house abruptly reversed course and ran back they way they came. They attempted to fire at the gun position as they did so. Cindy retook her position and shot the second man in the team. Along with the wound he already suffered in his shoulder the man staggered and veered left. He hit another mine and joined his colleague in a fiery death. The final soldier made the wall but a shot from Cindy's AR 15 tore into his leg as he disappeared around the wall.

Meanwhile, the second man in the frontal assault also hit a mine and suffered the same fate, but an uninjured Berry ran even faster toward the house rather than slowing down. Ralph dropped the man in the rear as he prepared to fire his grenade. The grenade went off tearing along just above the ground until it exploded against the wall, creating another hole in Ralph's wall. Ralph dropped the third man with a bullet to the head, but Berry somehow managed to avoid the mines and reach a position against the house. Ralph couldn't see Berry in his new position. Quickly removing his pack, Berry placed an explosive charge against the front door and blew it off its hinges. Then he threw both a tear gas canister and a stun grenade inside. Donning his gas mask, Berry ran inside looking for a target. When Berry did not see one, he began to shoot at selected places in an attempt to flush Ralph and his daughter into the open.

Ralph anticipating the man would come in the front door shooting tried to get a clean shot at the man but the tear gas and stun grenade slowed his response. Both he and Cindy attached a gas mask on their belts but it took time to put it on their faces. Also, as designed, the stun grenade distracted Ralph. With a little luck, the hardened soldier managed to put a round close to Ralph's head. When Ralph finally had a chance to shoot. Berry had already managed to slip into the next room, a small study. Ralph cautiously followed the shooter to the small room, making sure the lead soldier did not have a firing position on him. Some of the tear gas had seeped into this space making the siting of his target difficult. As he slowly moved forward, Ralph heard a noise to the left. He instinctively moved in that direction but did not do so completely. Ralph had many times thrown something on the opposite side to attract an enemy from this position. Unfortunately, the split second cost Ralph. The lead soldier from a concealed position just inside the door, shot a bullet through the door striking Ralph's lead hand. Unable to hold his AR 15 effectively, Ralph dropped the weapon and started to withdraw his 9mm with his left hand, but the move cost him precious seconds. Seizing his brief advantage, Berry quickly appeared in front of Ralph with his assault weapon trained on him. Ralph could not bring his 9mm up to a firing position in time.

"Drop you weapon now." Berry yelled.

Ralph reluctantly did so to buy himself more time. In this game of death, you delayed the inevitable as long as you could. Berry continued,

"Well now the great Ralph finally dies. You have killed most of my men. Now you and your daughter will pay the price. Any last words."

"I lived as a soldier, now I die as one."

"I would have said the same. Now death comes for you." Berry replied.

But before Berry could fire, a bullet struck him in the forehead. He collapsed shooting his weapon into the ceiling. Cindy stood behind Ralph with her AR 15 issuing a faint puff of smoke. Cindy ran to her father and hugged him.

"Dad you are hurt. I am glad that I got the drop on him. This GI Joe would have surely killed you and me if he could. I came toward your position as soon as this GI Joe breached our front door."

"Yes he would have. But now we are truly a team. You saved my life and made the correct move toward the door. Also you have an injury. I hoped I'd never see your blood spilt."

"Just paying you back for the many times you saved mine. As to the injury it is nothing. I am a long way from the many injuries you have suffered over the years. I used to fantasize that you were the dashing man with a sword cut on your face, but your face may be one of the few places you don't have a scar."

"Cindy the men you shot in this battle including this man are your first kills. I did not want this life for you, but now you have done something that makes you unlike most people. You have taken the lives of other human beings. There is no turning back from this. I'm sorry. As to the face scar, I may have one of those before too long."

"Don't be sorry over my situation. I have already seen death many times. I accept it and have no qualms about killing a man who would take everything I care about from me. I lost my innocence when Ted tried to kill me as a child after murdering my parents. But I do differ from you in not wanting any more scars. I am a girl after all."

"Cindy, I suppose this makes sense, but naturally I want to protect you from the nasty world out there. The cops will be here any second. Let's deactivate the minefield and drop our weapons. We have to look like victims here, even though most of the attackers died. We will greet them arm and arm with our hands raised. Anyway, I will need treatment for this hand wound. It hurts like hell. Something tells me that I will need to use this hand again. "

18ᵗʰ Birthday

The raid on Ralph's home created many problems. Although no civilian sustained injuries, the mines and 50 caliber guns used by Ralph to defend his home violated several laws. Ralph fought a series of criminal indictments and lawsuits but in the end, Ralph, a decorated soldier, and his 16 year-old daughter fought an assault team of terrorists and won. Had he not possessed these advanced weapons, both he and daughter would have been killed. So Ralph had to pay some heavy fines and accept a probationary sentence of 6 months but his legal problems seem to have finally come to an end. No one wanted to punish Ralph for defending his home and daughter.

Two of the assault team of 15 men survived, but revealed very little about their military unit or its purpose. Only their dead leader knew all the details of their assignment. They seemed to be a collection of mercenaries from several parts of the world engaged in war and assault for hire. Who hired them remained a mystery but Ralph's history naturally led investigators back to Afghanistan and its new ruler, a cousin of the last one. On the threat of the US pulling out of Afghanistan made by the US Secretary of State, the new Afghan leader promised he would not engage in any military activities in the US but never admitted to hiring the mercenaries.

Another 1 1/2 years passed with life returning to normal for both Ralph and Cindy. Ralph came home from work a little early to celebrate Cindy's 18ᵗʰ birthday. He massaged his stiff left hand, which had now gained almost its entire function after two operations but still hurt Ralph at times as did his many injuries collected over the years. They both knew what the birthday meant but had not discussed it. Ralph and Cindy just continued to talk about other men and women but never acted on their discussions. Ralph purchased a stunning designer dress for Cindy after a great deal of research for her 18th birthday. Cindy for the most part, dressed like a soldier or a boy. Despite her wearing casual clothes, several companies had wanted her to model for them. Cindy showed little interest in doing this. At Cindy's insistence, the little party they had planned did not contain an invite list. Only Ralph and Cindy would attend.

Cindy loved her dress and insisted on putting it on for the rest of the party. Out of luck and careful attention to what Cindy said, Ralph bought Cindy exactly what she wanted. She looked like she had just walked off the catwalk at Vogue. Cindy had become the very beautiful woman everyone expected she would become. The conversation flowed nicely between Cindy and Ralph as the evening wore on until Cindy suddenly looked into Ralph's eyes and said.

"Ralph, I have loved you from the moment you came to that warehouse and rescued me. With my parents murdered, you have been my whole world. At first, I loved you as a daughter loves a father but over time, I have come to love you as a woman loves a man. I can't explain it nor do I want to try. Our age difference is just a number. It means nothing to me. I am as I have said before ready to become your lover and your wife if you will have me."

"Cindy I feel exactly the same way. When I came to the adoption agency you looked as if you walked out of a dream. You were the most beautiful little girl I had ever seen. You have now turned into the most beautiful woman I have ever seen. But it is much more than that. You are my soul mate and my companion. I can't imagine myself ever being with another woman. You are everything to me. I will marry you today if you want. I have stopped trying to predict my future or yours. We should finally be done with all the attacks but I've said that before. I can only offer you the life you already have. I hope it is enough."

"As I just said, I will marry you, the sooner the better. I have everything I want in you and our life. Now we must make love and keep making love in the time life offers us. Neither one of us have any guarantees we will survive for very long. We seem to be everyone's favorite targets. I want to stay as close to you as I can. Oh and one more thing. I want to have your babies. When I lost my family, I have longed to build another one. Life has not allowed either of us to have a normal life, but I sure want to try and build one."

"I would be happy to oblige you my future wife. Our children will learn how to protect themselves and carry on with what we have done. We cannot allow our past to dictate our lives any longer."

"I have no doubt our children will learn how to protect themselves. In our family, you must." Cindy laughed as she grabbed Ralph's hand and led him upstairs.